CHERGUI'S CHILD

JANE RIDDELL

CHERGUI'S CHILD

By Jane Riddell

Published in 2015 by Jane Riddell

Cover Art: Lisa Firth

Copyright © Jane Riddell

DEDICATION

To my son Jamie, the inspiration for this story

ACKNOWLEDGEMENTS

I would like to thank the following people whose time and engagement with the book have helped me improve it in countless ways:

Jennifer Young, NaTasha Bertrand, Natalie Mera Ford, Anjana Chowdhury, David Stevenson and Marianne Sevachko for commenting on plot and characterisation;

Jamie Gray and Anjana Chowdhury for helping me with the precision of the French language;

Lisa Firth for designing the cover;

My partner Peter, for his continuing encouragement of everything I do.

1

This is my memory of the beginning: shivering passengers, a leaden sky, shrivelled leaves cavorting in the wind. A rainbow striped woollen scarf, a dropped crimson glove – welcome darts of colour amongst the monochrome. Resigned passivity from people who'd done this journey too often. A scene easily envisaged as an Impressionist painting, gracing the walls of London's National Gallery, a scene entitled: *Wintry Afternoon at St Alban's Station*.

When my phone rang, I ignored it, reluctant to hear James apologising for his behaviour of the night before. An edgy conversation with my on/off boyfriend would have drained my limited energy. When the phone sounded a second time, announcing my father, I answered. Despite the crackly line, I could make out Dad's voice, the urgency of his message.

Ninety minutes later, I hesitated at the door of room twelve of the Medical Assessment Unit at St Thomas' Hospital. Through the glass panel, diminished as if a magician had shrunk her body, lay my aunt, her hair, nightdress, everything, colourless, like the bleached hospital bedding. Except for the intravenous drip, there was no equipment, and the pale grey bed and bare locker top gave off a detached vibe, as if awaiting their next occupant. I pictured the ward orderlies cleaning and disinfecting the room for another patient, wished I'd stopped for freesias, red and yellow ones, those with the strongest and sweetest scent.

My throat tightened as I recalled Dorothy's gravelly smoker's voice, 'We bought a fondue set at Sainsbury's. Half price. William's preparing the Gruyère and a Riesling is chilling in the fridge. Taxi's on its way to your flat. No arguments...'

Dad rose as I tiptoed to the bedside. 'Olivia!'

'How is she?'

He shook his head as if he'd been asked the same question innumerable times. 'It was a massive stroke.'

I went round to the other side of the bed and hugged William, before inspecting the notes on a clipboard at the end of the bed. 'Morphine – nothing else?'

'No point, darling,' Dad said, his face impassive, the way it often was in stressful situations.

'There's t-PA. It's a drug which–'

'Dottie is dying,' William said through tight lips. 'I don't want them giving her drugs.'

We stared at him, grasping his wife's hand, mottled cheeks twitching.

'Your mother's fetching Dorothy's things, don't know why,' Dad added.

William's face contorted. 'I don't want Nora here.'

Dad frowned at him. 'They *are* sisters.'

William tightened his grip on Dorothy's hand. 'It's our anniversary next week. Five years.'

I sat beside the bed, studied my aunt's other hand, its

sunspots and prominent veins, its flaking burgundy nail varnish. 'It's me, Olivia.'

Her white/brown hair clung in wisps to her face and the skin on her left cheek was distorted, as if yanked by invisible string. I didn't want to, but I recognised the odour. Nurses call it "the smell of death". Involuntarily I pulled back, imagining freesias, as if able to exchange the smells in my mind. I glanced at William, wondering if he'd fully accepted that his beloved Dottie was leaving him, us.

The door opened, revealing Mum, holdall in one hand, yellow carnations in the other.

William stood, wobbled. 'You have no place here, Nora.'

Lips pursed, she transferred two brushed cotton nighties, a pair of slippers and a box of paper hankies to the locker. 'I had to call in at Marks and Spencer. Dorothy had nothing suitable at home.'

'Go away,' he said, his higher tone barely concealing emotion.

Mum shut the locker door. 'Don't be ridiculous.'

As William lurched forward, Dad and I caught him.

'I don't want you here,' William said to Mum, with renewed energy, pulling himself free of our impeding arms.

She straightened. 'Find a vase for the flowers, Olivia. Don't make a scene, please, William.'

'This is your fault,' he moaned.

'I think you should leave, Nora,' Dad said as William pointed his finger at her.

William hobbled over to her. 'It's your fault Dorothy is like this. *Your* fault.'

'Nora, please,' Dad said, taking her arm.

Before they reached the door, she turned to star/me at William, as if appealing to him. His eyes were watery but bright with determination. As a nurse appeared, Mum started to speak, reconsidered and left.

'Dad?'

He scratched the eczema on his arm. 'You know your mother and Dorothy... A squabble, I expect.'

William stroked his wife's hair, his expression reflective. 'We've been married five years. I should have bought her a wooden carving. A Barbary ape, maybe. She liked those when we were in Gib.'

'It's the thought that counts,' the nurse said, adjusting the morphine drip.

In the adjoining bathroom, I splashed water over my face. My hair had escaped its combs, and my eyes – green like pistachio nuts, my aunt always described them – were dull.

The bathroom contained no crumpled towels, no splodges of shampoo or toothpaste. Only a wooden hair-brush, and a plastic container with her false teeth. As I removed strands of hair from the brush, their auburn tint almost grown out, the scent of her homemade peach hair spray filled my nostrils. I knelt, rested my elbows on the chair and buried my head in my hands.

While daylight succumbed to darkness and lights emerged in surrounding buildings, I willed Dorothy to regain consciousness. Even briefly, so she knew of my presence. It was impossible to imagine an end to our impromptu evenings watching Bridget Jones DVDs, an end to the last-minute phone calls requesting I meet her in Oxford Street to advise if a dress made her look too old.

My throat burned with unshed tears.

Staff checked her pulse. Shifted pillows. Changed her catheter. Sometimes they watched us, wondering, perhaps, if we were aware of how little time remained. Once or twice, a young nurse hovered, maybe fresh from training on communicating with relatives, yet unsure of what to say. The wail of ambulances and police cars occasionally punctured the silence. A doctor appeared, asked if we wanted to discuss anything and, interpreting our silence to mean that we didn't, left immediately.

Before dawn, my aunt's cheeks quivered, then she opened her eyes. I glanced at William, asleep in an easy chair, a blanket draped over him. 'Letter,' she rasped, as I bent my head to her. Again came the hoarse word, 'letter'. I squeezed her cold hand, aware now of a shadowy figure in a white coat waiting in the corner. As I stood, intending to wake William, Dorothy's face relaxed and she closed her eyes for the final time.

TWO DAYS later as I handed a £20 note to the taxi driver, I could still visualise my aunt's pallid, dying face.

'Hey – your change,' he called after me.

I took the money, scrambled up the steps and pressed heavily on the brass doorbell of the lawyer's office. In reception, I removed my jacket and perched on a leather armchair, wondering again why I'd been summoned. What was so important it couldn't be discussed over the phone?

The paintings on the drab green walls did nothing to lift my spirits: cherubs hovering round a tormented loin-clothed man; mountains tumbling into a murky lake. My fingers drummed the armrests as my thoughts reverted to the evening before. James had arrived late, and from the window of my third floor flat, I'd watched him adjust the metal coat hanger that served as an aerial for his Citröen. His perfunctory peck on my cheek irritated me. When he left early, claiming a headache – from my incense, of course, not his smoking (nothing that happened to James was ever his fault) – I'd been relieved.

Exhaustion permeated me: no Dorothy, and the funeral to endure tomorrow. 10:15 am. Where was the lawyer? I flicked through a *National Geographic* article about Iceland, closed the magazine. The door opposite opened, two men shook hands and one of them left, smiling at me as he passed.

'Miss Bowden, I'm Charles Minto. Apologies for summoning you at such short notice and for keeping you waiting.'

I followed him into a large, sparsely furnished room, sat down and surveyed my surroundings, wondering if their soothing cream colours eased the stress of divorce, financial worries and problems with neighbours. Outside, the wind buffeted leafless trees and the sky showed no inkling of sunshine.

'I am sorry about your aunt's death,' he said, smoothing back his white forelock. The glare from his specs reminded me of my former headmaster, but the lawyer's aura was calmer.

'I didn't manage to talk to her. I was in St Albans when she had her stroke.'

'Your father told me. I contacted you to tell you about Dorothy's Will.'

How much more caring he sounded, using Dorothy's name. 'Her Will?'

He nodded, studying me with sudden intensity as if I were a specimen in a lab. I wanted to parachute myself home, to work, anywhere.

'She changed it the day before she had her stroke. You are the main beneficiary.'

My pulse raced. 'But... this isn't... What about William, what about my mother? Does she know? Will I have to tell her?'

His eyes softened. 'Your aunt was adamant you have the money. She has provided well for William but the rest has been left to you. The figure is about £700,000.'

I imagined Mum's outrage. £700,000!

'There's something else. Dorothy dictated a letter to you when she changed her Will.'

'A letter?'

He handed me the envelope. 'Take your time – the contents are... unusual.'

My heart clamoured for escape. I wanted Dorothy, not her money. I didn't want to read a letter, I didn't want to discuss finances. All I yearned for, in fact, was my cosy duvet and sleep.

After peering at my name on the envelope, I opened it and scanned the letter. Then I reread it, the letters dancing like pixies. When finally I glanced up, the green and maroon circles on Mr Minto's tie were swirling.

He waited for a moment, then handed me a glass of water. 'Drink this. You're in shock.'

THE FOLLOWING MORNING, I contemplated the soberly clad people as they collapsed and shook umbrellas before entering the church. Around me, rhododendrons dripped, their reds and corals subdued in a leaden sky. Soggy clumps of saffron and violet crocuses leaned to the side. I identified with them. A blister from new shoes hindered my walking, and my head and eyes ached from crying, both for Dorothy and the letter.

For what I now knew.

Since its revelation, I'd experienced a floating sensation when moving. Shock, I supposed. Questioning, too, about my aunt's mental state when she dictated the letter the day before her stroke. For the moment, however, there were social obligations, I reminded myself, bending to slip a paper hanky behind my left heel. I fastened another two coat buttons, inhaled deeply and advanced to the church entrance.

As I walked to the front of the packed church, each step resounded on the stone floor and each movement of my blistered heel provoked a wince. Slipping into the second row, I avoided eye contact with Mum who'd turned at the sound of footsteps. My heart went out to William, slouched between my parents, the shoulders of his suit jacket shiny and a tad crumpled. While I attempted to focus on the lily-adorned coffin, Martin swivelled round to wink at me and I wished we were sitting together.

After wriggling out of my shoes, I became conscious of a commotion – Martin edging his way out of the front pew into mine to join me. Anger emanated from Mum's rigid back, the net trim of her black hat trembling in support: both children ignoring the custom of sitting with the immediate family.

There would be raised eyebrows. Comments.

'Dearly beloved,' the vicar's voice resonated, reminding me of his former success on the stage. 'We are gathered today to celebrate the life of Dorothy Roxburgh. Let us begin by singing Dorothy's favourite hymn, *For All the Saints*.'

The organ's rousing swell distracted me from the damp collar chafing my neck, from my sore foot. Everything would be okay. I would keep breathing, minimise contact with

Mum, protect my space. While the vicar paid tribute to Dorothy's life – her commitment to the arts, her voluntary work with homeless adolescents – I studied my mother, her composure. I thought about women in Varanasi congregating by the Ganges to weep openly for their loved ones, how much healthier these customs were than our buttoned-up Western ways.

At the end of the service, I waited for the front row to disperse. On my way out, however, despite keeping close to Martin, I couldn't prevent an elderly woman from questioning me about Dorothy's death, during which time my brother disappeared. Outside the church, while my parents and William thanked mourners for attending, I slipped away. The rain had stopped and I spotted Martin leaning against a beech tree, rolling a cigarette. As I approached him, he frowned.

'Don't start. Nora's been banging on about it since I got back, making me go into the garden,' he said. 'I am trying to stop, anyway.'

'Give me a hug.'

His navy wool coat was damp but his strong arms reassured me. Had anyone calculated the extra comfort of an extended hug? I wondered. A standard cuddle might provide ten minutes of solace. An additional ten seconds could propel you through the day.

His lips brushed my hair. 'I've missed you.'

'I didn't think you'd make it, if you'd get a flight.'

He exhaled and followed the trail of smoke with his eyes. 'Cancellation... Had to go from Sydney, though. Didn't you get my text? Zoë says "hi" and when are you coming to visit?'

Had Mum mentioned the Will to him? Whatever she said, he'd be loyal to me, but would it be untimely to broach the subject now? Make sure he knew I hadn't influenced Dorothy?

'Dad said you were with Dorothy when she died. Must have been grim.'

'We have to talk, Marti, I mean, really talk.'

'Let's go to the pub, get bombed out.' He wiped his spectacles with his scarf, peered to see if they were dry.

I reached into my bag for the liquorice toffees. 'Want one?'

'You still eat these,' he said, gloved fingers struggling with the wrapper.

The taste of liquorice returned me to childhood days: two ten-year-olds ensconced in an armchair, wrapped in Dad's holey cardigan, taking turns to read aloud; trying not to hear his muffled crying from the adjacent study after an onslaught of Mum's criticism, or from the floor above, the plaintive noise of the vacuum cleaner. The toffee's flavour, its softness from the warmth of my mouth, had restored me to peace. Still did.

'Where's James? Or have you split up again?' Martin asked through a mouthful of toffee.

'He's away – work,' I said, despising the lie but unable to admit my suspicion that James felt superior to our family. 'Don't look at me like that.'

'Like what?'

'Your "yeah right" expression – when you met, you didn't see him at his best.'

Martin yawned. 'I know – something in the pub made his eyes sting. Anyway, I did try...'

He can be kind,' I continued, 'When I had 'flu he read me *Wind in the Willows* for hours... Oh God, here's Nora.'

Mum was bearing down on us, a black dress and

matching coat accentuating her height. I braced myself. Even in the wind, she seemed in control.

'We expected you to travel with us in the funeral car, Olivia,' she said. 'And you know perfectly well that it's normal practice for the immediate family to shake hands with people who've made an effort to come to the funeral. I was most embarrassed that neither you nor Martin was prepared to do this. I can't imagine what people must be thinking.'

As I searched for a satisfactory reply, the shiny beads in her veil winked at me, conspirators. Fortunately, just then the vicar trundled over to us, his poodle-like black curls still damp from the earlier rain.

'Olivia, Martin, how nice to see you – despite the circumstances.'

'We'll expect you at the house,' Mum told him.

'Yes, yes. Though not for long, I'm afraid. Another service.'

He walked away, Mum striding after him.

Martin rolled his eyes. 'She should have been in the army. Come on, Liv. Must do our bit.'

'These are the arrangements,' Mum announced during the return journey to Greenwich. 'Dad and Martin will organise the drinks. Marjorie will hand round food – sandwiches and fruit loaf. I don't expect anyone will stay long on such a ghastly day. Olivia, I'd like you to show people to the guest room to freshen up, please.'

By the time we reached my parents' home, cars were drawing up outside the house, the rain had reappeared and water from a blocked drain flooded the pavement.

'Do hurry,' Mum said. 'We don't want people hanging around in this frightful weather.'

In my old bedroom, I rearranged my charcoal dress,

wishing I'd worn black tights to minimise my chubby legs. As soon as was polite, I'd leave. Then, back home, if the rain had stopped, I'd run in the park.

While peering out of the window, I noticed a man approaching our house and momentarily my heart stopped. When the figure drew closer, though, I realised it wasn't Richie. Of course not. Nevertheless, the thought of my ex caused my pulse to race. Despite what he'd done. *Cut*, I told myself, observing my fierce expression in the mirror. *Cut*, I repeated, conjuring up the image of a cleaver-armed butcher hacking through a slab of meat, the unwanted bit landing on an enamel tray.

I inspected my face, wondering if my demeanour had changed since reading Dorothy's letter. If people would notice. After combing my hair and reapplying lipstick, I left the room, as Mum appeared with the first guest.

The dining room and sitting room smelled of sherry and damp clothes. Mum now bustled about, taking drinks orders, passing them on to Dad who, like a butler on a trial period, meekly appeared with glasses of whisky and sherry. Impressively focused, Marjorie circulated with a tray of meticulously trimmed sand-wiches. Several times I managed to slip away as she approached, the determined glint in her eye conveying her desire that no one go hungry. Martin hovered by the fireplace, his muscly figure appearing cramped in its grey suit; his hand delving into his jacket pocket, reap-pearing empty, transferring its energy to fiddling with a paperclip.

'How are you, Dad? I asked, catching him during an off-duty moment. In my new shoes, I was nearly as tall as him. Tall and with blistered heels. I could feel the rawness of eroded skin, dampness from seeping liquid.

He shrugged, his smile resigned. 'Your mother has everything under control.'

'And what are you conspiring about?' Mum challenged from behind. 'Sonja and Hamish need their glasses refilling, Ronald – the medium dry.'

As she strode away, I observed Dad's bland expression. My inheritance would further fuel her anger, as if her past disappointments weren't enough. He would bear the brunt, of course – he always did. An urge overcame me to whisk him and Martin away from this room of restricted behaviours. On our own in the pub, we could de-corset, I'd confide in them and feel less alone, less indecisive.

Noticing Marjorie with a tray of shortbread and fruit loaf, I did another body swerve. While guests welcomed more food, I wondered how many of them realised the calories they were consuming.

Mum sighed and I knew why – disapproval of the escalating noise. It wasn't appropriate to stay long on such occasions and one of the guests should be initiating departure. A conversation by the window seemed particularly loud and I recognised a florid-faced neighbour. Resembling a teacher about to reprimand a rowdy pupil, Mum strode over to him, clasped his arm. 'George, let me introduce you to Ruth. She's also going to China this summer.'

'I'd prefer to finish our conversation,' he responded, removing his forearm from Mum's pearly pink nail-varnished fingers, returning his attention to his companion. I suppressed a gurgle of laughter.

Across the road, lights were appearing in front rooms. When could I leave? William sidled over, saying, 'I want to go home. I don't like fuss.'

Martin was now next to me, nodding. 'I'll drive you. Olivia will come too. Settle you in.'

I helped William with his coat, catching Dad's envious eye.

By the time we arrived at my uncle's terraced house, the wind and rain had subsided, the sun casting shards of light on the sitting room walls, highlighting a resilient cobweb, a discoloured rectangle where a painting had been removed. The room was filled with vases of flowers, some surrounded by a cluster of decaying petals. A film of dust covered the mantelpiece and bookcase, and a pile of unopened envelopes lay on the coffee table.

William sank into his armchair, scooped up the cat and closed his eyes, his hand stroking Tibby's apricot fur.

'I'll put the kettle on,' I said, kicking off my shoes. What relief. Now to find Elastoplast and antiseptic.

My uncle opened his eyes: 'You'll put me in a home, won't you?'

I knelt beside him, touched his arm, frail through its jacket and shirt. His fingers appeared gnarled. Was he taking his pills? Tibby shot me a reproachful glance for disturbing her, then slithered under the bureau.

'Dorothy will be back soon,' he said, searching for the cat. 'She always plays bridge on a Tuesday. Comes home at five. It's nearly five now. She'll be back soon and she'll make the tea. We always have soup and sandwiches when it's a bridge day.'

In the kitchen, I switched on the kettle, and helped myself to Dettol and cotton wool. After cleaning my blister, I stuck an Elastoplast on it. When I returned with the coffee, William clutched the stick propped against the chair, hoisted himself up and shuffled towards the window, his tall, angular figure as caged-looking as his grief. 'I'm watching out for Dorothy. She likes to see my face when she comes back.'

Martin ran his fingers through his hair. 'Drink your coffee, William.'

William twisted round, his expression anguished. 'She's gone, isn't she, my lovely Dottie?'

As my brother and I caught each other's eye, I detected sadness in his expression that I sensed was connected with more than Dorothy's death.

'Did she suffer?' William continued. 'I can't bear to think of her suffering. She was so beautiful on our wedding day... she had flowers in her hair... and her dress was ivory satin. She could have been twenty-five, not sixty-five. She wanted you to have her engagement ring, Olivia. Fetch the box – it's in the attic.'

Dusty air encircled the attic, and the floor creaked as I squeezed between a sideboard and a camp bed covered with shoeboxes, snagging my dress on a splinter of wood from a chest of drawers. To my left, an open drawer overflowed with porcelain dolls attired in antique Christening robes, and nearby on the floor were a couple of wooden tennis rackets with broken strings. A soapy smell was catapulting me back to childhood, and next to the rackets, I noticed a faded box of Mornay's *French Fern* soap. Through the skylight I heard the cawing of crows.

Several more minutes elapsed before I spotted, on top of an old trunk, a blue velvet box with the letters DJV stitched in gilt thread. I peeked inside then snapped the lid shut – I didn't want an emerald ring or ebony beads. I wanted Dorothy. Lowering myself onto a rocking chair, I draped a blanket over me. It smelled of mothballs and was scratchy but warm.

I woke to a crashing noise.

'Bollocks,' Martin said, rubbing his elbow. 'What are you *doing*? Did you find the box? Please come down. William keeps wandering over to the window to look for Dorothy. It's doing my head in.'

'Nora will have him in a care home before summer and he'll be miserable.'

Martin's eyes flashed with anger as he ran his fingers through his hair. 'You seem knackered. What's the rumpus with her and the Will, anyway? She's so cranky at the moment – don't know how Dad stands it 24/7.'

I flicked a spec of fluff from the blanket and fingered the torn wool on my sleeve. 'Dorothy's left me most of her money.'

'Jeez.'

'£700,000.'

'Holy Dooley.'

Neither his eyes nor voice conveyed jealousy and I loved him for this.

'I can't believe it,' I continued. 'Most people divvy it up. But there's a reason. A reason why she's done this.'

'What? Tell me.'

He tilted his head, regarded me appealingly. When we were children, we'd done this if wanting something of the other. What must it be like not having a twin? Not experiencing sharing a womb? I dragged myself from the rocking chair and hugged him, feeling his tension as I did so.

I returned to the chair. Since reading Dorothy's letter, I'd thought of little else than its revelation. But now the words eluded me.

'Jeez, don't do this to me. What is it, Liv? And please stop rocking.'

'She wrote to me. I'll show you her letter.'

'Tell me.'

'*My dearest Olivia,*' I read. '*I am unwell and know that there is a chance I might not see you again. I am leaving you most of my money. But there's a reason...*' Aware of a strange sense of observing myself, I dropped the letter.

'Don't stop,' Martin said. 'Please...'

I handed him the letter. Watched his eyes widen in astonishment.

2

_____

even years earlier

Seen years earlier
Olivia looks up from wiping the table, to observe a customer who's just seated himself and is transferring his meal from tray to table. From the open window she can see an unblemished blue sky, white tulips, and pink hyacinths. Today London zoo is mobbed with all ages, several schools having brought their year 7s. Many fathers are here with young kids and she remembers her visits with Dad.

'Spring's arrived, finally,' the man says. 'Bet you wish you weren't working.'

She smiles. 'I finish in an hour.'

He squeezes a sachet of mayonnaise over his salad. 'Then what?'

'Then I'll try out my new zoom lens.'

His eyes sparkle. 'Here? I'm interested in photography, too. What kind of camera do you have?'

'An Olympus *OM 10* with a manual override. It takes brilliant photos. Pity they don't make them anymore.'

A school party arrive and she catches the eye of another

waitress as the children gabble away while retrieving their lunch boxes. The teachers point to the long table reserved for them, try to rein in the more hyper kids, while they slide into seats and peer in delight or dismay at the contents of their meals lovingly prepared by dad or mum. At this point, she approaches an elderly shaky woman, offering to help her move to a corner table, where she'll be more comfortable.

As Olivia clears other tables, she senses the man's eye on her, and despite the fact he must be twice her age and wears a wedding ring, his interest isn't unwelcome. Later, while photographing the gorillas, she thinks about him: his high forehead and straight fair hair, the dark eyes which sparkle when animated.

The weeks pass, her gap year disappearing more quickly than she had envisaged. In six months' time, it'll be autumn and the start of university.

A month after first meeting the man, she is volunteering as a tour guide. It being a large group, she doesn't notice him initially. Then, while the party is absorbed by a mother hippo snorting and grunting as she nudges her calf into the pool, a voice says, 'You're good at this.'

She turns to see him, conscious of the others now observing them. When leading the party to the monkey house, she loses her ability to answer questions fluently, all too aware of his presence.

At the end of the tour, the man says, 'Fancy a coffee? I'm Richie.'

He takes her to a coffee shop near the zoo, buys millionaire's shortbread for him and carrot cake for her. They are the only customers, and whenever Olivia glances at the counter, the waitress is watching them.

'It was my father who suggested I apply for a job at the

zoo,' Olivia tells him. 'When I was a child, he took me here often.'

'My dad never had time to take me anywhere. He was a carpenter. He had a workshop at the bottom of our garden, and I loved the smell of the wood and the oils and varnishes he used.'

Richie stops and gazes past her before continuing, 'He always made something for my birthday and for Christmas – even when he was busy. It was partly because they didn't have much money, you see. For a while, I sort of looked down on these things. Then when I was older, I realised the effort and love he put into those toys.'

At his wistful expression, she places her hand on his arm.

They discuss the pros and cons of digital cameras; the best filters to use; how much editing of photos they permit themselves to do on iPhoto. To her relief, when they part company, he doesn't suggest meeting again. Over the following months, they bump into each other a couple of times, exchange a few words.

When she begins studying for nursing, she gives up her waitressing job but continues doing the occasional guiding tour. Although she doesn't see him again, she always thinks of him when at the zoo.

Six years earlier

It's late afternoon as Olivia slips her notepad into her backpack, discreetly observing Richie behind his desk. In this light he could pass for thirty but she knows he's recently celebrated his fortieth. With his wife. A fellow student met them leaving a Nepalese restaurant, and shortly after, a message circulated on Facebook about the hunky Richie having turned forty.

It took a while, for them to recover from recognising each other when she began medicine, further adjustment required when he became her tutor in third year.

'You've got to grips with free radicals and antioxidants, then,' he now says.

She nods. 'The book you recommended: Baynes and Dominiczak – it's easy to understand.'

He smiles. 'I expect it was heavily edited.'

'For dummies, you mean?'

He opens his diary. 'That's not what I meant... Fancy a drink?'

She considers her tentative plan to meet Jo and Tom in the pub, a notion of tackling an assignment due in the following week.

'I should get home.'

Outside, autumn leaves swirl in the breeze and light on the campus lawn heightens the green. Honeysuckle fragrance, pungent after an earlier rainfall, wafts through the open window.

He is now standing close to her. Even with closed eyes, she'd sense his presence. 'Just one,' he promises.

He helps her into her jacket and stands aside to let her out first, bending to retrieve the bus pass which has fallen from her pocket. It's the old-fashioned courtesy that does it, she thinks.

The pub is mobbed with Manchester United fans glued to the telly. Her eyes sting from the veil of smoke, and inter-mittent roaring punctuates surrounding conversations.

He returns from the bar with two vodkas and orange. Her hand trembles when he gives her the glass.

'Are you enjoying medical school, then?' he asks.

'I am now. It took a while to get used to studying again.'

He leans forward, rests his chin on his hands, expression curious.

'It's nothing odd,' she says. 'I trained as a nurse then worked for a while. I'd originally planned to do medicine, but when I was sixteen, I had bad asthma and had to repeat the year.'

She pauses, remembering the year of struggling not to fall behind with schoolwork, worrying that asthma would always blight her life.

'Afterwards I didn't think I'd be fit enough for medicine, so I did my nursing training, then changed my mind, and here I am.'

'Is it working out?'

'It all felt quite removed from being a doctor, until I did my first placement.'

He sips his vodka. 'Well yes, it would. Where was it?'

'University College Hospital.'

His eyes shine. 'UCH – my old stamping ground. I loved that hospital. Even though it was falling down when I worked there. The new site is very grand.'

They discuss London hospitals and a Berlin conference where he's presenting a Paper. He orders more drinks. She knocks hers back quickly, stands. 'I'd better get home.'

Two weeks later, she taps on Richie's door twice before he answers. He's at his desk, surrounded by papers and books. As he twists round to the shelf behind his desk, his elbow upsets a pile, knocking it to the floor, and he swears while retrieving the bundle. 'You'd think with email, there'd be less paperwork. Have a seat. How's it going?' His phone rings. 'Dr Williams? No, sorry. I have a tutorial.' He turns to look at her. "So, where did we leave off last time?"

She explains.

'I'll use the whiteboard.'

He scribbles facts, explaining while he writes.

'Can you slow down?' she asks after a while.

He looks puzzled, as if reminded of where he is, what he's doing.

Ten minutes before their session should end, he snaps shut a textbook and contemplates her. 'I'm hungry. Fancy an Indian meal? There's a place recently opened in Kensington.'

'Dr Williams, I know you're married.'

She awaits the usual clichés but he says nothing. She remembers the Nepalese restaurant where he supposedly celebrated with his wife. Perhaps it wasn't his wife.

In the Indian restaurant, he strokes her hand. 'I've always liked you, you see.'

Their table is white and candlelit, the single rose real and scented. Sitar music plays in the background, stirring her more than she'd expect. Her eyes dart to the silver band on his left hand. He notices and points to a plate. 'Have a pakora.'

She takes one. 'You're not assuming we'll... sleep together?'

'How can you prove whether at this moment we are sleeping, and all our thoughts are a dream; or whether we are awake, and talking to one another in the waking state? Plato... Is this what you'd like, Olivia? To sleep with me?'

Of course she should tell him this isn't what she wants. His expression is raw, however, and she would like to hold him. As a comforter. More than a comforter, if she's honest. The waiter delivers their main course and returns to ask if

they are happy with their food, if they'd like another drink.
She glances at Richie, wishing they were on their own,
yearning to touch the hollow below his Adam's apple, to feel
his hand on the small of her back.

'Aren't you hungry?' he asks, head tilted. He helps
himself to more chutney. 'What do you plan to specialise
in?'

'Paediatrics.'

'Really? Can be tough. You're caring for the parents as
well as the child.'

'I thought nurses provided the pastoral care.'

He reaches for her hand. 'A skilled doctor is more than
solely a clinician.'

When he drops her off, he leans over, fingers her throat.
It would be so easy. So wrong. As her left hand rests on the
door handle, she resists the urge to touch a tiny scar above
his lip, wrenches open the car door, leaves without looking
back.

On the morning of her next tutorial, Richie texts to cancel.
She endures lectures, struggles to concentrate, not to worry.
Clutching her phone like a safety raft. At lunchtime she
hovers near his office.

'Coming to Lill's?' Roz and Tom ask after zoology. She
shakes her head.

'After your tutorial, we mean,' Roz adds.

'It's cancelled. I need to get back.'

Roz grabs her arm. 'Liv?'

She pulls away.

At home she eats last night's leftovers while watching
the news, her flat seeming chilly and impersonal. She

resists the temptation to text Richie. She's crossed the Rubicon.

She hears no more and assumes their next tutorial will proceed as planned. Time drags until the day. By five o'clock, her right thumb aches from checking her phone, willing him not to cancel. When she knocks on his office door there's no reply. Ten minutes later, as she's about to leave, she hears running. He appears, tie flapping, hair dishevelled.

'Sorry,' he says, unlocking the door. He stands back to let her past, follows her in, dumping his briefcase and jacket on his desk. The sweaty smell of him heightens her desire.

He steps forward, cups her face. 'Olivia.' He presses his lips to hers. He tastes of apple.

She takes a taxi, he drives. In the flat, she rushes around the sitting room, grabbing stray clothes and chipped mugs, shoving dead freesias and paper hankies in the bin. She opens the bedroom window, bundles dirty clothes into the laundry basket, makes the bed. When she answers the entryphone, her body trembles at the sound of his voice, despite having expected it.

He embraces her, unbuttons her blouse, then stops.

'It's alright,' she says, leading him to the bedroom.

'But if you love and must needs have desires, let these be your desires:

To melt and be like a running brook that sings its melody to the night.

To know the pain of too much tenderness,' he says. 'Kahlil Gibran.'

When she wakes during the night, he's gone, the woody scent of his aftershave on her pillow, the sole evidence he's been here. Clutching the pillow to her cheek, she falls asleep again.

Autumn whizzes by, a blur of classes, essays and Richie. Apart from their tutorials, Olivia never knows much in advance when they'll be together, as he constantly seems to be preparing for conferences, working on research. Her mobile phone, secure in her jeans pocket, acquires a heightened importance, part of her always alert to its announcements. When she hasn't seen him for a while, she imagines she feels the phone vibrating and whisks it from her pocket, to find no new messages. On the off chance of a rendezvous, she cancels friends, postpones accepting invitations to a family Sunday lunch.

Being with an older man excites her: no amateurish fumbling, no need for hand signals. He is eager to please, instinctive, his style relaxed and paced, occasionally frenzied. It's like riding a wave, exhilarating, risky. He brings Valpolicella and Sicilian chocolates. She wears floral dresses, twists her hair into a French roll, buys satin French knickers and concocts facial masks from oatmeal and yoghurt. She cooks: tagliatelle with mushrooms, moussaka, focaccia bread with parmesan and basil.

'This is fabulous,' he'll comment, mouth full. 'My wife is allergic to wheat. Occasionally I buy bread and biscuits but there's no one to share them with.'

The temptation to cook the things he can't eat at home is irresistible.

They sit across the table from each other, not saying much, and as the evening progresses, her longing for him increases. The lead-in seldom varies: he finishes his coffee, snuffs out the candle, the air filling with the smell of wax, sometimes freesias. He pulls her to her feet with hands radiating heat. Caresses her throat, his wedding ring cool against her skin. He kisses her forehead, pushes a deviant strand behind her ear. 'Such fabulous hair,' he says, enfolding her. As he leads her to the bedroom, she pirouettes under his arm.

Afterwards, they lie together. They don't discuss his marriage, the future. The word "love" is seldom mentioned, though frequently she finds it difficult not to declare her feelings. Once she questions why he doesn't shower before leaving, why he risks being discovered. 'My wife doesn't mind,' he says. 'Provided I'm discreet.'

When the flat door clicks shut, she immerses herself in the telly, until she feels distanced from him.

SEVEN WEEKS INTO THEIR RELATIONSHIP, on a raw December evening, he doesn't appear.

She picks at the wilting salad on the table. Starts on the wine. Inspects her phone repeatedly for missed messages. Has she mistaken the date? Has he? She opens textbooks, but all she can conclude – while eating the cheesecake they would have shared – is that finally he has tired of her.

At eleven o'clock, when she's resigned to his not showing, the buzzer goes. Perhaps it's a neighbour pressing the wrong bell, she thinks, bracing herself for disappointment.

'It's me,' Richie whispers.

'Sorry,' he says, when he enters the flat. 'My wife booked tickets for a concert, as a surprise, you see. Brahms. I had to go... And she fancied having supper afterwards.' He shrugs. 'I made the excuse of having forgotten to bring home my laptop. Can't stay long.'

'I... you told me she didn't mind.'

He fidgets with his tie, and as his eyes focus on the open bedroom door, she witnesses his indecision.

She pictures him at the concert with his wife, exchanging smiles at certain moments during the performance. For the first time, she perceives the wife as an entity. Someone who buys tickets for concerts. Insists on an intimate meal afterwards. She imagines red leather banquette seats and bracket lamps dispensing gentle light. Post-concert talk. Jealousy sears her: the parts of him exclusive to his wife. She visualises her, smooth and fragrant, in a silk nightgown, awaiting her husband's return.

She turns away. 'It's late, I need to get to bed.'

He hesitates. 'Well, yes, I just wanted to explain.'

He leaves the flat, his visit having lasted barely five minutes. She crawls into bed, counts the cracks on the ceiling, telling herself for the millionth time that she must end her relationship with him.

3

'You're on compassionate leave,' Anya said firmly but not unkindly, when I appeared in the duty room the day after my aunt's funeral.

'All I do is wander around my flat, doing nothing. Besides, with Jess being ill...'

Except for the orderly desk, the manager's office resembled a storeroom for broken chairs, drip stands, and sphygmomanometers awaiting recalibration. On the bookcase, three empty mugs smelled of Arabic coffee. She must have started early that day. In the garden I heard a clipping noise from the gardener's shears pruning back the berberis.

Anya studied me. 'How did the funeral go?'

'The usual tributes, tear-jerking hymns. I know Dorothy was elderly, but she was so much fun, so spontaneous – she'd get those crazy ideas...'

I felt in my pocket for the letter I'd taken to carrying around like a talisman. Ironic, when it seemed more like a crossroads with no direction signs.

Anya's expression was sympathetic. 'Okay, you can stay,

but no group work. I suggest you help in the gym this morning.'

As I turned to leave, she called me back. 'Four hours, Olivia, no more.'

Lightheaded from having ignored breakfast, I found some bread in the staff kitchen and spread two slices with a thin layer of butter. After eating half a slice, I chucked the rest in the bin.

In the large, newly painted gym, Kirsty, a sixteen-year-old suffering back injuries from a motorbike accident, slouched on a medicine ball, fiddling with her iPod.

'Sit straight, Kirsty,' Gill called from the other side of the room. 'This is about strengthening your core muscles.'

I winked at Kirsty. 'Darren been in touch?'

She shook her head. 'Not even a text. I hope his bike's a write-off.'

'How's your back?'

'Bit better.'

'Gill's right, though. You need to sit properly. Like this.'

Positioned near Kirsty was Ben, strengthening his shoulders and arms with a bar.

When one of the forklift trucks at the storehouse broke down, this feisty ginger-haired lad had been forced to lift crates and was currently embroiled in a legal wrangle about liability for his damaged shoulder.

Gill put on George Michael's *Too Funky* and immediately Ben abandoned his exercises, to hip-hop. Gill supported Kirsty's arms while she stepped from side to side.

'Will I ever walk properly again?' Kirsty asked.

Gill nodded. 'You'll be moving like Ben in a month or two.'

'You really think?'

Kirsty seemed so unconvinced that I put my arm round her, pecked her cheek.

Against the rules, of course, but sometimes it was too hard to hold back. This was why I loved my job – the opportunity to get to know the patients, most of whom were long-stay.

Outside, the wintry sun dispensed a glorious misty light over the gardens, the fields, the distant hills and I wished I had my camera.

At lunchtime, I followed Gill to the staff dining room.

'Smells like cauliflower cheese,' she said. 'I'm starving.'

I searched for the salads but couldn't see any.

When I made to leave, she grabbed my arm. 'Aren't you eating?'

'I had a huge breakfast.'

When Gill returned from lunch, I helped her support a fourteen-year-old boy walking his first steps since a road accident. My lack of food and broken nights' sleep were taking their toll, however, Gill noticed, and after we'd helped Rob back to his room, she turned to me. 'Go home and rest.'

During the train journey back to central London, I scrutinised passengers, wondering if they were observing me, thinking how dumpy I appeared. Then an overweight woman of similar age to me, got on, clutching a polystyrene container. While the train rattled along, she devoured her ketchup-smeared chips, making throaty sounds when munching. I watched, perplexed. Might I become like her, chubby cheeks and double chin reducing my eyes to piggy size?

Eventually I moved away, avoiding another passenger crunching on a giant-sized packet of nachos. At the next station, I noticed a restaurant advertising an "all you can eat" buffet.

The UK had become obsessed with eating.

BACK AT MY FLAT, I phoned Martin. While waiting for him, I cleaned the wardrobe mirror with Windolene, then inspected myself from all angles, clothed and naked. When the buzzer chimed, I scrambled into my tracksuit and ran to answer.

'I can't face the birthday dinner,' I told him.

'You didn't ask me round about this, surely? We could have talked on the phone.' He moved to sit beside me on the sofa. 'You don't need to tell Nora anything about the letter. Not until you're ready, anyway.'

'It's not the dinner, Marti.'

'Then what is it? I'm starving, shall I make some pasta?'

'I've eaten. Besides, I'm going for a run later, so I don't want to eat before then.'

When he returned from the loo, he said, 'There are two bathing suits in the bathroom.'

'Your point?'

He wandered through to the kitchen, opened the fridge door and the cupboards. When he reappeared, understanding flooded his face. 'It's come back, hasn't it? Oh Liv...'

Now I regretted contacting him. I didn't want to talk, I wanted to run until I dropped. It had taken him an hour to get here, however, so I couldn't ask him to leave.

'Probably the shock of Dorothy's letter – stress can bring on anything,' he added.

'I can't go back to The Priory.'

He tugged the knee of his trousers. 'Stop rushing ahead. What's been happening?'

'Same as last time.'

'Make an appointment to see Dr Wilton.'

'I can't go to the surgery. Not like this...'

Martin sighed. 'He might be prepared to add you to his house calls, I suppose.'

When Dr Wilton arrived, I explained about my reduced appetite. When pushed, I admitted thinking I was fat, and when further pushed, confessed about my obsession with exercise.

'Can you identify the triggers?' he asked.

My life, I thought. Mum. Being a failed medical student. Dorothy's letter.

'My aunt's death, being in my parents' home, my mother. I never feel good about myself when I'm around her.'

His expression was compassionate. 'Is this fairly recent?'

'And we have our birthday celebration dinner this weekend,' Martin added, running his fingers through his hair.

'As you know,' Dr Wilton said, 'when you've experienced one episode of anorexia nervosa, it can be easy to relapse. Have you still got a copy of your "preventing relapse" programme?'

I had no idea where it was.

He leaned forward. 'What I suggest is referring you to Dr Barak and making an appointment to see the dietitian who looked after you before. And find your relapse prevention plan. Make an appointment at the surgery for the end of the week and we'll take it from there.'

'I can't cancel the birthday dinner. My mother will...'

He stroked my arm so gently that my eyes filled. What was it about kindness in men that touched me so much?

'Practise your coping strategies,' he advised, glancing at his watch.

Martin showed the doctor out and returned to the sitting room. 'Prevention plan, Liv, where is it?'

I rummaged through my desk drawers, eventually locating it tucked into a cookery book in the kitchen. It must have been there for five or six years.

'Got it,' I said, ripping open the envelope.

'Develop a support system – and use it!' I read out loud. 'It is important to surround yourself with people who love and encourage you. These can be members of your family, your friends, or your care providers. They will be there to help you when you are struggling with a difficult situation...' I broke off reading. 'So, can you imagine me turning to Nora for support?'

He rolled his eyes.

I scanned the rest of the document. 'Try to get rid of any negative influences in your life. Including people who make you feel bad about yourself.'

He grabbed the sheet from me. 'Identify your "triggers". '

'Number I: Family dinners,' I suggested.

'Anyway, this is helpful stuff, Liv.'

When Martin left, I stared for ages at the cheddar in the fridge, finally cutting off a small chunk to eat with rocket and tomatoes.

Dr Barak offered me a consultation two days later. Arranging to see the dietitian proved more difficult – Rachel had left her post and confiding in another nutritionist didn't appeal.

'What about Hilary?' Roz suggested. 'Remember she specialised in mental health, and she's always been interested in diet. She came to see you at–'

'I hardly need reminding.'

Hilary had been lovely, easy. One of the few people who avoided platitudes or clichés. If there was a single person who could help my self-esteem, it was her.

She visited the following afternoon, focusing on devising an eating pattern and coping techniques for stressful situations, specifically the celebration dinner.

'Don't forget that psychotherapy will help you recover from your relapse,' she said when leaving.

I told her I'd arranged to see Dr Barak and she gave the thumbs up sign.

MARTIN WAVED as I searched for him in the pub. The day had been cold and blustery, requiring me to raise the TV volume to drown out the moaning wind. Now it was a relief to leave the flat. Have company.

'I should have collected you,' he said.

'I'm loads better. Verging on normal. Imagine!'

'Nora asked how you were. She was upset about not being allowed to visit.'

I laughed. 'Which would have sent my stress levels rocketing. I am much better. Hilary helped me plan – only one hour's exercise per day, weigh myself once a week max, *and* we put together a seven-day menu which, amazingly, I am sticking to. Fingers crossed, this continues.'

'Good for you.'

A group of women in tight black or red dresses and spiky heels appeared, reeking of cheap perfume and laughing raucously. Some of them were about to light up before being reminded of the smoking ban. Fags and lighters in hand, the loudest of them clicked their way outside, stumbling, apologising effusively as they bumped into customers. A hen night, perhaps. Suddenly I felt old. Clapped-out.

Martin returned from the bar with a glass of red wine for me, a pint of Beamish for him. 'Did you remember the letter?'

'Of course.'

'Read it to me, will you?'

His preoccupied, sad expression had retreated – for the moment – yet I hesitated before retrieving the crushed envelope from my bag. I read out loud:

'*This will come as a shock to you five years later, but I have found out one of your babies survived. You left the hospital so quickly – I know you were in a state. They weren't able to get in touch with you to let you know. They managed to contact Richie, and he claimed the baby girl and gave the impression you were his wife.*

'*I'm sure you will want to find your daughter and I am leaving you most of my money to help you do this. This inheritance will provide you with a financial cushion to raise a child. You have been like a daughter to me, Olivia, and I am sure you will make a wonderful mother. I wish you all the luck in finding your little girl, if this is what you decide to do. I'm only sorry I probably won't be with you to support you through a difficult time.*

Your loving Dorothy.'

Martin stared at me. 'You are a mother!'

4

'It was easier to believe she was dead... easier than knowing she's being brought up by someone else.'

A dreadful comment, although true. I'd progressed in accepting the deaths of my twins, but Dorothy's letter had ripped open the wound.

Martin took my hand. 'You can get her back. She's yours.'

'I'd be a crap mother.'

'You'd be brilliant.'

'She's got a mum and dad. They're what she knows. Besides, I couldn't... I can't barge into her life after five years. Even if I knew where she is.'

Better not to try than fail.

Martin's voice deepened. 'You must find her. You can't not try.' He tugged at his trouser knee, and the sad expression returned. As if conscious of my scrutiny, he straightened, swigged his drink.

'I'm weak, Marti.'

'Vulnerable. Not weak.'

I searched his face. 'You don't mind, do you, about the

money? About Dorothy leaving me so much, although, if I'm not going to use it for... Oh God, what a mess.'

'Course not, silly. I've enough wedge, anyway.'

Our conversation continued: his reasons why I should search for my child, my views on why I shouldn't. When we'd exhausted the subject, before I could ask what was going on with him, he stood abruptly, saying he'd promised to phone Zoë.

In time he'd confide in me.

THREE EVENINGS LATER, I paused outside my parents' home in East Greenwich. Staring at the redbrick terraced house, with its freshly painted window frames, its pruned and weeded front garden, instinct urged me to plead illness and return to my flat. If the decision had been Martin's and mine, we would have celebrated our birthday in a restaurant, where, distanced from dominant home territory, Nora would shelve her moans and disappointments for an evening.

'Come in, come in,' Dad said, gallantly cheerful. 'Happy birthday, darling. Martin's on his way. He's been shopping.'

The smell of cooking lamb permeated the hall as I wriggled out of my coat, tucked rebellious strands of hair behind my ear. In the sitting room I plonked myself on the sofa, stomach churning. If only Zoë had accompanied Martin to London, or William had been invited for dinner. Anything to swell the numbers, deflect attention from me... I should find Mum. Get the greeting over.

'You're looking fit, Dad. Still swimming each day?'

'I was in the sea at Hastings last Sunday.'

'Cool!'

'Freezing, actually. Your mother wouldn't even leave the car.'

On cue, like an actor appearing on stage, Mum strode into the sitting room.

'Happy birthday, Olivia. What a lovely dress, it's so nice to see you wearing something colourful.' She glanced at the mantelpiece clock. 'What has happened to Martin? I said half past seven. The lamb will be overdone.'

I drifted through to the dining room, studied the table with its red and blue dinner set, silver candlesticks, cruets and gleaming napkin rings. *Cut*, I instructed myself, as images of Richie surfaced. *Cut, cut.*

When the front door opened, bringing with it a welcome breeze and a tantalising link with the outside world, I rushed into the hall. Martin flung his jacket over the bannisters. 'Sorry I'm late. Happy birthday, Liv.'

We hugged.

Dad produced champagne flutes, glasses tinkling against each other when he set the tray on the sideboard.

'Finally, a reason to open this,' he said, uncorking a bottle of Veuve Clicquot.

The cork shot out, spraying tawny liquid, and we laughed. My breathing reduced.

I knew my mother would propose a toast, and twisting through me, like a serpent searching for an exit, was a notion of announcing I had a daughter and my parents were now grandparents.

Mum raised her glass. 'We have two things to celebrate. Olivia and Martin's birthday, of course, and Peter Foyle's promotion. He's now Head of the Geography Department – I didn't mention this, did I Ronald?'

Dad's expression was one of sweet tolerance, but a vein in his temple pulsed. 'Many times, dear.'

'Pamela's delighted, of course. He's worked so hard since joining that school. It wouldn't surprise me if he becomes head teacher.'

I studied Mum's face – handsome, rather than beautiful, with its high forehead and piercing large blue eyes. This evening, her usual red lipstick coated the thin lips, and her Greek nose seemed longer than normal. A mauve tint had been applied to her wavy grey hair and the customary pearl necklace, worn to conceal a thyroidectomy scar, was yellowing.

'Time to eat,' she said as the aroma of lamb grew more pungent.

When we seated ourselves at the table and she opened the hostess trolley, my brow beaded with sweat. I recalled Hilary's advice: distract myself with conversation; don't think of the food too much; be assertive, but not rude, about portion sizes and second helpings.

'Why aren't we talking about Dorothy?' I asked while Mum served the soup, an orange mixture, garnished with fresh coriander leaves.

She passed me the jug of sour cream. 'Help yourself.'

I gave the jug to Martin. 'Mum?'

'Grief is a private thing.'

I shook my head. 'We all loved her and we're here, pretending nothing's happened. You must miss her terribly. I do.' Stupid comment. If my mother already knew about the Will, the only feeling she'd have about her sister would be anger.

'Great soup,' Martin remarked, chucking me a sympathetic look.

Mum nodded. 'Thank you, dear. Organic carrots. And I soured the cream in advance. You haven't tried my rye bread – I made it especially for you. Ronald, give him a slice.'

Darkness had fallen, and from the neighbouring house we could hear the faint sound of piano music, Brahms probably. One of the candles on the sideboard had gone out, filling the air with the scent of wax, a smell still indelibly associated with Richie.

While Mum retrieved lamb, sautéed potatoes, broccoli and parsnips from the trolley, Dad opened a bottle of Cabernet Sauvignon.

'Olivia, pass me your glass, darling.'

As he poured himself a glass, Mum laid her hand on his arm. 'You know very well what the cardiologist advised, Ronald – three units a day, maximum.'

'This *is* my third,' he said.

'Cardiologist?' Martin asked.

She sprouted an uncertain expression, aware, perhaps, of having sounded harsher than intended. 'A routine blood test, nothing to worry about, but your father needs to be sensible. How many potatoes, Olivia?'

'One, please.'

I stared at my plate: three slices of lamb with glistening gravy, two potatoes, broccoli (negative amounts of carbohydrate) and parsnips – 25 calories per ounce.

Placing both hands on my lower abdomen, I concentrated on deep breathing. Inhale, exhale. And again. Once my breathing had slowed down, I visualised a garden heady with scent; lizards scrambling on warm stone walls; the hum of bees around exotic flowers. To my relief, my body was responding, breathing becoming regular. I'd tell Martin about this later – my taking control.

'How's school?' my brother asked.

Dad smiled. 'I have a few promising pupils this year. Makes all the difference.' His expression distanced, as if back in the classroom, describing a horse's bones.

'They're lucky to have you, anyway – you're so passionate about teaching,' Martin added.

Mum pursed her lips. 'If you'd applied for promotion, you'd have been Head of the Science Department now.'

Dad replaced his wine glass, rubbed the throbbing vein on his temple. 'Not this evening, Nora, please.'

'You always say that, Ronald. *Not this evening.*'

'It was eighteen years ago. I like teaching zoology. I've never wanted to manage a department.'

For a while, silence reigned. I scanned the sitting room – its varnished floorboards now covered with a thick pile carpet; the perfectly functional sash windows replaced with bland side-hung ones; the leather chairs now upholstered. More than ever, I longed for the painted floorboards and jungle of plants in my flat. A sense of life. My heart raced, my breathing became shallow. *Inhale, exhale.*

'There were so many sacrifices,' Mum continued, warming to her litany of complaints. She would load her fork with food, lift it, then replace it on the plate and deliver another rapier thrust at my poor father, before raising the fork again. Each time she lifted her fork, he'd lift his, too, his movements slow, mechanical.

She helped herself to more mint sauce. 'We could have bought a bigger house. And we'd have been spared those frightful holidays. We could have gone to Tuscany or Nice, like our friends. Instead of that ghastly hotel where–'

Dad shoved aside his plate, scratched the eczema on his arm. 'The children loved those holidays. And so did you, when we first went there.'

'We never wanted to leave Treyarnon Bay,' Martin said. 'I bet most of Cornwall is too built up now.'

A vision flashed before me of playing with my daughter on the same beaches where Dad had played with

Martin and me. I saw a bright red bucket, a yellow fishing net.

Mum sniffed. 'More lamb anyone?'

There was silence.

She frowned. 'What has happened to your appetites?'

My brother and I caught each other's eye, his expression despairing, mine sympathetic. Poor Martin, staying here. No escape when the evening ended.

'I'm having more,' Mum said, sliding open the trolley door.

Chest tight, I hurried from the dining room into the garden, to the unseasonably mild night air. There, I sat on the bench under the beech tree until my thudding decelerated. Knowing I'd exhausted my agreed hour of daily exercise helped convince me it wasn't essential to go running now, that it would be more helpful to think of something positive. Concentrate on deep breathing. As the sweet fragrance of early-flowering hyacinths reached me, I plucked one of the flowers, holding the waxy bell-shaped bloom against my skin. My breathing improved and soon I felt composed enough to return to the dinner.

After letting myself into the house again, I listened for sounds from the dining room.

'I tell you, Ronald, she'll be back in hospital again. Have you noticed how thin she's got?'

'She seems fine to me,' came his reply.

'She is fine, Mum, if you'd stay off her case,' Martin added.

When I opened the dining room door, Mum said to me, 'If I upset you, I apologise.'

'We've taken on a new jillaroo on the ranch,' Martin said. 'She's great with the cattle.'

Mum looked blank. 'Jillaroo?'

He rolled his eyes. 'A jillaroo's a trainee stockwoman. You know – jackaroo, man, jillaroo, woman? I thought you'd know this.'

'I hope Zoe's father knows how lucky he is to have a stockman of your calibre.'

'I know how lucky I am with my father-in-law.'

Dad smiled sweetly and my heart ached for him. He would make a lovely grandpa. I observed the deep lines surrounding his green eyes, the more pronounced pouches under his eyes, the lonely strands of hair straddling his scalp. My gaze then shifted to the wedding photograph on the sideboard: him in morning dress, his shoulders too narrow for the jacket, the breast pocket carnation too small for impact; my mother in cream lace and satin, and flat shoes to minimise her additional inch over him, smiling for the camera.

Mum distributed crystal glasses of chocolate mousse, offered whipped cream. When she popped through to the kitchen, Martin reached over and took a large spoonful of my pudding. I smiled my gratitude. Twelve minutes past nine.

After we'd finished, Dad busied himself with the coffee percolator, a task entrusted to him.

'Those are the wrong coffee cups, Ronald. You know very well I prefer the green set,' Mum pointed out.

'Jesus Christ!' he said so vehemently that I jumped, knocking over my glass. As the wine bled into the table-cloth, I reached for the salt cellar and poured its contents over the stain. He retrieved the green coffee cups from the sideboard.

'How's William?' I asked, abandoning my efforts with the salt, sneaking another peak at my watch. Twenty-three minutes past. Discussing my uncle might take us to a quarter to ten. Then I could leave.

Mum paused from clearing the pudding glasses. 'I've arranged for Meals on Wheels while I research care homes,' she said, her voice sharp, challenging a flurry of criticism.

Dad replaced the percolator. 'I keep pointing out – he could live here. William would hate a nursing home.'

Mum's voice went quiet. 'Don't you think I've done my share of caring for the elderly? All those years of attending to Mother, when Dorothy was gallivanting round the world. No-one appreciates my sacrifices.'

'Even so, Nora, I think William should live here, or have help at home – someone checking on him several times a day, Meals on Wheels, too. Or he could move to supported accommodation, have his own flat.'

Martin left the table. In the gathering wind, trees were swaying, our childhood swing clanging against its frame. Then the strains of Faure's *Requiem* drifted into the dining room, a stream of soothing sound. My brother returned with a large box of mint chocolates. Mum filled and refilled coffee cups. We laughed when Martin recounted stories about a disastrous ranch hand his father-in-law had employed. Even Mum's lips twitched. Now my stomach no longer churned. Furthermore, I hadn't needed to vomit, or take refuge in running. Hilary would be impressed.

'There's an interesting documentary on television,' Mum announced. 'Then you can open your presents.'

In the sitting room, I kicked off my shoes and curled my legs under me, ready to watch the programme about Zimbabwean wildlife. Martin produced his pouch of Drum, teasing and twisting strands of tobacco. Having disappeared for ten minutes, Dad returned, seemingly more relaxed.

For an hour or so, our attention focused on lumbering

elephants, elegant flamingos and peachy red sunsets. The chocolates did many rounds.

Five minutes after the documentary finished, Mum appeared with a trolley bearing Madeira cake and tea things, and I noticed Dad's wary expression. As she moved her arm, the silver blade of the cake knife glinted like sheet lightning.

'By the way, Olivia, you'll be receiving a letter from Dorothy's lawyer,' she declared.

Fingers of icy steel gripped my stomach.

She handed me a slab of cake. 'I am contesting the Will.'

5

L ater, back at my flat in Sussex Lane, I sank onto the sofa and kicked off my shoes. Mum could at least have discussed with me her upset over the Will? Attempted a compromise. How could she prioritise money over our relationship? Risk bad publicity? Headlines flashed before me: *Mother contests daughter's legacy*. And the gutter press would be less merciful: *Mum's dash for cash; Cash thicker than blood.*

When the doorbell rang, I trudged through to the hall. Mrs Driscoll, the widow across the stair, clutched a letter.

'Sorry, luv, opened this by mistake – half-asleep when it arrived.'

'Don't worry,' I said, taking the white envelope. 'Did you sort your boiler problem?'

'Had to get a new one. No summer holiday this year, now. Sorry about the letter.'

In the kitchen, I studied the white envelope with its green WMD logo. Mr Minto's letter explained that my mother's challenging the Will was due to an earlier version having named William and her as principal beneficiaries, and her conviction of Dorothy's confusion when she changed it. Despite his view of Dorothy's lucidness when she dictated the letter prior to her stroke, her GP was required to express an opinion as she'd seen him that day. The lawyer ended by conveying his sympathy about my distressing family situation, pointing out that if my mother understood the circumstances, she might reconsider her stance.

So Mum *was* serious.

I removed my damp clothes and showered, lingering under the hot water. She could have the money. If I didn't search for my child, I didn't deserve the inheritance. While changing into comfy nightwear, I turned on the radio, to hear the presenter say, 'More and more adopted children are searching for their birth parents once they reach adulthood.' I changed station but the words lingered, pursuing me round the flat as I did dishes, put on a wash, cleaned the kitchen floor. One day my daughter might be pursuing the truth – hurt, bewildered, determined.

Martin was right – I must find her.

I drew the sitting room curtains, switched on the gas fire, and starting compiling places to search on my laptop: UK universities, those in other English-speaking countries, countries and areas where French was spoken. His home. London teaching hospitals. Already I regretted the time I'd wasted since learning of my child's existence, berated myself for my indecision, my lack of spirit.

As I sipped my coffee, reality hit. To travel far I'd need loads of money. Furthermore, such a search could take years, and if successful, might involve legal action. If Mum won her challenge I'd be far more restricted in what I could do.

MARTIN WAS SEATED at a corner table in the pub when I arrived, a newspaper propped on his scarf and gloves, a gin and tonic surrounded by a garland of cashew nut packets. So like old times, before he met Zoë and moved to the other side of the world.

'I hate Sundays,' he said. 'You've changed your mind, haven't you?'

'She's my daughter!'

'Good call.'

'You think so? It'll be even more difficult... with Nora challenging the Will. I can't believe she's done this.'

He shook his head so vigorously that his hair appeared windswept. 'She can't possibly win. The lawyer would have known if Dorothy was loopy.'

'Yeah?' I so wanted to believe my twin. Only a few days had elapsed since taking my monumental decision, but it felt like I'd been on this track for weeks.

'Yeah, Liv. Definitely. Anyway, if you run out of money, I'll help. And if I get stuck, I can always borrow from Zoë's Dad.'

'This would make it so public.'

'You sound like Nora,' he said, laughing. 'What *would* the neighbours think, Ronald?'

'I wonder if I should tell her why I was left the money. I'm sure she's still angry about Dorothy helping me buy my flat, and now this.'

He grabbed a handful of nuts. 'Dorothy chose to pay the deposit. Anyway, it might not make any difference if you explain about the Will.'

'How could Ritchie deceive me like this, how could he do it?'

'I know, I know. A crap thing to do.'

'It's all I can think about, Marti. What she looks like, the sound of her voice.'

It wasn't all, though. Guilt at abandoning her, expecting her to die, consumed me. My unworthiness to be a mother.

Martin rolled a cigarette. 'How's the eating?'

'Hilary's been brilliant. It's weird, but perhaps the news about my child brought on the relapse, and focusing on finding her now, has helped me get over it completely. Fingers crossed.'

He pointed at my glass. 'Do you want another?'

'I've been through the UK uni websites,' I said when he returned with the drinks. 'And I tried my old university – he doesn't work there anymore and no one seems to know where he moved to. God, it's so cold... I can't believe it's April. And I have to try the hospitals. Richie might not be teaching biochemistry now – maybe I need to try different faculties. And he might be in France, or anywhere they speak English or French. It's so overwhelming, I mean–'

'He's bilingual?'

'His mother is Parisian.'

'What about LinkedIn and Twitter?' He glanced at the pub wall advertising free Wifi. 'I've got my iPad. We'll do it now.' Seeing my hesitation, he added, 'Why not? Are you afraid of not finding her or afraid of finding her?'

I didn't know.

The snooker on the telly portrayed deeply tanned faces and a garishly green tablecloth, and I wondered why no one adjusted the colour.

I studied my brother, admiring his "get on with it" approach, the gene I hadn't inherited.

'Richie's wife couldn't have children – did I tell you? She had loads of miscarriages.'

Martin produced an iPad from his backpack, 'Zoë's had one – last month.'

I stared at him, now understanding his recent demeanour. 'Why didn't you tell me before? And you've been listening to all my stuff.'

He removed his specs, peered at them and straightened one of the arms. 'It was early on – about eight weeks.'

'Even so...' I broke off, remembering my ambivalence around this time in my pregnancy, rebuking myself now for not welcoming the situation wholeheartedly, despite the circumstances.

Perhaps I didn't deserve to find my little girl.

'She's okay, I think,' he said, scratching his hair. 'I wouldn't have come over, otherwise. Don't say anything to Mum and Dad. Anyway, you must be systematic in your search for Richie.'

'Tell Zoë I'm so sorry.'

He examined a loose thread in his jeans. 'She keeps telling me to stop smoking. I know she's right.'

We were silent.

'Anyway, Richie,' he eventually said, switching on his iPad, logging into LinkedIn. 'What's his full name? There'll be hundreds of Richard Williams.'

'Richard P – God, I don't even know what the "P" stands for... Richard P. Williams.'

Martin scrolled through a list. 'There are at least 30 here: 20 in the UK. An architect, a screenwriter, retired minister etc. etc. No doctors.'

'Try the ones in the States.'

As he did this, I wondered why he continued to smoke, when knowing of the dangers in pregnancy. Likewise, I forced myself to admit, if I'd behaved more positively, courageously, at that faraway hospital, how different the outcome could have been.

Maybe we were all born to self-sabotage.

'No one,' he said.

'I've been putting off trying his home. Not quite ready.'

'He wouldn't be stupid enough to stay there. You need a lawyer.'

Martin now wore his determined expression and I pictured him in cowboy boots and hat, herding cattle, dust swirling under an azure sky.

'I'm seeing Mr Minto about the Will.'

'Hire a private detective.'

I laughed. 'Yeah right – a man in a raincoat, hovering, a damp cigarette hanging from his mouth, a half-eaten ham roll in his brief case... She'll be five and a half.'

'You've been watching too many black and white movies. I'll try Twitter... You know I've never actually understood the appeal of Twitter. You don't tweet do you, Liv?'

'I tried but I couldn't take it seriously. Remember when I had the terrible cough?'

He laughed. 'You paid a fortune for a disgusting treacly Chinese brew.'

'I tweeted about spending the day in bed watching Dorothy's Downton Abbey DVDs and eating jam sandwiches. I closed my account after. It was frothy, even by my standards.'

He looked up. 'There's no one here called Richard Williams who fits his description. I'll try Facebook.'

'Leave it for now.'

Patrons were leaving and the barmaid was wiping the evening's special courses from the blackboard. I thought of my empty flat.

Martin inhaled deeply from his roll-up. 'Will you tell

Dad?'

I shook my head. 'Not fair to him, to keep that from Nora.'

'You know she's found a care home for William? Poor old sod.'

'She can't take over his life.'

'Bollocks,' he said, running his fingers through his hair. 'She hardly does anything else. She couldn't even trust us to learn enough at school. Remember the maths coach? What a waste. I will always be a wally at maths, anyway.'

'At least you didn't have mock interviews for med school.'

Into my mind floated the memory of Nora at the dining room table, firing questions about my motivation to become a doctor, the brass buttons of her chunky cardigan gleaming in the overhead light.

Martin was studying me. 'Does James know what's happened?'

'He wouldn't understand.'

'For God's sake, Liv, if you can't talk to him about this, why don't you dump him?'

'Should be getting back,' I muttered.

'Do you know why you stay with him?'

'Because he's a demon on the dance floor and he can be kind. He cares about me more than he realises, I know he does.'

Martin rolled his eyes. 'He's a control freak. Fast-forward four years. Can you see yourself with him, still?'

'I don't want to turn out like Nora. Making a man miserable... You'll be gone in four days.'

'Why don't I stay at yours 'til then? I can help you make a plan. It would be easier returning to Oz if I knew you had one.'

He looked appealingly at me and I remembered his sadness over Zoë's miscarriage.

'You'd trade the luxury of East Greenwich for my sofa?'

YELLOW ORANGE LIGHT from street lamps hardly penetrated the fog that had hovered all day and bestowed a spookiness on the evening. Across the road, 32 Portman Terrace lay in darkness, curtainless windows revealing no signs of activity. It was nine o'clock. I buttoned my jacket, abandoned the flask of bland tomato soup, and switched on my iPod. Another half-hour then I'd call it a night.

As I was dozing off, a taxi stopped on the other side of the street and a plump woman in her thirties emerged, followed by a girl of about nine. Seconds later, the ground floor of the Victorian terraced house filled with light, and shortly after, lights emerged on the upper floor. My heart pounded while I deliberated. It was mid-week, during the school term, too late to knock on the door. At least I now knew who occupied the house.

And it wasn't Richie.

When I returned to Portman Terrace the following afternoon, the house was awash in sunlight, the stone building soft and welcoming. In jeans and sweatshirt, the woman who answered the doorbell seemed younger today. An aroma of homemade bread wafted through the hall.

'We've just been here four months,' she told me.

'You didn't buy this house from a Dr Williams?'

'No. Watkins – I think. He'd died. His daughter was selling it. But we never met her. The sale was carried out through the estate agents and lawyers.'

'Do you have an address for her?'

The woman tilted her head. 'What's this about?'

'Sorry, I should have explained. I'm trying to get in touch with this Dr Williams. It's important.'

'The person who sold the house lives in Scotland. The agency would know – I've got their business card. Come on in – it's freezing, despite the sun. I'm Kate, by the way.'

I followed her, wrestling a surreal sensation. This had been Richie's home, and my child would have lived here, even briefly, while he made plans. Anger flared as I surveyed the hall with its chest of drawers, its coat rack and umbrella stand. He had no right, no bloody right, to do what he'd done.

'Here it is,' Kate said, handing me the card. 'I've just made tea. Do you want a cup?'

I hesitated.

'Come through, please.'

A large oilskin covered table dominated the kitchen. The burgundy Aga added cosiness, and the large green-framed railway clock on the wall emitted a loud and strangely reassuring tick.

She removed a bundle of papers from the table. 'Excuse the mess. Do you like homemade bread? I could make us a sandwich.'

Again, I hesitated, but the smell of fresh bread was too much to resist, further evidence of my improvement.

'One slice, please. Are you always so kind to strangers knocking on your door?'

Skirting the kitchen, was a garden with a swing, a rabbit hutch, a child's bike with muddy wheels, and a vegetable patch. Richie and Alice would have purchased this house with a family in mind. I tried to find sympathy for Alice, for what she'd been through, but at least she'd had five years of raising my child.

Kate smiled. 'I'm a single parent. I adore Sophie, but occasionally I crave adult conversation... Ham and cucumber okay?'

Such unexpected hospitality triggered a surge of emotion, and I blurted out my story. Kate's keen attention made me even more emotional.

'You must do everything you can to find your child,' she said, when I'd finished, and it was then I noticed her stroking a cuddly elephant.

I bit into the sandwich, sipped my tea. We chatted about London, the approaching Olympic Games and Sophie's desperation to watch the athletics. Sheets twirled on the washing line.

An hour later, Kate stood. 'I need to collect Sophie from school.'

Reluctantly I left the comfy chair, the homely kitchen. 'Sorry I've taken so much of your time. Thanks for being so kind.'

'Do you want a lift? I go past the agency.'

'I need time to think.'

She hugged me. 'Hope you find Dr Williams and your daughter.'

I strolled along the road to the tube station, invigorated by the bracing wind and clouds whisking across the sky. Kate's hospitality had restored my belief in people.

IN THE GREEK RESTAURANT, I surveyed the posters of the acropolis in Athens, the whitewashed houses of Mykonos. Waiters wove between tables, bearing plates of stuffed vine leaves and lamb stew, the aroma of cinnamon, dill and cloves pungent, making me hungry. When catching sight of my reflection on a large wall mirror, I didn't cringe. I *was* recovering.

From my bag I retrieved Roz's Christmas present, *Men – do we really need them?* I ran my fingers through the first two chapters, curling a few pages, creasing one, so that it seemed less pristine, less unread.

'Sorry, sorry,' Roz gasped as she reached the table and threw off her jacket, emitting a waft of Lacoste *Femme*, her trademark perfume. 'You do *not* want to know what happened... You look nice... Have you ordered?'

As she freed her hair from its scrunchie, she noticed the book. 'Ah, finally you're reading it... Lawdy, what a day. Did Martin get off all right yesterday?'

'I hated saying goodbye at the airport. Even more than when he first left.'

'Wish I had a twin. The estate agent wasn't much help, after all?'

'The current owner bought the house from someone who sold it on behalf of her father and wasn't involved in buying it. I've tried her number four times and no luck.'

Roz sipped her water. 'It's unlikely she could help, I reckon. What about Richie's friends? I'm so glad you agreed to a meal, by the way.'

'I *am* better, but I'll stick to one course.'

'Sure, sure. Richie's friends?'

'Didn't meet anyone. Besides, they all knew Alice, so...'

And yet, Richie had assured me his wife didn't bother about his affairs. That she valued her independence.

Familiar Greek music now wafted from the bar. Roz and I rolled our eyes. 'Remember Mykonos?' I asked, and we sank like soufflés with laughter. 'Kefi in Ketavia,' we sang repeatedly, before collapsing again.

Roz sighed. 'All those gay men – some of them were at least bi, the way they eyed us on the beach.'

'Eyed you, you mean. Most bikinis aren't quite so lacking in fabric.'

'Can't wear anything like that now. Never know when we might bump into a parishioner.'

No one had been more gobsmacked than me when Roz fell in love with a man of the cloth. When she didn't mind opening parish jumble sales or organising tea parties for church wives. Provided she could work as a doctor, retain a professional identity, she was happy to do her bit to support Brian. Although I didn't envy my friend her happiness, I often wondered if I'd find as compatible a partner. I also wondered why she continued to be so interested in problem relationships, if she didn't quite trust her chances of remaining happily married.

'What about Richie's colleagues?' she asked. 'Earth to Olivia? Hallo?'

'I tried the university – couldn't find anything.'

'I assume you've been to the police, and of course there are Missing Person Charities–'

'Been there, got the t-shirt,' I said, surprised by my light-hearted tone. All the laughing, I supposed. It had always intrigued me that the body produces different chemicals in tears of laughter than it does in those of grief.

I returned my attention to Roz, who was wearing her "tell me more" expression. 'But according to them, Richie can't be described as "missing" because he's an adult and it's unlikely he didn't choose to go wherever he's gone. Which rules out Missing Persons' Charities, too.'

She helped herself to more pitta bread. 'What about the Electoral Roll – but I've a feeling people can opt out of being in the full list – which is the only one you can buy. Have you tried the golf club?'

'He was captain when I knew him.'

And how proud he'd been. A handicap of two at the age of sixteen – no mean achievement, especially when hailing from a family without the wherewithal for luxuries.

'There'll be photos, Liv – they might give you a clue. Brian's praying for you every night, by the way.'

'I wish I believed.'

She reached for my hand, gripped it hard. 'Try the golf club. These guys talk to each other in the bar afterwards. How about a wine bar after we're finished here?'

I nodded, surprised by how much I'd enjoyed the meal, unsurprised by Roz' ability to lift my spirits.

As I GAZED at an expanse of meticulously cut grass, the smell catapulted me back to childhood, listening to the gentle whirring noise when Dad strolled the garden with his hand lawn mower. He would wash blades of grass, blot them dry with paper towels and show me how to whistle, pulling the blade tight to form a reed and blowing through the hole.

I felt weary. There was zilch to show for trawling through websites after a demanding shift at The Grange, and with Martin gone, Roz remained my sole face-to-face confidante. And Dr Barak. Not that there was much exploratory work filling our sessions. For once, I was clear: I must find my daughter, I must find Richie.

'Ladies' hours don't start until three,' a man in a royal blue Pringle jumper informed me.

'I'm trying to find work. Can you let me in please?'

He frowned. 'Women aren't allowed in this part of the clubhouse.'

'I need to speak to the barman – please?'

He opened the door. 'Upstairs, on the left.'

Once the man was out of sight, I descended the stairs and advanced along the corridor, peering at photographs. There was Richie in the middle of the front row. 2005. Again in 2006, his hair shorter. The 2007 photo was missing, the 2008 one revealed a different captain. As the customary ache for him surfaced, I visualised it evaporating, like a handprint on a steamy window.

'Can we help you?' a voice asked.

I turned to see two younger men – no Pringle jumpers, no checked trousers. 'I'm trying to get in to touch with Richie Williams. He was captain.'

'He left,' one of the men told me. 'When, Dave?'

Dave considered. 'Four years ago? Perhaps longer. It was sudden. Who are you?'

'A friend.'

'Try Eddie Caldwell,' the first man said. 'He's on the eighteenth green. Should be finished any minute. But be inconspicuous.'

'I know. Too early for ladies' play.'

Outside, chiffon clouds whizzed across the sky and the smell of manure drifted over from a nearby field.

'I did see Richie again,' Eddie said. 'On Oxford Street. His wife was pushing a buggy. Didn't even know he had a sprog. My lass was pregnant and he was around when I talked about being chuffed to become a father. Never said anything and–'

'When was this?'

'When? Daniel was born in November 2006. It would be shortly before then. Who did you say you are?'

'Colleague – ex colleague. He left the department suddenly and...'

Eddie scratched his nose. 'He was going abroad. France – to work in France.'

'You're sure?'

'I was so flummoxed about the baby... Yes, it was France, definitely France. A town beginning with P, I think. Not Paris, I'd have remembered if it was Paris. We had our honeymoon there... Is he in trouble?'

Eddie's close-set eyes were hungry for gossip. Something to share with his golfing buddies while they downed their post-match beers.

'We were working on a project.'

'You're a researcher then?'

I took a deep breath. 'Yes. Please try to think where he was going. It's important.'

The distant hills beckoned. It would be lovely to amble there in such beautiful afternoon light. Perhaps I should text James, cancel this evening.

'It was in the south, I think – he said it would be hot. Think it might have been Perpignan...' Eddie paused, then continued, voice raised in excitement. 'Near mountains. Near the Spanish border. How about a drink? I might remember more.'

'Women aren't allowed in the bar.'

He eyed me like I was a fish slipping off a hook. 'There's a pub across the road.'

'Can you think of anything else?'

'He said he might go to Canada afterwards. I don't think it was a permanent job. He was thinking about when it finished. Try Perpignan.'

'Perpignan, Perpignan,' I hummed as I left the golf club. Finally, progress. I'd go to France. I'd go to Perpignan.

6

When there was no reply from James's apartment, I realised there'd be time to intercept Dad on his way to choir practice. I'd been grateful for Mum's wisdom tooth extraction, and – God forgive me – for the complication requiring post-operative treatment, allowing him and me three precious days together. Mum was home again and it would be lovely to see him once more on his own.

I recalled my rush of emotion on discovering him in a Bovril oilskin apron, frying sausages and mushrooms, humming *Once in Royal David's City*. Despite it being out of season. Still remembered the glorious sound of his choir rehearsing Brahms' *Requiem,* drinking Dubonnet with him afterwards at the pub. We'd even managed to inject some fun into the frantic vacuuming and dusting, and disposal of convenience food containers before Mum's return.

On the point of leaving, I heard the front door to James's building click open. When I entered his flat, no smell of cooking wafted from the kitchen, which meant a takeaway, and, fingers crossed, Indian – yum.

I dumped my jacket on his hall chair. 'So, what have you ordered? Nepalese or Indian?'

'I've eaten,' James said.

'You invited me for dinner.'

He frowned. 'Did I? Oh... I could make you a toastie.'

'How can you forget you've invited someone to dinner?' I asked.

'I didn't realise you were serious about France,' he said, scraping off some white bits from the cheddar. 'You didn't even ask my opinion. Most people would think you're flaky, leaving your job to go travelling. Personally, I think it's nonsense.'

'Nonsense?'

'And where do I fit into all this, Livvy? Am I permitted to visit you?'

'Would you want to?'

'I have to say I'm surprised you've chosen to put your travels before us.'

'Us? What exactly is "us"? James, this is more off/on than a tap. Besides, you always introduce me as a "friend". It's been five years. Don't you think we're a bit stuck?'

'We see each other regularly and–'

'Nick and Annabel moved in together after six months, Ingrid and Tom got engaged after a year. You haven't even introduced me to your mother and you won't meet my parents.'

'Do you want the cheese sliced or grated?' He rummaged in the cutlery drawer. 'It'll have to be grated. The slicer's gone.'

'I bet you introduced her to Charlotte.'

He laid grated cheese on the toast and placed it under the grill. 'She knew Charlotte's aunt.'

'Yeah, right. And that's the only reason? James, does your mother know I exist?'

'I've mentioned you.'

The kitchen was closing in. On such a beautiful evening, I wanted to find a green space, or even a square, listen to African drumming, or musicians playing panpipes. I needed to smell the recently moistened earth, the spring-flowering bushes, perhaps buy a bag of samosas.

What I wanted most was space to daydream about being with my child.

I bit into the toasted cheese. 'C'mon, let's go out.'

'Actually, I have work to do.'

'I'll watch telly while you're working, then we can go for a walk, or dancing, the new club – you remember, Annabelle recommended it.'

'I'm tired.'

'So, why *did* you invite me round?'

His face contorted, then he turned away. 'Now look here, Livvy, if this is how you're going to be, you might as well leave. I have an important meeting tomorrow and the last thing I need is you rattling me.'

He left the kitchen, banging the door. After several moments, I found him in the sitting room, seated in the tattered leather armchair, face obscured by the *Guardian,* right hand squeezing a putty ball the physio had given him for tennis elbow.

'James?'

'Do your gallivanting. But don't expect me to be waiting for you to return.'

'Can't we at least talk about this?'

'Just go. But I want my *Wind in the Willows* back, and my salsa CDs. All of them.'

It was an unusually warm June morning when I stepped out of the taxi at St Pancras International. Meringue clouds whirled through the blue sky, trees, swathed in green, swayed in the breeze. As I paused to absorb my surroundings one last time before entering the station, a group of Japanese tourists laden with bulky cameras and Harrods' bags jostled me, interrupting my reflections.

I approached the Eurostar terminal, fed my ticket to the machine and glanced at the station clock. Not long to go. Until I'd tried everything to find my daughter, I would be in limbo. While studying the passenger lounge – suited people speaking earnestly into mobile phones; the huddle of Ashkenazi Jews with their thick beards, side curls and wide-brimmed fedora hats – I willed the clock to move faster.

Nearby, a twenty-something woman in flouncy skirt and gold pumps rushed over to a man and kissed him, his arms hovering restlessly on her tanned waist, as though such restraint was intolerable. I fingered the softness of my new leather jacket and smiled – the autumnal brown suited me. Dad's treat.

On the train, I stared unseeingly at my book, doubts resurfacing. Had I tried hard enough in the UK? What if the golf club bloke was mistaken and Richie hadn't gone to Perpignan? Did I have enough resilience to cope with what lay ahead? What if my money ran out? The questions continued, an unending conveyor belt of things I couldn't answer. It was one thing hearing Mr Minto's optimism about my inheritance being safe, another when I'd resigned from my job. Yet another when I'd realised that renting out my flat would barely cover the mortgage. Should Mum win her contest, I'd be reliant on my savings.

Nearly noon. James would be finished at the partners' meeting.

He answered his phone immediately. 'I knew you wouldn't go. You see, I know you better than you know yourself, Livvy. Now, tonight's busy but tomorrow we'll–'

I hung up, increasingly eager to be away.

Sunshine flooded my hotel bedroom the following morning. In the courtyard, a whooshing fountain gently reminded me of another day in full swing. Further away, my eyes focused on a vista of mossy pantile roofs, and beyond those, a backdrop of purple mountains, already hazy in the Mediterranean light. Something about the view threw me back to my self-imposed exile in Morocco, and several moments elapsed before I returned to the present.

As I walked through the university campus, I searched for Richie. Although it was officially the summer holidays, he might be here, writing lectures for the following semester or catching up with paperwork. Despite months of envisaging such a moment, however, I still had little idea of what to say if I did find him. In despairing moments, I imagined him running away. My giving chase. In optimistic mode, I heard myself assuring him I didn't want unpleasantness, simply access to my daughter. But how would I begin such a conversation? What if he denied knowing me? He'd been prepared to conceal our daughter's existence from me indefinitely. What else might he be driven to do?

'Yes. Docteur Williams was working here but he now not work here,' the university registrar, a tall, stick insect of a woman, informed me.

'When was this?'

She delved into a filing cabinet, produced a folder. 'Ah. Yes, he was here, but it was for small time – *un contrat à durée déterminée*, a fixed-term contract. He was here for two years only.'

'So, do you know where he went when he left, Madame?' I asked, removing my cardigan, noticing the unused fan in the corner of the room.

'Mademoiselle Croix. We have not this information. Why are you wanting to know this, please?'

'I am a... I'm a friend.'

She drew the window blind. 'This room, it is too hot at the summer and the fan, it does not work since yesterday.' Her brown blouse clung to her.

'It's important I find out where Dr Williams is.'

'*Je suis vraiment desolée*. I'm really sorry.'

I wiped my forehead. 'Would anyone else know? Can anyone give me information? Did you meet his wife?'

'His wife?'

'Or his... his child?'

'Why do you ask these questions?' she said, eyes narrowing, hand reaching for the phone.

I placed my hand on her bony arm. 'Please don't... Could we sit down, please, and I'll explain.'

She removed her hairband, freeing her straight hair, softening her face. 'Please explain me why you come here at the university.'

'Dr Williams has my daughter. Our daughter.'

'I do not understand. Please explain me the situation. Why is he having your daughter?'

'I thought the baby died at birth, she didn't, the hospital couldn't find me – they found him, the father. He... he collected the baby from Morocco.'

Mademoiselle Croix's eyes widened. 'Morocco? You have baby in Morocco?'

I nodded. Like a computer crashing, the energy left me.

'*C'est bizarre ça*. That is weird. He keep the baby? You have seen this baby never, your daughter?'

I retrieved my inhaler, puffed it into my mouth and leaned back on the chair.

'*Mon dieu*! My God! It is a wicked thing. *Alors*... perhaps it is possible I help you. There is here a person who knows maybe where Dr Williams go after he leave. I see if it is possible for you to speak with him.'

'Thanks. I...'

I swayed.

She opened a door behind a black lacquered screen. 'You are ill. Please, you lie here.'

'Can you speak to this person now? Please?'

She wrenched the window up several inches, allowing a trickle of air to drift in my direction. Immediately I revived. From outside came a faint hum of traffic, nearer by, a chorus of voices – a summer school class had finished. Such evidence of normality helped.

She spoke in rapid French on the phone, then finished and turned to me, voice keen with desire to help. 'Dr Hunckler, he not here today. But I think it is possible to speak with you tomorrow – at twelve o'clock. If you prefer, you come first here in my office then I go with you in his office and I wait while you are speaking with him.'

'That would be great. Thank you so much.'

The campus clock struck one-fifteen when I left the grounds. Twenty-three hours before gleaning more about Richie, twenty-three long hours, with no certainty of learning anything else. A current of loneliness ran through me. My chest ached from yearning.

As I wandered around the citadel south of the old part of Perpignan, my feet halted by a bronze sculpture of a woman with an infant pressed to her collarbone. The mother was kneeling, her upper body bare, the cloth draped loosely over her legs, stopping mid-thigh. Her tightly braided hair was scraped off her face. One arm supported the baby's shoulder, the other, its feet and her expression conveyed both tranquillity and contemplation.

Later, calm and mellow from crying, a splint on the cracked part of my heart, I left my hotel room. Despite intending to walk in a nearby park, I found myself meandering by the shady tree-lined canal in Perpignan, until the sun set and rose light suffused the sky. I then made my way to a street of restaurants and twenty minutes later was presented with couscous and a carafe of Valdepenas. Fingers crossed, Dr Hunckler would have more information.

LOOMING OVER HIS DESK, Dr Hunckler seemed too big for his office, and an absence of paintings, plants or family photos, suggested a personality devoted solely to work. But his smile was genuine, his dark eyes conveying both warmth and sympathy.

'I have spoken with Mademoiselle Croix this morning,' he told me. 'She has explained me your situation.'

'Do you know where Dr Williams went when he left? Any information might help. I mean, did he return to England, did he go to another city in France?'

'He talks about Canada. He told to me that he has friends in Montreal.'

'He was always ambitious,' I said. 'Plenty of opportunities in Canada, of course.'

Dr Hunkler and Mademoiselle Croix exchanged looks.

'Is there anyone else, any other colleagues who might know more? Did you meet his wife? His child – my daughter?'

Before he spoke, I knew his answer. He shook his head. 'I did not know him much. He worked here for two years only.'

So Richie had left nearly four years ago. Four years. Only now did I become aware of how much hope I'd attached to talking with Dr Hunckler, how narrow the range between unmerited optimism and spirit-draining realism.

'You believe me, you believe my story?' I asked, standing.

He nodded. 'People do not lie about important things. I hope that you will be successful to find your daughter.'

I reached into my bag for my personal cards, handed one to him, another to Mademoiselle Croix. 'Please get in touch if you can remember anything else... Anything, right?'

Again, I experienced the aching place in my heart, where the need to be a mother had lodged.

While walking through the campus grounds, my phone went.

'How's it going?' Roz asked.

I updated her, each word heavy on my tongue.

From the end of the phone came the tinkle of glasses. 'What will you do now?'

'Return to London tomorrow, see what's happened with the Will, then head off to Canada... Are you in the pub?'

Silence, then she said, 'Canada's huge.'

'I know.' I dug deep for energy to feign pleasure. 'It's great to hear your voice. How's Brian?'

'Guess where we are... Menton. Brian's brother and sister-in-law have rented a villa. Come and see us. A few days won't make a difference.'

THE DOUBLE-DECKER TGV hurtled along the coast to Menton, past crowded but characterless beaches, palm trees, purple and deep pink bougainvillea, salmon and ochre coloured houses. I felt myself relax. The compartment was air-conditioned and quiet: no beeping mobile phones, hissing headphones, not even too many announcements from the guard. Intermittently I could smell lavender, when the train stopped and its doors opened.

When we pulled into Nice, I studied the frenzy of passengers on the platform – Friday evening commuters returning to coastal towns. Suddenly my eyes homed in on a man boarding the train on the opposite platform. A few seconds elapsed before I realised. I yanked down the window.

'Richie!' I yelled, at the moment my train moved off.

ix years earlier

S The January morning glistens with frost and there's an exhilarating bite to the air. Sauntering to work, Olivia savours the previous night with Richie – she's never experienced so much intensity, never felt so overwhelmed by passion that she was almost relieved when he left, fearful of doing or saying anything to spoil the mood. Afterwards, she'd lain in bed gazing at the honey-scented pink cyclamen: his gift.

As she walks, she is conscious of searching for someone to smile at. Of tolerating normal irritations – people bumping into her, gratuitous car honking. Despite having already breakfasted, she treats herself to an onion bagel with cream cheese.

This is the second week of her community placement – a health centre decorated in relaxing pastel greens and blues. Feng Shui input. The GPs are friendly, the health visitors and practice nurses happy for her to observe their clinics. Perform simple tasks like weighing patients, taking blood pressure, testing urine for diabetes.

So far, she has sat in with three GPs to observe different consultation styles. Today and tomorrow, she is working with the senior partner, Dr Fraser, whose patients, rather than be treated by another doctor, choose to wait two weeks for an appointment with him. She loves his room – its avocado plants framing the window; the yellow and orange geometric Paul Klee prints contrasting with apple green walls.

'I'll introduce you as a fourth-year medical student, and ask if it's okay, your being here,' he explains.

Two hours rush past. A young man presents with tonsillitis, who Dr Fraser permits her to examine. She reports the existence of white spots in his throat, indicating a streptococcus infection, and recommends a broad-spectrum antibiotic. An accounting student requires more time: contraception is destroying her libido. He studies the case notes, further probes her medical history, and prescribes a different pill, suggesting if this one doesn't suit, she might wish to consider other methods of contraception. Olivia is thankful she herself can manage on a low dose pill. That reduced libido is a nonissue. An overweight middle-aged woman experiences constant fatigue, several people complain of diarrhoea and vomiting, and a patient with an immunoglobulin deficiency believes his monthly injections aren't helping.

Being listened to is affirming. Furthermore, all the patients have addressed her, as well as Dr Fraser, while discussing symptoms and asking questions. She likes the fact that, in most cases, GPs can help immediately – advice, reassurance, a prescription. Instead of paediatrics, she wonders about specialising in general practice.

At eleven o'clock, a female receptionist appears with coffee and Jaffa cakes. 'I haven't been off the phone because

of the diarrhoea and vomiting bug. All the emergency
appointments have been taken.'

Dr Fraser scrutinises his diary. 'I'll extend the afternoon
surgery by half an hour. See if Maria and Alison can do the
same.'

After coffee, he reads the case notes of the next patient.
'This lady is nine weeks pregnant, with a history of miscar-
rying,' he tells Olivia. 'If it were more straightforward, I
would get you to examine her abdomen, but she is anxious,
understandably, so I should conduct the consultation.'

Olivia swallows her second Jaffa cake, aware she herself
wouldn't want an inexperienced medical student involved.
Even for the simplest aspects of her pregnancy care.

'Could I nip to the loo?'

'Yes. But I'll call her in. Don't want to get behind.'

When Olivia returns, the patient is lying on the couch.

'Everything seems fine,' Dr Fraser says. 'Have you a date
for the booking-in clinic?'

'Next Wednesday... Would you take my blood pressure?'

'Certainly. You've had high blood pressure before.' He
lifts the sphygmomanometer from his desk. 'Try to relax.
Easy for me to say, I know.' The woman smiles, inhales
deeply.

'Are you working?' he asks, wrapping the pressure cuff
round her arm.

'I've reduced my hours. I'm doing two short days a week.'

He inflates the cuff, checks the reading. 'There's nothing
to worry about with your blood pressure. But make sure you
don't gain too much weight.'

The woman's face clouds.

'What is it?'

'I'll leave,' Olivia offers.

'You don't need to. I know everything is confidential... My husband is glad I'm pregnant, of course. We've always had – not exactly an open relationship, but from time to time he... the flings never last long and I haven't minded too much. But now it matters.'

'Have you told him how you feel?' Dr Fraser asks.

'He's always busy. What with work and... other things.'

'He's based at University College Hospital, is that right?'

She shakes her head. 'Not any more. No, Richie's lecturing in biochemistry and he's much happier now. Better suited to theory than practice, he says.'

Olivia grabs the sides of her chair. Richie! It must be her Richie. Oh God!

Dr Fraser replaces the sphygmomanometer in its box. 'Do you think Richie is involved with someone at the moment?'

The woman sighs heavily. 'I'm not sure.'

'I could prescribe a small dose of imipramine for your anxiety. It won't harm the baby.'

'I think I should take it.'

Olivia excuses herself, stumbles to the loo where she retches in the basin. She's never asked Richie if his marriage still includes sex. However, it's one thing him sleeping with Alice, another that she is pregnant. Yet another meeting her, witnessing such anxiety.

She has no choice but to end this affair.

'Thank you for leaving,' Dr Fraser says, when she returns to his consulting room. 'Poor woman, she is in a state. I wish I could tell her husband to get his act together. The stress could jeopardise her pregnancy, and he should know this, being a doctor. But I'm not his GP, and even if I was, I couldn't breach patient confidentiality.'

After the afternoon surgery, Olivia flags a taxi. At home, she texts Richie, asking him to call. He doesn't.

That evening, she drives to his house, waits on the other side of the street, pondering whether to phone his landline. She even considers ringing the doorbell. But this would be crazy, not least of all because Alice might answer. Eventually a black Peugeot pulls up and his wife emerges but he remains seated. As Olivia is about to get out of her car, however, Alice wheels round, calls to her husband. Cold, and consumed with self–disgust, Olivia goes home.

'You were quiet yesterday afternoon,' Dr Fraser comments the next morning. Olivia hesitates, part of her wanting to confide in him. Professional suicide.

'Was it Mrs Williams? The situation with her husband? Horrible place to be.'

Olivia gulps. 'Is there anything you can do?'

'If her husband were my patient, I could suggest he talks to his wife about anything which is bothering her. But no more than that. It's the same for priests. The impossible Code of Canon Law. One of the most difficult things about medicine, especially general practice, is to acquire the right balance of detachment and involvement. Too detached... well, you appear to be cold and disinterested. Too much involvement, and it's impossible to remain objective and you might miss something important.' Dr Fraser pauses, looking at her intently. 'My father retired from general practice in his early fifties. Burnt out... The task for you, Olivia, is to put aside anything difficult about yesterday.'

Today shouldn't be so hectic, he tells her, while they inspect the surgery list. Ironic though – being busy would be easier. All she wants is to see Richie, find out how he really feels about her.

In the evening, she receives a text. 'At conf Rome. Back Mon. B in touch.'

She grabs her jacket and goes to the cinema where she watches a second-rate movie, comforted by a bag of liquorice toffees.

RICHIE VISITS THE FOLLOWING WEDNESDAY. Olivia spends the day in a tizzy, not sure she can bear to break things off.

'Have you eaten?' she asks, when he arrives. It's after eight o'clock and wet; he smells of damp and polo mints.

He examines the headline of the newspaper on the table. 'I'm not hungry.'

For the past week she's been wondering how to get him to tell her his wife is pregnant. 'How are things... at home?'

She's never posed this question before.

He tugs the hairs under his watchstrap. Since arriving, he's hardly made eye contact.

'Alice has miscarried.'

Her forehead beads with sweat. Despite her love for him, despite everything, she didn't want this to happen.

'You didn't tell me she was pregnant.'

'The obstetrician told her it's highly unlikely she can carry a baby to term. She's miscarried before, you see.'

The timbre of his voice is different. Reedy.

'She had a bleed last night,' he continues. 'At the booking clinic today they told her the baby had died.'

'Shouldn't you be at home with her?'

The room feels cold so she switches on the fire. As she watches the rain pattering against the window, mixed with guilt about what's happened, is an inexcusable need to know he still loves her.

He flops onto a chair, tugs his tie, swallows hard. 'She's at her sister's... You know, she's always been quite tolerant of–'

'Your indiscretions... Perhaps things have changed for her, perhaps she found out about us and it upset her.'

She must be careful. Not reveal she's met Alice.

He stares at the gas fire. 'I'd hate to be responsible, you see. For what's happened. The sex is mechanical. Not like with you. But we're close, in some ways... She won't give up.'

'What do you mean?'

'She's so desperate to be a mother, you know. I shouldn't be talking to you about this. I'm sorry... I don't know what to do. I've never seen Alice like this before – this awful mixture of grief but determination.'

She wants to hug him. She wants to be able to exonerate herself from guilt. 'I made corn chowder soup.'

She escapes to the kitchen. Hearing him talk like this convinces her he still loves his wife, so she must do the decent thing – end the relationship. But he seems fragile. While waiting for the soup to heat up, she leans against the worktop, trying to regulate her breathing. She locates an inhaler. It's magic, she thinks, how speedily this little canister relaxes the muscles around her airways, enabling her to breathe properly. The soup is bubbling and the room now smells of bacon. She fills a bowl, butters a slice of bread, her movements heavy. Food won't change a thing.

He eats mechanically. She sits on the sofa, he remains at the table.

Eventually he stands. 'I'd better get home, I suppose. Alice will be back from her sister's.'

After he's gone, she sits on the sofa, despising herself for lacking the courage to end their relationship. She pictures

Alice discovering the blood, lying down in the hope that rest will save her baby, dreading the sensation of more wetness between her legs. She wonders if Richie accompanied her to the obstetrician.

Will this tragedy bring him and his wife closer or drive a wedge between them?

8

'You seem weird,' Roz remarked when I disembarked at Menton half an hour later.

'I've seen him... Richie.'

'What?'

'Getting on a train in Nice. I'm sure it was him – his hair, the way he hopped onto the train like a deer. He has a moustache now... My train pulled out before I could do anything.'

She hugged me again. 'Well, at least you don't need to go to Canada... What will you do now?'

'He may not be living here. He might have been on holiday and been leaving France. He could have been heading for the airport to fly to Canada... I need a drink.'

'Contact the station – see if you can work out which train he was on.'

'Could we do it now?'

'We're meeting the others on a swanky boat... I'll text Brian.'

'I need alcohol before I do anything.'

As afternoon sunshine yielded to dusk and lights gradually appeared, the old town of Menton throbbed. Buskers tormented violins, gypsies peddled roses. Smells of fish soup and garlic emanated from shuttered windows.

'This'll do,' Roz said. 'We were here two nights ago.'

We entered the bar and ordered a bottle of wine. I knocked back two glasses in minutes.

'And you were all set to go to Canada,' my friend remarked.

Her voice was cheerful, a hockey captain raising team morale when competing against formidable opposition – her way of decompressing me, helping me return to a more manageable place.

'To be so close. If my train had arrived even a moment earlier, if–'

'Don't waste time on the "what ifs". At least you've seen him. I'm assuming he was on his own?'

'Didn't see anyone else.'

But they might already have been on the train. Alice and my daughter. I could have been within fifty feet of my child.

I stood. 'C'mon, I need to go back to the station, see if they can find out what train he was likely to be on.'

'Hang on,' she said. 'The American barmaid speaks fluent French. We'll ask her to contact the station.'

I provided the woman with my journey details and she agreed to call. Ten minutes later, she appeared at our table. 'The train on the opposite platform to yours was the TGV to Paris. It stops at various places until Marseille, then it's non-stop to Paris.'

'Thanks,' I said, slipping her a ten-euro note.

'Progress,' Roz said.

'But he could have got off anywhere in this area, or gone to Paris, and he could have been flying anywhere from there or from Marseille. It's one thing seeing him board the train, quite another finding out where he lives. Where do I begin?'

She slung a tanned arm round me. 'By spending a few days with us. Relax. Then see what your head tells you.'

'I've missed enough of her life already... Okay, two nights... And thanks.'

Later, in the shower at Roz and Brian's villa, I concluded that the logical starting point was finding where Richie had been in Nice. If he'd attended a conference or meeting, he would have stayed in a hotel – and, most likely, one belonging to either of the two chains he favoured.

TWO DAYS LATER, I approached the Ibis Hotel in the centre of Nice. Relieved to escape the crowded street, I followed the sign to the ladies where I inspected myself in the mirror, approving of my reflection. The beige and red dress seemed appropriate for my mission: its neckline, while flattering, not too low. I combed my hair, reapplied lipstick, took a deep breath and emerged into the foyer again.

At the desk, several couples waited to check out, a young man delivered flowers. The female receptionist was scrutin-ising a bill, but the male clerk's attention was on a commo-tion outside. When I turned round, I saw a fracas across the road: two young men punching each other, a third joining in, shouts of "*putain,* whore" filling the air. A siren wailed and seconds later a blue van appeared, four baton-armed policemen leaping out to restrain the men.

I waited until the couples settled their bill and the flowers were whisked off to their recipient. With luck, the female receptionist would disappear into the office.

Both clerks remained there, however, now checking computers and sorting through the mail. Then, to my relief, the woman scanned the foyer and returned to the office.

Hoping no other guests would appear, I approached the desk. The man smiled.

'*Bonjour, Madame*'

'*Bonjour Monsieur, je cherche cet home*. I am looking for this man.'

'I speak English,' he replied.

'I know you're not supposed to give out information about your guests,' I continued, 'but I'm trying to get in touch with this man. It's important. His name is Richard Williams. Dr Richard Williams. Can you tell me if he's stayed here over the last few weeks?'

The man studied me curiously, and appeared to be waiting, so I shoved a ten-euro note over the counter, his hand deftly covered it and slipped it into his pocket. He flicked through the computer. 'There is no one of this name registered here since four weeks. I can't look back more now.'

I handed him my photo of Richie. 'And you don't recognise this man?'

He shook his head, turning round when the female clerk appeared.

After trying four hotels, I'd made no progress. Richie hadn't stayed in any of the ones he patronised and no one knew of recent medical conferences hosted in Nice. There was one place left to try but my head ached. Perhaps I'd leave this one until tomorrow. I found a café, ordered a *croque monsieur* and coffee, and while waiting, refreshed myself in the loo. Already, in the air-conditioned building, I felt less sticky.

While hovering near the Radisson Hotel, I observed a maroon-jacketed doorman emerge with a clothes rack on wheels, followed by a woman in a tailored dress and stiletto heels, issuing instructions. An agitated porter then appeared, trouser legs spattered with what looked like milk, trailing behind him three resisting Siamese kittens on a single lead. I reached for my camera and took some photos before the woman gave me a filthy look.

Avoiding the doorman's eye, and hoping to emulate a poised guest, I stepped under the blue striped awning into the marbled floor foyer. At my approach, the yawning receptionist jumped to attention.

When I explained my quest, he replied in a broad Scottish accent, 'We're not allowed to give out information about our guests.'

'I've an important reason for asking.'

'I finish in fifteen minutes. Why don't we go for a drink and you can tell me your story.'

Registering the misty need in his eyes, I said, 'I'm not here to be picked up.'

His expression hardened. 'Didn't say you were. Do you want to go for a drink or not? I might remember seeing him, later.'

'Would you at least check the computer... please?'

When he remained silent, I added, 'Then I'll have a quick drink with you.'

As we sat at a pavement café, surrounded by Marlboro smokers and the roar of traffic from the nearby thoroughfare, I waited for David to make this drink worth my while.

'I went through the computer again, and our visitor book,' he told me, 'but there's no one registered in this name. Have you tried other hotels? There are over 500 in Nice... Why do you want to find him?'

I stood. 'It's a long story.'

'Do you want to get a bite to eat?'

'Thanks for your help.'

I flagged a taxi, and back in my hotel room, lay down and fell asleep immediately.

ENTERING the agency was like stepping into a fridge, and I happily slipped on the lightweight cardigan I'd carried around and hadn't needed until now. Having ascertained I was looking for nannying work, a harassed woman shoved an application form at me, explaining that she was on her own today as her assistant had a stomach bug. During the ten minutes it took to complete the paperwork, the phone rang six times.

The door then flew open, admitting a blast of heat and a small, heavily pregnant red-haired woman in a billowing pink dress.

'Madame Chevalier – *ca va bien?* Is everything okay?' the agent asked.

The woman collapsed onto a chair and wiped her face with a sleeve. 'No, Delphine, *je ne vais pas bien.* I'm not okay. The girl you found for me – Julie – has broken her leg. She was meant to be arriving tomorrow. Didn't she phone you? This is a disaster. The children have finished school, I have the café to manage and I'm pregnant – the doctor says I've not to do too much. And Bertrand can't take time off work.'

Delphine handed her a glass of water. 'I have not spoken with Julie. I am sorry that this happens, but the timing is perhaps not so bad. Here is Olivia Bowden. She wishes to work with children.'

Madame Chevalier scrutinised me, blinking hard. 'Could you start now?'

'Madame, you must first make the interview, you must verify the references,' Delphine said, rubbing her watery brown eyes.

'I can do it here. This is an emergency, it is.'

Delphine swept a ring-bedecked hand through her

wispy brown hair, glancing from me to Madame Chevalier as if pressed to make a life-impacting decision. 'There is a place which you can use.'

She showed us into a back room and opened the shutters. Dust motes drifted between filing cabinets and the corner basin tap dripped, but at least the place was cool. A half-eaten ham baguette smelled of rancid butter and with a practised arm, she swept it into a bin before rushing to answer the phone.

Madame Chevalier sank onto a chair and turned to face me. 'Right, Laura, you ask me questions, while I get myself together.' Her pale blue eyes gradually focused on me, suggesting that she could be lax then suddenly snap, wrenching someone out of complacency.

'It's Olivia... How many children do you have, Madame Chevalier?'

'Cerys. Call me Cerys. Never think of myself as Madame Chevalier, like to retain something of my Welsh origins. Henri is nine and Odette is seven.' She patted her stomach. 'And this one's due in September. Bertrand, my husband, is a doctor. We live in Villefranche. Do you have references? Have you been a child-minder before?'

I detailed my babysitting experience and voluntary work at a children's home, touched on my nursing job in rehab and she nodded vigorously.

'Great,' she eventually said, bestowing a plump smile on me.

In her pink maternity dress, with her unruly wavy titian hair and youthful skin, she resembled an overgrown primary school girl who'd won a prize.

'You're obviously suitable. You'd have your own bedroom and en suite bathroom.'

'What about days off?'

I'd need enough time to search for Richie. During the week, too.

She sipped her water. 'Most weekends and every second Tuesday. What's your French like? There are classes in Villefranche. It would make life easier if you could cope in French when you have to. We tend to speak English at home. Can you drive?'

'Yes. And my French is reasonable. I speak it better than I understand it. But I learn quickly.'

With the benefit of preparation time, I could have promoted myself better, but there were other agencies to try if Cerys didn't offer me the job. Nevertheless, the sooner I began working, the sooner I'd have some income and free accommodation. I couldn't afford to assume Mum's challenging of Dorothy's Will would be unsuccessful. And living with a half-French family might help me in other ways. As for embellishing my ability to speak French, I reckoned I could get away with that.

She blinked. 'Right. Here's my email address – for your references.'

I gaped at her while she unpacked and repacked her shoulder bag, muttering about *Intermarché*, Henri's clarinet lesson and Bertrand's evening clinic.

'Shouldn't I meet the children... see if they like me?'

'They'll like you. And there won't be any problem with Bertrand. When can you start? Have a think and I'll phone you this evening. What's your mobile number?'

'Shouldn't you wait for my references?'

'There isn't time, Lau – Olivia. I can judge character.'

After she left, I filled in more forms, my cynical side reminding me that good things don't happen so easily. The children could be obnoxious. I might have to work so hard there'd be no energy left for finding my little girl. On the other hand, although Cerys might talk me to death, she seemed decent enough.

Outside, the light was less bright, throwing into relief a small garden with a cabbage palm and a patch of faded grass. From the open window, I imagined I could smell the sea. It would be cooler now, too – the perfect temperature for a stroll along the waterfront.

'Arrangements do not usually be made so quickly,' Delphine told me when I left.

'It'll be fine,' I said, venturing once more into the July afternoon.

THREE DAYS LATER, I squinted in the midday light at Villefranche station, my throat parched, legs damp under my trousers. As I searched for Cerys, I noticed to my right, the port of Villefranche with its picturesque terracotta and salmon buildings, their shuttered windows and balconies. By the harbour were pleasure boats of varying size, further out, yachts. The agent had been right: it was lovely.

'Sorry I'm late,' Cerys said, appearing by my side. 'Called into the café – big mistake, of course, got sucked into sorting out endless problems, I did. The car's double-parked, but it's unavoidable. We use this beach often. At least you see all shapes. Even cellulite. Not like some beaches where there isn't a gram of unnecessary fat.'

I surveyed the crowded scene: reclining bodies; infants shielded by umbrellas; children splashing in the water. The air smelled of petrol fumes and rotting food from overfilled litter bins. As a helicopter circled overhead, I visualised paddling in the sea with my daughter, clasping her hand and laughing while waves tickled our feet.

'Come on,' Cerys called.

I followed her to a green Renault Clio.

She flung sandals and sweet wrappers from the passenger seat. 'Right, quick tour of Villefranche.'

With skill she negotiated the traffic, pointing out a church here, a restaurant there. 'Traffic's a nightmare at this time of year. Fifteen years in France and I haven't got used to the way they drive.'

She swerved to avoid a car cutting in front of us. '*Cythraul!* Demon!'

'What?'

'Welsh. If you have to swear, choose a language no one else understands.'

I shifted position, mopped my brow, wondering if the house would have air-conditioning.

'We live there, on the *moyenne cornice*,' she said, pointing at the mountains. 'It's close enough to drive to town in a few minutes, and the views are fantastic.'

It would be cooler there, thank God.

She turned left, drove along a narrow road and parked by the harbour.

'Let's have an ice cream,' she said, heaving herself out of the car, like a buffalo emerging from a swamp. 'This is Place Amelie Pollonaise, the heart of the town. Over there's Cap Ferrat. You can take a bus there or walk, if you're energetic. What flavour do you want? It's all homemade.'

'The children are dying to meet you,' she continued while we ate our ice creams. 'Henri's nine. He's bright and can be a monkey. Loves pulling apart radios and reassembling them and making elaborate spaceships from the weirdest things. He's football-mad and he plays the clarinet. Odette's quiet, she is. Reads a lot and loves dancing, loves the garden – not so confident, needs more reassurance.'

Amidst Cerys's conversation, I thought of my Wednesday routine – finishing my shift at five, debating whether or not to grocery shop on the way home, if I'd work out or run. If I'd phone James.

Edgware Road would be heaving: last minute shoppers plundering corner shops for dinner ingredients; pub goers overflowing onto the pavement with their pints and fags; window boxes spilling forth daisies, marigolds and baby's breath; floral scents mingling with spices from Indian restaurants; residual heat radiating from brick-fronted buildings. My ground floor neighbour would be watering his dahlias, or scrubbing the steps, hoping for an opportunity to chat.

'We always have an au pair over the summer,' Cerys was saying as I retuned into her monologue. 'Odette and Henri adapt quickly. All the girls have loved them, of course. Did you do medicine at one of the London colleges? I studied domestic science there. London, I mean. My parents wanted me to stay in Cardiff but I was keen to move on. Lots of emphasis on puddings and cakes and elaborate sauces, things to make you an eligible wife. The lecturers were from the dark ages. Lots of old-fashioned advice. Everything's changed now, of course, no longer the push to find the "right" man, not that I believe there's a "right" man.'

To my relief, she didn't talk much on the homeward journey.

'Here we are,' she said eventually.

I slid out of the car and studied the cream coloured house. Its upper two floors were fronted by intricate wrought-iron balconies with window boxes of red and purple geraniums, and on either side of the front door, palm trees extended the height of the building. Ensconced in a newspaper on the patio was an olive-skinned man, and a girl splashed in a kidney-shaped pool.

To my right I could see Villefranche, and straight ahead the wooded peninsula of Cap Ferrat slumped like a sleeping animal. Fingers crossed, my room would face this calming vista.

'This is my husband, Bertrand,' Cerys said as the man strutted over. He was tall and dark and would have been handsome, had his hazel-flecked eyes not been a mite too close together. Nevertheless, he looked fit in his swimming shorts and yellow polo shirt.

He extended his arm. 'Welcome in our house.'

'Odette, come here, *cariad*, love,' Cerys called.

The child scrambled out of the pool, tugged up her bathing suit and ran over to me, proffering her cheek for a kiss.

Cerys slipped a hand into her daughter's, introduced us.

As I processed Odette's brown, shoulder-length hair and large brown eyes, a wave of grief struck me. I didn't even know what my daughter looked like. And, with renewed force, it hit me that despite her being a bit older than my child, it might be too painful looking after Odette.

'The children are bilingual – they go to the international school in Nice,' Carys was saying. 'We normally speak English *en famille* but Bertrand uses French on his own with them. I've probably told you all this already... Where is Henri?'

'The Agency told me you teach at Nice University,' I said as Bertrand led me into the house. 'What do you lecture on?'

'It is dermatology. Come, I will show to you your room.'

When we reached the landing, a fair-haired boy appeared.

'You must be Olivia, I'm Henri,' he said, pushing past his father to open the door.

'Do you like it?' Henri asked.

I glanced at the spacious room – its double bed with hand-painted ends, the large fitted wardrobe and matching chest of drawers – before heading for the balcony. The view greeting me was of red pantile roofs and the sea. To my right, the harbour of Villefranche stretched out, the citadel at the far end just visible; to the left was the forested Cap Ferrat. YES!

Then, like a balloon deflating, I remembered my purpose here. This wasn't a gap year or a career break. It wasn't about experiencing another country, sightseeing until I dropped. Already the surrounding landscape seemed more muted as I stepped back in.

'*Maman* let me choose the paint,' Henri said. 'She says I understand colours. We both liked this pale yellow. You have your own shower and toilet. In here.'

'We have taken out the clothes from the wardrobe,' Bertrand told me, frowning at his son who was now circling the room, arms outstretched, voice imitating an engine's whine.

'Bertie, Bertie,' came the sound of Cerys's voice from downstairs. Bertrand scowled and left the room with Henri. I flopped onto the bed, but minutes later a knock on the door interrupted my thinking.

'I'll show you the rest of the house, then you can have lunch,' Cerys said. She'd changed into a russet coloured dress that complimented her hair and skin tone. In the right colours she was pretty. I followed her into the landing. Flinging open a door, she swept me in with an aura of pride. 'This is Odette's room.'

I received a fleeting impression of pale grey floor tiles

and a blue and green patterned bedspread, partly obscured by teddy bears. The view was similar to mine.

Cerys opened another door, closed it immediately. 'You can see Henri's room later.'

The master bedroom also overlooked the sea. By the window an exercise bike still sported its label, a mound of bulging plastic bags lying beside it. The air smelled stale.

'Great bike,' I said.

'Once *bambina*'s born, I'll use it. Each pregnancy, the weight's piled on. I don't even check in the mirror any more. Come and have lunch. The children ate earlier with Bertrand and I'm not hungry. Tend to nibble at the café. I was skinny before I had children.'

'You're having a girl, then.'

Cerys grinned. 'Don't tell Henri and Odette. I want it to be a surprise.'

I smiled when I saw the kitchen: its solid, oak table; its two trough-shaped fireclay sinks and iron range; the earthy orange walls and brown flagstone floor which made a pleasant, tapping sound under my feet. A huge wooden dresser was crammed with bottles of wine, olive oil, vinegar and spices, and the windowsill brimmed with herbs and cuttings, miniature green bottles and seashells. A family room...

'I'll show you the playroom later,' she said. 'Once I've tidied it.'

Having swept the table clear of unopened mail, Plasticine and paintbrushes, she produced a bulging baguette and a glass of pink liquid from the fridge.

'The baguette is goat cheese and salad, and the drink is Odette's lemonade. It's terribly keen, she is, for you to try it. She's worried she didn't add enough sugar... Do taste it and then I can put her mind at rest.'

I sipped the drink and gave the thumbs up sign.

She grinned. 'She'll be delighted – I'll go and tell her. If you want to rest after you've eaten... I expect you're struggling with the heat. It took me years to get used to it.'

After lunch, I unpacked, then, drowsy from sun pouring into the room, lay down, rearranged the long bolster pillow and turned to face the window and unbroken expanse of blue sky.

Outside, Cerys's rapid Welsh voice and Bertrand's equally fast French one, filled the afternoon air, accompanied by children's laughter and squeals and the scoosh of a garden hose. '*Non, Papa; Maman, aide moi, aide moi!* Mummy help me!' I heard Cerys's high-pitched giggle, a car engine revving, a dog barking.

Later, I was roused from sleep. From the window I watched the children in the pool, Henri trying to push Odette off her plastic dolphin, both squealing and laughing.

'You said you'd be here this afternoon,' Cerys's voice floated up to the bedroom.

'I must do a lecture,' Bertrand replied. 'Guillaume is ill.'

'Why not one of the others? It doesn't always have to be you. Promised you'd cook tonight, you did. Dr Brimé said I've not to do too much.'

A thud of rap from a passing vehicle obliterated Bertrand's response. Then came the crunching of gravel and her voice calling after his car, 'Don't be late, Bertie. Please.'

I fell asleep again soon after, thinking of Morocco.

It was nearly five when I awoke. After showering, I peered in the bathroom mirror while towel drying my hair. For most of my thirty years, people had remarked on my similarity to Mum. Today, to my relief, I observed more of Dad in me – the brown wavy hair and oval jawline.

At six o'clock, I joined the family at the dining room

table, accepted a glass of wine. Cerys refilled hers and glared out of the window, her rust coloured dress now resembling a collapsed marquee. From the kitchen came clattering sounds and humming.

'We're having a simple meal,' she said, her tone both exasperated and resigned. 'Bertrand had to work this afternoon and he was going to cook a Provençal dish. But we'll have this tomorrow, to welcome you.'

When he appeared with a soufflé, Odette and Henri stared at it.

Cerys clicked her teeth. 'I would not give you thank you for eggs right now, Bertrand Chevalier. And you know this. Did you make a salad?'

'*Bien sur. C'est dans la cuisine.* Of course. It's in the kitchen.'

Odette whispered in her mother's ear.

'She wants to sit beside you,' Cerys told me. 'Swap seats please, Henri.'

'*Maman!*'

'Please, Henri.'

Odette swapped chairs and gazed at me shyly.

I smiled at her. 'Your lemonade was yummy.'

'*Maman* showed me what to do,' she said, sticking her tongue out at Henri.

I helped myself to salad and vinaigrette.

'Don't forget the oil,' Cerys pointed out. 'Not watching your weight, surely?'

Was it too soon to ask when my first Tuesday off would be? I must continue searching, my perception of time already skewed, hours of doing nothing seeming like days. My hand flew to my mouth. In addition to searching for Richie, I could check if there were any five-year-old girls with the surname "Williams" at the international school.

During my first private moment with them, I'd ask Odette and Henri.

When I raised my head, Bertrand was observing me, almost as if he'd guessed my purpose here. With effort, I held his gaze until he redirected it to Odette.

Between bursts of conversation, the children studied me – Odette with furtive glances, Henri more openly. They were attractive: Odette resembling her father with her brown hair and eyes; Henri inheriting his mother's colouring, his floppy strawberry blonde hair and lopsided grin lending him an impish appearance. His blue eyes were intelligent. When they'd finished eating, Cerys sent them to bed, impervious to their protests and delaying tactics.

Bedtime rituals completed, she returned flushed and breathless, and plonked herself beside me on the sitting room sofa. 'I'll tell you about our routine. Bertie, please don't smoke in here. It's bad for the baby.'

He stood. 'To drink wine is bad also.'

'Tired, he is,' she said when her husband had left the room. 'One of his colleagues is ill and he's been covering for him.'

Later, she followed me upstairs. 'I hope you'll like it here with the children. There's plenty to do, with the beach and their friends. Henri plays football and Odette has a weekly dance class. I expect you're glad to get away from London – such a big, impersonal place. Hope you'll sleep okay – the bed's comfy. I hope there isn't anything important I've forgotten.'

'There'll be time in the morning.'

'There will, yes. I don't have to be at the café until eleven. Two things you should know about France: most shops close for several hours over lunchtime, and nothing is open on a public holiday. Took me years to get used to this. Good night, then.'

WHEN I AWOKE the following morning, it was after nine. During the night I'd been aware of heavy rain, and the scent of wet earth now drifted through the open window.

Cerys was spooning paté into plastic containers when I appeared in the kitchen. 'Morning. Sleep okay?'

'I didn't mean to get up so late.'

'I have to leave in forty-five minutes. Henri, take your Lego through to the playroom, *cariad,* love. Don't want to trip over bits.'

After she'd gone over the routines she'd described the previous night, I located the children in a small room off the kitchen, sorting through their beach toys.

'We should throw this spade out, Odette,' Henri said. 'It's broken. And it's pink.'

She grabbed the spade from him. 'It's my favourite.'

'It's useless. The handle's cracked and there's a nail sticking out. You know said it could be dangerous. Put it in the dustbin. No, don't. Maybe I could make it into something.'

'Are you going to stay with us all summer?' Odette asked.

'Yes, she will,' Henri said. 'Like Amanda did last year. Olivia will be here until school begins, then Fabienne will be with us at Christmas until the shop closes. Then next summer someone else will look after us.'

I examined the condemned spade. 'Do you mind having different people?'

He took the spade from me and shoved it into the bin.

'It's interesting. Let's play in the paddling pool, but I want to show you our den first.'

'Sunhats, sunscreen, children,' Cerys called from the car. 'Remember what *Papa* said about protecting your skin. It's getting hot.'

After making sure Odette and Henri were covered in sunscreen, I followed them into the back garden. A den painted in army colours occupied one corner. In another, a hammock stretched between two pine trees. Smothering the wall enclosing the garden were red and pink bougainvillea, pale-blue plumbago and purple clematis. I edged myself onto the hammock and rocked from side to side, appreciating the rush of air, the feel of canvas beneath me, the manure-like smell and roughness of its connecting ropes.

As the children filled the paddling pool, I joined them. 'You both go to the international school in Nice, right?'

Henri nodded. 'But we get taught some subjects in French.'

'So, do you know any girls with the surname "Williams"?'

Odette shook her head. Henri pondered, causing my heart to race. 'There's a girl with the name "Williamson".'

'Are you sure it's "Williamson"? How old is she?'

He shrugged. 'Guess so. She's bigger than me – I think she's about 11.'

After lunch, Odette clutched my hand. 'Do you want to see where *Maman* keeps clothes for the new baby?'

She took me into the utility room, where she wrestled with the middle drawer of a pine chest, finally pulling it out triumphantly, and producing a blue polka dot baby grow with red feet.

'*Maman* told me I wore this when I was a baby. I think it's lovely.'

The contents of a different drawer entered my mind: a tiny green cardigan which had taken four months to knit, a clutch of Winnie the Pooh bibs and a horse-shaped rattle.

'WHAT ARE you doing on your day off?' Cerys asked, watering the basil on the windowsill. 'Leave that, you're officially off duty.'

I paused from loading the dishwasher. 'I'm going to look around Nice.'

'Could give you a lift in later, if you want. Odette has a dance class.'

'Thanks, but I'd rather go in this morning.'

'Watch out for pickpockets. They're rife, especially at this time of year, and they can spot a tourist a mile off.'

As I hovered outside the Université de Nice Sophia-Antipolis, my stomach fluttered. Inside the main building, I paused at the reception window, peering at an empty room. I pressed the buzzer and waited. No one appeared. I rang again. Nothing.

I then walked along the ground floor corridor of the Faculty of Medicine, scrutinising names on doors. From one room I heard the whirr of a photocopier, from another, jazz. An aroma of soup wafted from a third room. At the end of the corridor, a board displayed photos of faculty staff. I studied it carefully. No photo of Richie. Two young women appeared.

'*Excusez–moi,*' I said. '*Je cherche quelqu'un. Connaissez-vous l'homme dans cette photo?* I am looking for someone. Do you know the man in this photo?'

They inspected the photo and shook their heads. '*Désolée.* Sorry.'

Several more people appeared, but again no one recognised the photo. This was a waste of time. Besides, I'd already trawled the university website for Richie's name.

On my way back, I paused at reception. A woman came over. '*Oui?*'

'*Je cherche l'homme dans cette photo. Est–ce que vous le connaissez?* I am looking for the man in this photo. Do you know him?'

She glanced at the photo, shook her head and returned to her desk.

It was barely two o'clock, too early to return to Villefranche. Instead, I strolled around the fruit and vegetable markets of the Cours Saleya, amongst rows of shining avocados, juicy mangos, purple and red grapes. Later, having searched in vain for a restaurant that was open, I settled for a pavement café, spirits lifting when my teeth sank into a fathomless mound of chocolate patisserie.

After leaving the café, I struggled not to think about Richie, unable to shift the cleaver from its chopping block in order to obliterate the onslaught of memories. What he'd done was unforgivable, but the babies had been conceived from love.

At the Promenade des Anges, I spent ten minutes dodging roller bladers and cyclists, then gave up. The only thing that would relax me was to go running this evening, regardless of the weather.

9

I leant against a rock and timed my pulse. Not bad. As the sun descended, a rosy- gold pervaded the sky, a faint breeze ruffling my hair, cooling me. Nearby, a couple stretched out on a rug. Further away, a man threw a stick to his dog. I finished my water and shook the sand from my shoes.

Peace was splintered by my phone: James. I ignored the call. The phone rang again.

'When are you coming back?' he asked tetchily. 'I actually had hoped you'd have got this out of your system by now. You don't need to stay away just to make a point... I don't even know where you are.'

The sky was changing by the second. 'I'm in France, near Nice, *and* I have a job.'

'You're working?'

'Nannying for two children.... It's a glorious sunset here, you should see the light on the water.'

'Nannying! Hardly a career. What about us?'

'We've been through this.'

'Through what?'

'You know – your difficulty in committing. Besides, you're too controlling and–'

'Controlling? Me? Now look here, Livvy–'

'Bye, James.'

After ringing off, his scathing remarks about being a nanny lingered in my thoughts. My wages from the Chevaliers wouldn't take me far. And if Mum won her challenge of the Will...

Perhaps I should have stayed in London, hired a private detective to find Richie. But this would have cost a fortune, especially if the investigator had to travel to Canada or even further afield.

The sun hovered on the horizon, the corniche high above dark and eerie, shadows ever-growing. I lay on my side, hypnotised by the crimson globe and its reflection on the smooth water. As sea swallowed sun, the ochre of the harbour buildings surrendered its intensity, the deserted beach now an expanse of gold. Glancing to my left, I saw the couple strolling away, figures gradually shrinking. I wondered what they'd do when they got home.

During my meander back to the town centre, Moby's *Why Does My Heart Feel So Bad?* played and replayed in my head. In Villefranche, I perched on the harbour wall, feeling its residual warmth through my shorts, listening to the starlings' evensong and the lapping water. Gazing out to the cruise liners, I visualised passengers changing for dinner and dancing.

Smaller boats now approached, holidaymakers venturing ashore for sole stuffed with mushroom purée – the French translation, *Sole farcie Sainte Marie*, sounded more romantic – or lobster-stuffed ravioli in a seafood cream sauce. (Translated to *les raviolis de homard à la crèmede crustacés*, I might choose this on a significant date.) After eating, the tourists would trawl the harbour shops for Provençal herbs and fridge magnets, before returning to base for a nightcap, followed, for couples, by a reassuring if predictable lovemaking, or snuggling beside a body they knew as intimately as their own.

In darkness, I ascended the *moyenne corniche*. At the Chevaliers, Cerys was slicing quiches in the kitchen, her movements slow. Her bump seemed larger, accentuated by the horizontally striped dungarees.

'Shall I finish this off?' I offered.

'Would you? They go into these containers, once they've cooled. Try to make the slices evenly sized.' She handed me a Sabatier slicer.

After I'd stacked the last container in the fridge, Bertrand appeared.

'Your shoulders are bad,' he said, placing his hands on them, massaging.

He continued kneading and the dull ache retreated, then, as he moved closer, an intake of breath made me turn. Cerys was standing by the kitchen door, in pyjamas, hair tousled from sleep.

'Bertrand?'

'I do a massage with the shoulders,' he said, continuing to work on me, but edging back.

I forced myself not to step away.

She yanked the fridge door open, reached for a carton of orange juice, and banged the door so hard it opened again. She shoved it with her foot, before pouring the juice into a glass, spilling some on the worktop.

'That's better, thanks, Bertrand,' I said, hoping to convey innocence. 'Night, Cerys.'

I traipsed upstairs, straining for sounds of conversation in the kitchen but hearing only the back door open and close. On the balcony, I gazed at the lights of Villefranche, at the moon's reflection on the sea. Tomorrow I'd explain to Cerys what had happened, that what she'd witnessed was innocuous.

As I stepped back into my room, I noticed an envelope lying on my bed.

'I apologise for taking so long to write to you,' Mr Minto wrote. *'There have been ongoing problems in contacting the GP who saw Dorothy shortly before she dictated the letter (the day before she had her stroke). I hope to speak with him soon, to see if he can vouch for her state of mind when she added the codicil to her Will. I have also spoken with your mother to see if she would withdraw her objection to the Will. Unfortunately, she is adamant she won't do so. Despite this, I am confident her challenge will be unsuccessful.*

'My colleague is in the process of winding up your aunt's Estate and estimates this will take another month. Either way, we hope things can be finalised by the middle of August.

'I trust things are going well for you in France and would be pleased to hear how you are getting on in your search for your little girl.

'I remain yours...'

So, I'd have to continue being careful with money. Perhaps Mr Minto had been right. Perhaps I should have explained the situation to Mum.

Was he as confident as he'd stated?

THREE DAYS LATER, I navigated Cerys's Renault out of the Chevalier driveway. My guidebook's description of the Languedoc – vineyards, somnolent villages, rocky outcrops and montane scrub – had sharpened my appetite to see another region of France. Furthermore, during the weekend I would put my search on a back burner – rest my eyes and mind. Refuel.

'How long will it take to get there, Olivia?' Henri asked.

'Depends on traffic and how often we stop. About five hours.'

'*Maman* said we can go to the festival dance with *Tante Antoinette* and *Oncle Fabrice*. And there's a donkey race,' Odette said. 'Did you pack my boots? *Maman* said it's muddy at the farm. I wish she and *Papa* were coming with us.'

'They'll join us tomorrow for the dance, sweetheart, but I don't expect *Maman* will be able to do much.'

Odette chatted on, Henri interjecting occasionally.

When conversation finally ran dry, I put on a tape, which, along with stopping for snacks, kept the children occupied. By four o'clock they were asleep so I switched off the music, welcoming silence and a chance to observe the changing countryside uninterrupted.

Fabrice and Antoinette were in the garden and rose to greet us as I slowed to a halt. Bertrand's brother was tall and dark, with a shy but warm smile. His wife was also tall, with prematurely grey hair cut in a bob that accentuated her cheekbones and dark grey eyes. After helping the children carry their weekend bags into the house, she suggested Fabrice give me a guided tour.

'The farming houses traditional in the Provencal have windows and doors which are pointing in the south, for that they protect us from wind in the winter and in summer the sun,' he explained, when he showed me round.

'I've heard about these... mistral winds.'

'Since twenty years we are working hard here. There are trees with olives and there are trees with fruit and we grow also the grapes. Antoinette, she is doctor in the next village.'

'Please come into the kitchen,' Antoinette invited, after he'd shown me the immediate farm buildings. 'I have made coffee.'

At the kitchen door, I paused. To one side, lay a rectangular glass topped table. Everything else was made of chrome or stainless steel, even the worktops.

'You were expecting a kitchen that is more traditional,' she said, reaching into the freezer, producing several plastic containers. 'I am a family doctor who has too much work. I don't have the time to put oil on the wooden surfaces when they have water on them. Or to put polish on the terracotta tiles.'

After dinner, Henri and Odette went to bed without their customary stalling techniques, Henri falling asleep instantly his head touched the pillow, Odette yawning while she attempted to read. I kissed them goodnight and retrieved their clothes from the floor, pausing by the open window to inhale the warm, lavender-scented air and gaze at a starless sky. Apart from the distant wasp-like sound of a motorbike and the intermittent barking of a farm dog, silence reigned.

In the kitchen, Fabrice was attacking a baking tray with steel wool, Antoinette reading a book with a front cover depicting a clinched couple. Eyes fixed on her novel, she said, 'In the Philippines, the women hurry to the harbour when these books are delivered. The romantic themes help them to escape the depression of their lives. For me, it is an escape from what I see at work every day.'

I turned away.

'Another child will join us tomorrow for the weekend,' she continued. 'His name is Philippe – he is the son of the colleague of my sister.'

Later, I checked on the children, lingering beside

Odette's bed. Asleep, arms spread out on either side of the pillow, she seemed younger than her seven years. Conscious of a build-up of longing again, I retreated to my room.

At breakfast the following morning, Antoinette offered to show me their land. I hesitated, wishing the suggestion had come from Fabrice.

'I take with me children to the market,' he offered.

Twenty minutes later, in a jeep smelling of manure, she and I were hurtling through a landscape of silvery olive trees, distant mauve mountains sharply defined in the clear light, providing a foreground to the snow-crested Pyrenees.

'I wish I could paint,' I said.

She swung the jeep off the road. 'Often, when I have had a difficult week, I drive here.'

'What a brilliant life, you're lucky.'

She shrugged. 'People imagine there are no problems in the countryside. But always there are problems. If the harvest is bad, there is more stress for the farmers and therefore there are domestic problems – worries about money, psychological conditions. Difficult relationships become violent. It would surprise you how often my patients confide in me.'

I viewed the heavily fragranced lavender field, further beyond, a yellow expanse of sunflowers, small stone buildings dotted like loaves of bread in the arid heat. 'I'm not as naïve as you think.'

'Most people have romantic opinions of the Languedoc. They see the lavender fields and the picturesque buildings used for storing the hay. They imagine that everything is perfect.'

'So, how did you and Fabrice meet?'

She smiled, her face softening. 'I studied at the university of Nice with Bertrand and we helped each other with our studies often. We became close, then he introduced me to Fabrice and I discovered that I was with the wrong brother. Bertrand was successful, but Fabrice was kind. We have been married since twenty-four years, but he still asks me sometimes why I did not choose the clever brother.'

'Fabrice is so gentle. I love gentleness in men.'

'But you,' she continued. 'I think that you are not happy. There is a darkness in your eyes, when you think that no one is watching you.'

'You must be weary of hearing people's problems.'

'Often I suggest that they speak with a counsellor. I could not do all the work that is necessary if I become... involved.'

'Do you have children?'

'Two sons.'

'Do they live near here?'

'Alfonse lives in Amsterdam and Lucas lives in Moscow. We do not often see them... Fabrice finds this difficult. But me... I would prefer not to see them so often and to know that they are happy, than if they visit many times out of obligation and be unhappy with their lives.'

I thought of my daughter, settled with Richie and Alice. Was it selfish to search for her, disrupt her life? How would I have coped with this situation at such an age?

Antoinette handed me a bottle of water. 'It can be isolating living in another country. I was in England for three years.'

After I relayed my story, she said, 'I do not know many doctors in Nice, apart from Bertrand naturally. Have you spoken with him?'

'No. And you mustn't tell him. Or Cerys.'

'I meet sometimes with other doctors in the region. Do you have a photo you can give to me? Perhaps I can show this photo to my colleagues.'

'It's at a photography studio in Nice, having a beard and moustache added... in case he's changed his appearance.'

'*D'accord*, okay, I have another suggestion. My brother, Laurent, will come to the party this evening. He is psychologist at the Clinique Saint George in Nice. He might be able to assist you.'

Back at the farmhouse, Henri was spread across a plane tree. Odette was helping Fabrice plant seeds and when she saw me, she dropped the trowel and rushed over.

'We've been to the market. *Oncle Fabrice* bought me a candle with a lovely smell. And we made a tart. I added the sugar!'

While she was showing me the baking, a car stopped outside the house.

'*Maman* and *Papa*,' she cried, running outside, me following.

'It's not our car,' Henri called to me, scrambling off the tree. 'My sister is stupid.'

An olive-skinned woman in a white blouse and tailored black trousers emerged and glided towards us, stepping around the muddy parts of the farmyard.

'Hallo, Antoinette,' she said, air kissing both her cheeks. '*Renée, Clara, Philippe, venez ici. Come here.*'

The back door of the car opened and a dark-haired girl of about eleven cantered over, flapping her arms, offering her cheek to Antoinette. '*Salut!* Hallo!'

'Véronique, Clara, this is Olivia, the nanny for Odette and Henri.'

Clara kissed me on both cheeks, Véronique extended her hand.

An older girl and a small fair-haired boy followed Clara. Antoinette introduced them to me as Renée and Phillipe.

Philippe approached Henri. 'Do you like Buzz Lightyear?' he asked, opening his backpack. 'I've got all the characters. *Papa* bought them for me.'

Henri gave the backpack a cursory look. '*Toy Story* is for little boys.'

'I'm a little boy.'

Odette took Philippe's hand. 'Do you want to see the kittens?'

Without waiting for Philippe's reply, Henri headed for the barn.

Philippe pulled away from Odette. 'When is *Papa* coming home?'

Véronique tutted. 'Stop the complaining, please. *Papa* will return soon.'

'Coffee, Véronique?' Antoinette asked.

'No, thank you. Renée and Clara must arrive at the camp by five. *Clara, attention!* Be careful. She has changed her clothes already two times today. *Reneé, ne mange plus.* Stop eating... She will become fat.'

Antoinette surveyed Renée before switching her attention back to Véronique. 'At what time will you collect Philippe tomorrow?'

'I wonder, is it possible that he can stay with you until the next weekend?'

Poor kid. No wonder he whined – being farmed out, literally, like a pet, and not even with his sisters.

'Pascal suggests that I visit him in Florence,' Véronique added. 'We have not seen each other since three weeks. I have taken enough clothes for Philippe... Renée, *laisse la baguette, je t'en prie.* Put that baguette away, please... Pascal and I do not often be together.'

Antoinette laid her hand on Véronique's arm. 'I have a difficult week at the surgery and Fabrice will be busy working at the farm. Pascal would like to see Philippe, I am sure.'

'I want to see *Papa*,' Philippe said.

'He could stay with us,' Odette suggested.

'Véronique, this is a difficult situation...' Antoinette began.

Odette was jumping up and down. '*Maman* and *Papa* will say "yes" if you ask them.'

Véronique flicked some mud from her sandals. 'I will telephone you tomorrow before I make a reservation for a flight... Now I must go.'

Noticing his family leaving, Philippe flung his arms round Clara, then stared at his mother, who patted his head.

'Come and see the kittens,' Odette called to Philippe and me.

I wandered over to the barn, Philippe trailing behind. In the subdued light, Henri and Odette huddled round several tiny furry bundles and a larger one.

'Do you want to hold one?' Henri asked Philippe.

He shook his head, tugging at a piece of straw, bottom lip jutting out.

Shortly after we heard another car.

'*Maman* and *Papa*,' Odette and Henri shrieked, dashing out of the barn.

I followed, spirits plummeting when a single figure emerged from the car.

'*Maman, elle est òu?* Where is Mummy?' Henri asked, while Odette peered into the back of the car.

Bertrand retrieved a grip bag from the car boot. *'Elle ne vient pas. Elle est fatiguée.* She isn't coming. She's tired.'

Odette and Henri exchanged disappointed glances.

'Is anything wrong?' I asked Bertrand, while the children shuffled towards the house, their father's bag dragging between them.

'Cerys had the bleed. The doctor told her that she must rest in bed for some days.'

'Shouldn't you... someone be with her?'

'It is not serious. Odette and Henri must be considered.'

Shortly after Bertrand's arrival, I hovered unseen by the kitchen door. Fabrice was sharpening a carving knife at the table while Antoinette emptied the dishwasher. Bertrand was facing the window overlooking the yard. Fabrice replaced the knife on the table and spoke to his brother's upright back. Although I couldn't understand what he said, his disapproval was apparent and, sensing Bertrand's resolve weakening, I slipped out of sight. Seconds later, I heard his light tread on the stairs, then creaking from an upstairs bedroom. From the kitchen, Antoinette and Fabrice's conversation was muted.

Once Bertrand had left, I sat outside for a while. For the first time since arriving in France, my body felt light, my head calm. Fabrice I'd liked from the start, and gradually I was warming to Antoinette, aware of there being more to her than her brusqueness suggested. When we returned to Nice, searching for my child would become paramount again. At the moment, however, I was relieved to let it recede.

At six o'clock, Cerys rang. 'The bleeding's stopped,' she told me. 'But the doctor's recommended several days of bed rest. You mustn't worry. Honestly, it'll be nice to sleep and read. I've got the new *Marie Claire* and *Elle*. Perhaps I might get inspiration for after *bambina*'s born.'

'I'm glad the bleeding's stopped... Cerys, there's a child here called Philippe. His mother's dumped him for the week but Antoinette and Fabrice are busy. Odette wants him to come back with us. It's not an ideal time, I mean, but...'

'I've met Véronique. I don't mind but it'll mean extra work for you. Right, fetch Odette and Henri, I'm dying to talk to them.'

AT DUSK, the village square thronged, the air heavy with expectation. A band – six men in jeans and t-shirts, three women in folk dress – were installing equipment and accepting carafes of wine from onlookers. Fairy lights on the plane trees cast a soft glow on the surroundings: clusters of people drinking and babbling; infants asleep in buggies; older children cavorting to a flute, played by a boy barely older than Henri.

'It is a local band but it is excellent for dancing,' Antoinette said. 'People will visit from many regions in the south of France to this fête.'

Fabrice appeared with a tray of drinks and handed me a glass. 'Here is pastis.'

'It is made from nectar and vanilla and cinnamon,' Antoinette added.

I took a sip and choked.

She laughed. 'Drink some water.'

A screech of bagpipes and an oboe-like instrument ruptured the air. Immediately, Fabrice led his wife to the dance area and swirled her round, her striped skirt twisting and teasing like a kite on a windy day. Glancing at my capris pants, I wished I'd brought a dress.

Henri and Odette were dancing with other children, and Philippe sat nearby, tapping a block of wood with a stick, immersed in the rhythm. Next time I looked over, he was dancing with Odette, clasping her hand.

When Fabrice and Antoinette returned to our table, Fabrice asked me to dance.

'I enjoyed my tour of your farm,' I said as he took my arm.

He smiled. 'The life, it is perfect. I am not the same as Bertrand. He is clever, he go to university. When I am young, I leave school to work with my father. He was also farmer.'

Antoinette was now chatting to a slim, brown haired man.

'Is that Laurent?'

Fabrice nodded. 'He is Antoinette's young brother. He is coming here always for the dance.'

At the table once more, Fabrice and Laurent embraced, then Antoinette introduced me to her brother. Straight away he asked me to dance. As we moved to the dance area, I noticed his limp, but it didn't impede him and I was the one begging to stop, three dances later.

'I will bring you the paella,' he said while we pushed and squeezed our way back to the table.

Minutes later, he deposited a large plate of rice, fish, chicken and chillies in front of me. Fabrice took his wife's arm and led her off.

I took a mouthful of paella. 'This is delicious.'

'Do you like Villefranche?' Laurent asked, regarding me with keen appraisal.

Although I blushed under his scrutiny, it was pleasant

having this attractive man show interest. It reminded me of Richie, at the beginning of our relationship.

'Olivia?' Laurent asked, eyebrows raised.

'Villefranche? It's pretty, a bit small, perhaps. Occasionally it would be good to get further away, not just to Nice.'

'I could lend to you my moped... My sister told me your story. Maybe it is possible for me to help you to search for this man. I know many people in Nice.'

A generous offer, considering I'd met him less than an hour ago.

'It's overwhelming at times. There are so many places he could be working: teaching biochemistry at a university; working as a radiotherapist or a family practitioner. I've checked all the family practices along the Côte D'Azur. Nothing about him.'

Laurent nodded. 'It takes three years of training to be a family practitioner. If he worked at Perpignan University for two years, he would not already have finished his internship. I think that someone who is ambitious would not choose to work as a family doctor. He would prefer to have a more important job.'

'Maybe you're right. I'm impressed.'

He laughed. 'When I first qualified as a psychologist, I shared an apartment with someone who worked with criminal profiling. I learned many things from this man.'

Later, during the clearing up, Laurent scribbled a number on the back of a business card. 'If you wish to arrange a rendezvous...'

ix years earlier

S   Olivia perches on the loo seat, clutching the test stick, watching the clock. Outside, the wind moans, a reminder of ongoing winter. When a purple line shows in the control window, her forehead beads with sweat. When a second purple line appears, she drops the stick, retrieves it, peers at it. Rereads the instruction leaflet.

As dusk approaches, she sits at her living room window, her thoughts returning to earlier in the day – buying the pregnancy test at Boots (joking with the checkout girl); attending a matinée at the Electric Cinema, cosy in the red leather seats, mint chocolates at the ready.

She's never forgotten even one pill – but there was that evening...

The irony doesn't escape her: the despair of Richie's wife at her inability to have children, her own ambivalence about being pregnant.

The following morning, she skips lectures. At lunchtime, she texts Richie but he doesn't reply and when she dials his number, she reaches voicemail. Eventually she calls the university.

'Dr Williams isn't available,' his secretary says. 'Can I take a message?'

'When will he be free, it's urgent.'

'Are you in one of his seminar groups?'

'Yes,' she lies.

'I'll see what's in his diary.'

A rustling of paper, then, 'He has a seminar, after that, a department meeting until around five. But he might ring in for messages. Or you could leave one on his voicemail.'

'Please ask him to phone me.'

The woman's tone softens. 'If it's a crisis, you could try the student support service.'

Olivia struggles to sound calm. 'It's not a crisis.'

After the call, she slumps at her kitchen table, sickened by having breached the cardinal rule – spoken to Richie's PA. She switches on the telly, falls asleep during a movie.

It's well after eight before he appears at her flat.

'It's great to see you,' he says, grabbing her by the waist, kissing her hair. 'What's so urgent it couldn't wait until tomorrow, then?'

'I needed to talk to you.'

He fondles her breasts, murmuring, 'You're gorgeous!'

She is tempted to delay telling him, so that they can enjoy their evening. 'I'm pregnant.'

He stumbles back. 'You're on the pill.'

'I was.'

His expression is bewildered. 'Did you forget one, then?'

'You remember Brighton, when I was ill after the fish soup... and we didn't use any other precautions later?'

At the time, she'd mentioned the unreliability of the low

dose pill with stomach upsets, but he'd been so keen, they'd both been.

'Yes, well, yes, yes. Oh Lord. What are you going to do? I can't believe this, my wife can't carry a baby to term but I knock you up within months. What a mess.'

She gulps. It's one thing her thinking this, another him expressing it, and so bluntly. She searches his face for a softening, for anything suggesting he'll be part of her life – their life. He needs time to adjust, she reasons, remembering she's had several days.

If only he would hold her.

'It could be a false reading, I suppose,' he says. 'Do you have symptoms?'

She turns away. 'A horrible taste at the back of my mouth. Nausea.'

He starts to open the Valpolicella he brought, stopping halfway through, sinking into the armchair. 'How far on do you think you are?'

'Do you love me?'

His phone goes. He checks the screen. 'Oh God... Hallo?... Oh Lord, sorry love, completely forgot... Yes, I'm at the university... Okay, asap.'

He clicks off the phone. 'We're having people for dinner, you see. I thought it was next week. I have to go.'

'I need you.'

'I'll phone you. Don't tell anyone about this. Please.'

He leaves the building, already on his mobile.

Of course he should go home. Alice is his wife. They might be unable to have children, but they can host elegant dinner parties. She pictures the women's tailored dresses. Inhales their expensive perfumes. She hears conversations about public spending cutbacks, turmoil in the Catholic Church.

How does Alice handle her guests' discussions on their children's development? Or is there a tacit agreement to avoid this subject?

If only she knew Richie still cared.

FOR DAYS, Olivia remains closeted in the flat, ignoring texts, Mum's invitation to dinner. At her laptop, she struggles to augment her notes, a supply of Kit Kats ready for when nausea intrudes, lemonade for eliminating the metallic taste in her mouth. Her breasts ache. Her head aches.

One evening the buzzer goes. Finally! She presses the entryphone, bolts to the bathroom to brush her teeth and hair.

The door raps, she opens it. 'I'm so... Roz!'

Roz gawps at her. 'You look awful. Why haven't you been in touch?'

Olivia stands aside to admit her friend.

Roz wrenches open the sitting room windows, speaks again, tone gentler.

'What's going on, Liv?'

Olivia fingers her stomach.

'You're pregnant!'

'If the university finds out...'

'Is he putting pressure on you? It's your body, your life.'

Roz prepares a sandwich and stands over Olivia while she eats. She fills the washing machine, dumps the dead freesias and does the dishes, while Olivia paces the flat.

'I'll support you, whatever you decide,' Roz says. 'But you must see your GP.'

Olivia says nothing. It's been ten days since hearing from Richie.

By March, jeans won't fasten and the daylong nausea persists. In the surgery waiting room, she surveys the other female patients, wondering if any of them are pregnant, if they guess why she's there. She flicks through *Vogue* magazines, staring at skinny models in white lacy tops and designer hipster jeans, skipping through out-of-focus fields. At adverts for Christian Dior perfume, their seductive qualities conveyed by rakish men fainting with desire. She tries not to think of Richie.

'It must be your decision,' Dr Wilton says. He leans back, tilts his head. 'Olivia, I've known you since you were a tot.'

To her embarrassment, her eyes spike with tears. She explains there's no chance of Richie leaving his wife, how her parents don't know. Admits she can't study and fears being kicked out of medical school.

The consultation concludes with a referral to the booking-in clinic, and she feels calmer when she leaves. Like she and Dr Wilton are in cahoots. She doesn't check her phone.

IN MATERNITY WEAR of an Oxford Street store, she fingers drab blue dresses and roomy trousers with elasticated waistbands. Demoralised, she walks through the coats and jackets department. There, while inspecting a heather-coloured blouson, she spots a familiar figure by the entrance. When the figure advances, automatically Olivia pulls in her stomach.

'So this is why you haven't been home,' Mum says, eying her abdomen. 'Come on.'

'Come on where?' she asks, conscious of her raised voice.

Her mother looks round. Several feet away, two assistants are examining skirts at the cash desk.

'You'd better come home with me.'

Too weary to argue, she follows her mother out of the shop into the heavy rain. Her mother and another woman flag down the same taxi.

'This is an emergency,' Mum says, opening the taxi door before the woman can challenge her, bundling Olivia in. Throughout the journey, her mother stares straight ahead, lips clenched, back rigid.

'Put your jacket on, please,' Mum says when the taxi pulls into Chester Gardens.

'I'm hot.'

'Just do it.'

While walking along the path to the house, her mother scans the neighbouring houses. Inside, she whips off her coat, and sits down at the computer in the sitting room.

'For God's sake, Mum, what are you doing?'

Her mother scribbles a number. 'Looking for clinics. I hope you haven't told anyone.'

'I'm not getting rid of the baby.'

'A termination is better than an unwanted child.'

'I want the baby, and you can't stop me. This is *one* thing you can't control.'

Nora scrutinises her over her bifocals. 'You know perfectly well you couldn't cope with a baby *and* continue your studies. I assume you don't have plans to marry the father.'

'I can finish medical school later.'

'You've worked hard. You've invested so much in this.'

'You have, you mean. This is a child, it's part of me, surely you can understand, being a mother yourself?'

Olivia trudges upstairs to her former bedroom. Bundles

of Mum's clothes are strewn on the bed – heavy knit cardigans and striped blouses, silk scarves with floral patterns. She wrestles a desire to sweep them to the floor, crawl under the duvet.

A wave of nausea engulfs her and she dashes to the bathroom. Her pulse races afterwards while she rinses her mouth, the mirror reflecting a blotchy skin, dull eyes. This should be the radiant stage – a honeymoon period between morning sickness and exhaustion from carrying additional weight.

She yearns for Richie. To be cherished.

She trudges downstairs again, where she finds her mother on the sofa, gazing into space. Although it's daytime, lamps on either end of the mantelpiece emit a bright light. From the kitchen wafts Radio 4's *PM programme*, Eddie Mair interrogating Gordon Brown. When Nora looks up, a momentary tenderness tenanting her eyes, Olivia longs to slump on the sofa, feel her mother's arm round her.

'Mum, I know it was hard for you not being able to become a doctor, and I know you're keen for me to succeed, and I probably will become a doctor one day, but–'

Her mother stands, rubs the back of her neck. 'I need to start dinner. Your father will be home in an hour. Do you want to eat with us? He can give you a lift back later.'

'When it's dark and the neighbours won't see, you mean... This isn't the fifties.'

'I don't suppose you've thought of the harm this could do to Dad's reputation at the school.'

Olivia puts on her jacket, closes the front door quietly and walks down the path without looking back.

Her landline phone rings later and she doesn't answer, fearing the caller is her mother. Realising it might be Richie, she grabs the receiver.

'Your father and I have talked,' Mum says. 'We'll pay for the procedure. Afterwards you can join us on the cruise to Norway. They have vacant cabins. You can rest there and be ready for the summer term. Perhaps Martin will come, too – we haven't had a family holiday for years.'

Olivia tugs the connector from the wall. Retrieves some wine from the fridge.

TWO DAYS LATER, Olivia meets her father for lunch. The restaurant has a high ceiling and large windows decorated with floral motifs, reminding her of the Rennie Macintosh exhibition he took her to when she was recovering from a prolonged chest infection.

'I'm on a mission, I'm afraid,' he tells her.

'To persuade me to have a termination. So, do you agree with Mum?'

He sighs. 'I understand where she's coming from. Her ambitions for you.'

'It's unhealthy, her living her life through me and Martin. Besides it's... it's too much pressure.'

'It's the way she is, darling,' he says, refilling their water glasses.

'I won't lose this baby... How could I get rid of it and then go on holiday? I mean, it's not like having a tooth out.'

He nods. His face is strained, his cardigan sleeves baggy, and it occurs to her he might be ill. He has seen a cardiologist, after all. When she reaches for his hand, however, and he squeezes hers, his strong grip is reassuring.

'I suppose this will make things even more difficult for you at home.'

'I know I should stand up to your mother more. Even so, we must be careful of her health.'

'Her health? She's never been ill.'

Despite the silence while they eat, she feels close to him, and when they part she lingers in his arms, deriving comfort from the tweedy smell of his jacket, like she did in childhood.

Reluctant to face her empty flat, she meanders along the wet pavements of Oxford Street, heaving with Saturday afternoon shoppers. Up Tottenham Court Road she walks, past electronic shops and home furnishing stores, past Goodge Street Station. As she crosses the busy Euston Road, a watery sun appears. She continues along Hampstead Road, recognising the Camden People's Theatre, where Dorothy took Martin and her to an unusual interpretation of *Macbeth*.

In the Camden market she buys a punnet of Spanish strawberries, stifling her guilt when she recalls Roz's rant about the environmental dangers of strawberry farming in Spain. The patches of blue sky are increasing.

She walks up Haverstock Hill, Rosslyn Hill and Heath Street, finally turning left into Hampstead Heath, now in glorious sunshine. Kids ride their bikes, dads rescue kites from trees, chuck frisbees – every child seems to be accompanied by a father.

Surrounding her is the distant hum of traffic, cars returning to Brent Cross, Edgware and further north. Returning with or to families.

Watching the sun set over Parliament Hill, she reflects on her recent conversations with Dorothy and Martin. Their optimism. And while the park empties, she remains, aware of having reached a watershed.

She can't abort her child: already its face will be looking

more human, its eyes moving closer together. Its liver will be making bile, its kidneys secreting urine into the bladder. No longer is it an amorphous blob that can be sucked out of her.

It never was.

As she walks to the Tube station, her body seems light but solid. Grounded.

11

Henri had established a circle of posts in the back garden and was counting the number of steps between each one. Checking finished, he demonstrated to Odette how to hit the ball with the cricket bat, but her head was turned in Philippe's direction.

'Come and play, Philippe,' Henri urged.

Philippe shook his head, remaining seated on a log beside the gardening shed. Despite it being his third day here, regardless of how hard the children tried, he refused to join them, except to watch television. Even when Henri proudly showed him the den, he'd been more interested in a squirrel chewing nuts. He enjoyed swinging on the hammock, but his mood only lifted when he mentioned *Papa*.

Odette ran up to him and tugged his t-shirt until he allowed himself to be dragged over. Henri painstakingly explained the rules and handed him the bat. When Henri bowled, Philippe swung and missed the ball. This happened again. After his fourth miss, he dropped the bat and trotted back to the shed. Henri scowled, muttered to Odette and returned to his position. She lifted the bat, tapped the ball and dashed to the first post.

'Please come back. It's useless with two,' Henri called to Philippe.

As I was wondering whether or not to intervene, Bertrand appeared. 'I fish at Breil sur Roya. I go with the children.'

'Philippe, too?'

He shrugged. 'If he wishes to come also.'

Fingers crossed, he would. The barking dog had disturbed my sleep and I longed to nap. As Henri and Odette rushed to the shed to fetch their wellies and rods, I heard them encouraging Philippe to come, saw him shake his head.

Ten minutes later, they'd left. Four hours on my own with him – unless Cerys returned early from the café.

'So, what will we do?' I asked.

He neither moved nor spoke.

'Beach?'

He shook his head, his eyes dull, with a hint of sadness.

'The park?'

When he shook his head again, I suppressed my irritation. There must be something he'd enjoy doing. He reminded me of a wounded animal.

Unexpectedly, his eyes then lit up. 'I want to make a cake.'

'We could make scones. Go and wash your hands.'

I cleared the table, found the ingredients and equipment. He returned, displaying his clean hands for inspection.

While I measured the flour and weighed the butter, he played with the tiny weights of the vintage scales, clinking them from one hand to another.

'You mix the flour and butter until it turns into crumbs,' I said. 'Like this, right? Now you try.'

He blended the ingredients, lips clenched in concentration, forehead furrowed. I laughed as flour flew onto his face and hair.

'Now we'll add milk.'

'I'll do it, I'll do it,' he said, clutching the jug, shakily adding the milk.

While I transferred blobs of scone mix to the baking tray, he jumped up and down.

'Can we eat the scones now?'

'We have to cook them first.'

'I help *Papa* make gingerbread. Do you know my *Papa*?' Then his eyes faded. 'He's gone away for thirty days. I have a calendar in my bedroom and I put a cross on every day after it's finished.'

'You'll have loads of days to cross off when you get home again.'

'Will these days be finished?'

'Of course... Philippe, why didn't you want to go fishing with the others?'

'It's horrible to catch fish... When I've growed into a big man I'm not going to eat fish or meat. I'm going to be a vegibairn.'

Once the scones were baked and cooling, he agreed to visit a park recommended by Cerys. During the walk there, he held my hand and hummed, occasionally breaking into a skip. When we arrived, I smiled at our surroundings: a wooden play area painted in natural hues; the air fragrant with flowering shrubs and eucalyptus.

For over an hour, Philippe crawled through tunnels, span on car tyres and slid down chutes. Reluctant to embroil myself in explanations about our connection, I sat apart from the other parents, content to watch him. From time to time, he would run over, place his warm hands on my knees, saying, 'I like this place.'

We returned home to find Odette and Henri in the front garden, peering at an overturned bucket and two grey, shiny fish, on the paving stones. Henri held a garden trowel, but apart from his seething expression, seemed to be immobilised. Odette was staring at the sky, as if awaiting delivery from her brother's anger.

'You're just a stupid girl,' he shouted.

'I didn't mean to,' she cried, hands covering her face.

I scooped up the fish. 'Calm down, Henri. Go and wash your hands, both of you. Philippe and I baked scones. You can have one before teatime.'

Henri scowled at Odette. She stuck her tongue out at him and ran off.

Bertrand appeared, having changed into work clothes. 'You must cook the fish this evening.'

Philippe tugged my arm, whispering, 'I want to make scones again.'

I wanted to, also. But when? In a few days' time, he would be away. As I bent to hug him, sniffing his lemon scented hair, I suddenly yearned to read him Winnie the Pooh, or help him construct a spaceship from Lego. Displacement activity.

Unable to find my own child, I lavished attention on someone else's.

At teatime, Philippe chewed listlessly on a mouthful of pasta.

Cerys heaved herself from the table. 'He's tired, he is. I'll take him upstairs.'

'Can we get the paddling pool out now?' Odette asked,

when her mother left the room. '*Maman* said we can stay up until *Papa* gets home.'

I nodded abstractedly, savouring the yellow light in the garden.

'Bertrand wants me to go to Lyon with him tomorrow,' Cerys informed me when she'd put Philippe to bed. 'I'll flop while he's at his conference, then he's going to take me to the Botanic gardens. There's a huge collection of glasshouses – hope I don't faint from the heat.' She giggled. 'Could you manage the three of them overnight? We won't leave until late afternoon.'

'No probs.'

'Great. Right, off you go – you'll be late for your French class. Bertie'll be home soon and he'll put the children to bed. Try and get Henri to practise his clarinet while we're away. I promised his teacher he wouldn't let it slip over the summer. You can have tomorrow morning off to make up for working extra hours while we're gone. In fact, if you're back by two, that would be okay.'

CERYS AND BERTRAND left shortly after two the following day. Due to a downpour, the children snuggled together on the sofa in the playroom, watching DVDs and eating popcorn. Then, to my surprise, when Henri set up his fire engine Playmobil, the younger boy joined in, although he seemed tired.

By evening, Philippe had developed a cough and hoarse voice, so I bathed him and administered Calpol. His eyes were closed before I'd finished reading *Toy Story*. From the sitting room came the reedy sound of Henri's clarinet.

Shortly after nine o'clock, Odette and Henri were asleep.

When I checked on them later, nevertheless, Philippe was coughing and his forehead felt hot. I sponged his face with lukewarm water and swapped the duvet for a fresh duvet cover. Having propped him up with another pillow, I plugged in the humidifier by his bed.

In the middle of the night, I woke to a tugging on my arm.

'Wake up, wake up, Olivia,' Henri said. 'Philippe's making funny noises.'

I rushed into Henri's room and knelt beside Philippe's bed. A rasping sound accompanied each breath he took. His face was florid. 'Philippe?'

The child opened his eyes and struggled into a sitting position, triggering a barking cough.

'What's wrong with him?' Henri asked.

'We need to get him into the bathroom. Henri, turn on the hot tap in the bath and shut the door.'

Philippe gave a hoarse cry.

Henri gasped. 'Is he having a bath in the middle of the night?'

'No, but if we get the room hot, this'll help. Quickly, please.'

Philippe's breathing was becoming more laboured.

As I helped him out of bed, Odette appeared, hair mussed from sleep. 'What's wrong with Philippe?'

'He has an infection.'

Her eyes widened. 'Is he going to die?'

'No! But he needs medicine. You should go back to bed.'

She yawned. 'Will I phone and ask *Maman* to come home?'

'She's too far away, sweetheart. I'll call Dr Brimé. The most helpful thing you can do is go back to bed.'

I carried Philippe to the bathroom and placed him on a

chair, where he clung to me, expression bewildered. The room wasn't warming up, so I disengaged his arms and reached to close the tiny window near the ceiling.

'Henri,' I called.

He reappeared with a paper bag. 'He can blow into this, Olivia. It stops you from breathing too hard. *Papa* told me.'

'I need to phone Dr Brimé. Find the phone number in *Maman's* address book, and get my mobile? It's on the table in my room. Quickly.'

'Is he going to die?'

'*No*. Get the number.'

After contacting the cabinet, I held Philippe while the bathroom filled with steam, my anxiety increasing as his ribcage heaved to allow him enough oxygen.

When Dr Brimé appeared, he listened to the child's chest, timed his breaths.

'He was tired yesterday and not hungry,' I explained. 'This evening he began coughing but his breathing wasn't laboured until recently. Then he developed a barking cough and I think there's stridor – I can hear a high-pitched noise when he breathes. Is it croup?'

'You are a nurse?'

'I was, and I studied medicine for several years.' I turned to Henri. 'Go and sleep in my bed.'

'But Olivia–'

'Please, Henri. It's easier for Dr Brimé... Will Philippe have to go to hospital?'

The doctor replaced the stethoscope in its box. 'I think that it is the croup. You can see how difficult his ribcage must work... I will give to him a nebuliser of epinephrine that we might dilate the bronchioles. I will give to him also some dexamethasone that will decrease the oedema... If these do not help, then perhaps he must go to the hospital.'

As Philippe's arms flailed, I stroked his back, but he continued struggling.

'You must speak with his mother,' Dr Brimé said.

'She's in Florence, both his parents are away.'

He tutted. 'The child is too young to be without his parents. We will take him to his bed.'

'He will be okay, won't he?'

'If he does not respond to the medicine, we must intubate him. We must first try the nebuliser... Please remain calm. It is better for the child if he does not sense that you are anxious.'

The doctor carried Philippe through to his bed. The machine was now ready, so I placed the mask over the child's nose and mouth, but when I fed the strap over his head, his hand reached to pull it away.

'It's alright, sweetheart,' I said. 'This will help you breathe.'

Soon a fine mist of vaporised medicine appeared for him to inhale through the mask, and he calmed down.

I clasped Philippe's febrile hand, listened to his rasping breath and watched his indrawn ribcage. His fair curls were lank, the sprinkling of nose freckles more prominent on his damp skin.

After a while, Dr Brimé adjusted the nebuliser and pointed at the child's chest. 'He breathes better. The medicine works. I will now give to him the dexamethasone. He will remain like this for some days, but his breathing will become more easy and more quiet... You have done well. Perhaps it is a good idea to return to medical school.'

When the doctor departed, I moved my armchair into Henri's room and observed Philippe until the nebuliser finished. After removing the mask, I shifted his pillow and waited for his eyes to close again before falling asleep myself. Intermittently I woke to his muttering, sponged his feverish body, sang him into an uneasy sleep. Did Alice do this for my daughter when she was ill? I wondered. Or did Richie?

By dawn, Philippe's temperature had dropped, his breathing was less raspy, and he managed to sip some water before sinking into a more restorative sleep. Not until now could I relax enough to fall into a deeper sleep myself.

I WOKE to a touch on my hand.

'Is Philippe still alive?' Odette asked.

I inspected him: his improved colour, his quieter breathing. 'He's much better.'

'I'm hungry,' she said.

'I'll get you cereal... Is Henri awake?'

After preparing breakfast, I returned to Philippe. While I watched him, he opened his eyes.

'You've been ill,' I explained.

He looked startled. 'Am I going to die?'

'No, sweetheart, you're not. You're much better than you were last night and in a few days' time you'll be completely back to normal.'

'I'm thirsty.'

I held the cup of water to his lips. 'Are you hungry?'

'I dreamed you were here. And *Papa*.'

'I *was* here – looking after you. *Papa* will be back soon. He'll be longing to see you.'

Philippe smiled and fell asleep. Lying back, eyes closed, I became aware of Odette and Henri's raised voices from the garden, knew I should make sure they'd applied sunscreen and were wearing sunhats. I'd go down in a moment.

That evening, while I was reading to Philippe, Cerys bustled in. Her cotton dress was crushed and a whiff of stale sweat wafted from her, but in addition to displaying anxiety, her eyes glowed.

'Odette and Henri told me Philippe's been ill. I should never have gone away,' she said. 'How is he? Is it a throat infection?'

'Croup. He's much better now but it gave me a fright.'

She looked at him, nodded several times as if reassuring herself, then flopped into a chair and examined her swollen ankles. 'I shouldn't have gone. Leaving you with three children.'

'Actually, Dr Brimé was pleased with how I coped. He told me I should go back to medical school. Complete my degree.'

'Maybe you should. Go and rest – I'll sit with Philippe. I feel guilty for enjoying myself while this was going on.'

'Successful trip, then?'

She grinned. 'Pity we can't do this sort of thing more often: the drawback of being a parent.'

On surfacing the next day, I found Cerys by Philippe's bed, cutting out ads from *Marie Claire*. Philippe's breathing seemed more or less normal and to my embarrassment, my eyes filled.

'Don't expect any of these would make a difference,' she said, eyes feasting on a model sporting a leather biker's jacket over a floral-patterned midi dress. 'Philippe seems better today. If you want to stay with him, that's okay. Bertrand's gone to Carrefour with the children. I need to go to the café, but not until this afternoon.'

When Philippe woke that afternoon, I read him Winnie the Pooh. He squealed in delight at the illustrations of piglet, looked puzzled whenever Eeyore was mentioned and blinked repeatedly when Tigger appeared. Halfway through the story, he reached for my hand and held it until I finished. Afterwards, I bathed him, changed his pyjamas and took him downstairs to eat with Henri and Odette. Initially, they stared at him constantly, as if expecting a relapse, and it was only when he got stuck into his chicken nuggets that they attended to their own food. He seemed thinner than before, but beamed at everyone, his furry monkey on his lap. After dinner, I took him out to the garden and rocked him on the hammock.

I STARED at the Hôpital De L'Archet in Nice, wondering if this visit would propel me forward in my search for Richie. Surrounding me was the hum of lunchtime traffic, employees returning home for their protracted midday break. Palm trees in the hospital gardens were motionless beneath the pale blue sky, characteristic of a heatwave, and already my head ached from petrol fumes, not helped by eyes strained from googling for radiologists in universities and *cabinets*.

As I walked along the ground floor corridor, the reflection from polished vinyl made me dizzy, and the floor cleaner smelled particularly strong. It was half past twelve – perhaps food would help. I located the dining room, joined a long queue and eventually took my tray to the one free table.

Moments later, two women in lab coats appeared.

'*Est–ce qu'elles sont libres?* Are these places free?' one of them asked, pointing to the empty chairs.

When I finished my meal, I produced the photos. 'I'm

trying to find this man. He's a doctor. He may not have a moustache, he might have a beard.'

After viewing Richie's picture, the women shook their heads.

'We have been at the hospital only since two months,' the taller one explained. 'If you wish, we will ask our friends.'

In the coffee lounge, people huddled round the photo, shaking their heads – except for one woman, who studied it closely. 'I think I am seeing this man before.'

My heart thumped. 'In the hospital?'

'It was long time. When I am beginning my studies. Wait, please.'

She made her way to the window and showed the photo to a man. He came over to me.

'*Salut*! Hallo! I have seen this man before. He give us a conference.'

'A lecture,' the woman said.

'Yes, a lecture. I think that he is living in Paris.'

12

S everal times during that night, the barking dog woke me, and it was after nine before I finally surfaced. Time dragged, the heat worsened by tiredness.

When Roz phoned during the evening, I launched into a description of Philippe's illness and my worry.

'You said he was a pain,' she remarked.

'Not when you get to know him – all he needs is more attention, poor little mite.'

She hesitated. 'You are okay, aren't you? You're not...'

'I'm knackered, and I feel so guilty.'

'Guilty?'

'So much caring for someone else's child, he had to work so hard to breathe. I was terrified his heart might just stop beating... I mean, I would have sat with him for days 'til he got better, yet I deserted my own baby.'

'Liv, you're searching for your child. Don't be so hard on yourself.'

'I do have a lead, actually – Richie might be in Paris.'

I explained about the student who'd recognised Richie's photo. My resolve to go there asap.

'Why aren't you sounding more excited, Liv?'

'I think I'm getting closer, but then I've thought so before and it hasn't amounted to much... It's as if I'm almost scared to hope... So, how are you?'

Roz' voice shifted up a gear. 'I was at a *Women who Love Too Much* workshop last night. I went with Jess – remember I told you about the loser she's involved with? I'll email you my notes.'

'For God's sake, you're happily married. Can't you leave it at that? Besides, all I can think about at the moment is finding my daughter.'

Stepping onto the balcony, I heard glasses clinking and a bellow of laughter from a yacht. On a rooftop below, a cat stretched on the pantiles, relishing the residual heat. Nearby, people queued for the bus to Villefranche. How I envied them: normal people with normal lives.

'Talking of problem men–' Roz said.

'We weren't.'

'Have you heard from James?'

I swigged from my water bottle. 'Not recently. Hallo, I'm Olivia. I'm a woman who loves too much. I'm here for the twelve–'

'There *is* a twelve-step programme for this syndrome, by the way... Livvy, you'll be mad but I have to confess...'

I stared over to the boat again, engulfed by a longing for fun. 'I have to go, Odette's crying.'

After the call, I felt bad. Although Roz occasionally didn't tune in, throughout my pregnancy, and even before that, she couldn't have been more supportive.

∾

Today Véronique was collecting Philippe. Had circumstances been different, I would have hung around to say goodbye. As things were, I didn't trust myself to be civil to the woman who treated her child so badly. While helping him wash and dress, it felt like I was deserting him and I hoped his father would be home soon.

'Are you pleased to be going home?' I asked.

'I want to see my *Papa*.'

'And your mother?'

Silence. What did I need to know? If he loved his mother? If he was happy to be leaving us?

After breakfast, I informed Cerys I'd be spending my free weekend in Paris, requesting to swap Tuesday off for the Monday. 'My brother will be there,' I added. 'We don't see each other often because he lives in Australia.'

'You did well, nursing Philippe when we were away,' she said. 'I suppose you've earned it and better now than after the baby's arrived.'

'So, if it's all right with you, I'll nip to the station now, get my ticket.' I downed my coffee, keen to leave before she changed her mind.

'You know he's being picked up at ten.'

'I'll take the moped, won't be long.'

Cerys refilled her coffee mug. 'You could book it online.'

When I hugged Philippe goodbye, aware of the softness of his skin, its unblemished texture, he pulled back, asking, 'Will you come to my house?'

'If I can,' I said, knowing this was inadequate.

His face registered a mixture of stoicism and reluctant acceptance of his lot: an adored but absent father, an indifferent mother.

'Not waiting to see Philippe off?' Cerys asked when I

popped my head round the kitchen door to announce my departure.

'Weekend tickets sell quickly.'

'Olivia–'

While wheeling the moped along the drive, I turned to see him by the front door, so I waved and waited for him to rejoin Odette and Henri. He didn't move. It was nearly ten o'clock – Véronique could arrive any minute. Stifling my guilt, I zoomed away.

ON MY RETURN from Cap Ferrat the following day, I stopped the moped below the corniche and retrieved my water bottle. Beside me a car hooted. Irritated, I continued drinking. Then the car pulled onto the roadside and a man emerged.

'James!'

'I should have told you I was coming but you'd have said not to.'

'How did you know where I was?'

He tugged his shirt sleeve. 'Someone gave me your address.'

'Roz! I'll shred her.'

'The last conversation you and I had was inconclusive.'

I returned the water bottle to the pannier. 'Not for me.'

It was one thing him contacting me by phone, another simply turning up unannounced.

'Can we talk? Please, Livvy, it's important. Is there a café we could go to? Or a restaurant? Have an early dinner?'

'I should get back. Besides, I must be a mess.' I glanced down at my crushed trousers, my scuffed sandals.

'Please,' he said.

I locked the moped, got into the car and directed him to a small restaurant by the harbour. It was expensive but he could afford it.

'It's a bit cavernous,' he remarked, when we descended the steps to the basement.

'Atmospheric,' I said.

With the right person.

In silence, we scrutinised the menu and the blackboard for the evening's specials. I chose scallops with rice and fresh figs. He selected an entrée of shellfish, followed by casserole cooked in a wine sauce.

'Have a starter,' he said.

I shook my head.

'How often do I take you to such a fine restaurant?'

He laughed. I didn't, his teasing too wrapped in truth to be funny. While we ate, I awaited barbed comments about my child-minding post, interrogation about my plans to return to London. In the absence of conversation, I anticipated my trip to Paris the following day. What could be achieved over a weekend. It was a while, therefore, before I sensed his changed demeanour.

'So, how's work?' I asked, peeking at my watch. Six-forty.

He wiped his mouth with the linen napkin, missing a smear of grease above his upper lip. 'Mother's ill... cancer.'

I reached for his hand. 'I'm sorry.'

'The bowel,' he said, tugging his sleeve. 'It had been there for a while before she went to the doctor. Fear, I suppose.'

The waiter appeared. 'Everything is okay? Can I bring you anything else?'

'It's fine, thanks,' I said, taking a mouthful of rice to support my comment. 'Is she having treatment? I mean, can they do anything for her?'

James stared out of the window. 'They operated. But they couldn't remove all of it. Her face is yellow. Probably not eating properly. I should arrange for a cook to come in.'

Yellow skin – jaundice – which meant one thing: liver metastases. He didn't realise the implications, not the type to question a doctor. He'd listen, but he wouldn't probe. Ironic, for a lawyer. Poor James.

He recounted how he'd learned of his mother's condition: the cancelled concert, a postponed lunch. How eventually she'd admitted what was going on. He described her weight loss, her lack of energy, the stomach pain and nausea, and now this horrible colour she'd turned. I remembered Dorothy's pallor at the end.

'This is why I need you to come home,' he said plaintively.

'I can't, not yet.'

'Nannies are two a penny.'

I stood. 'Back in a minute.'

In the ladies, I sank onto a bamboo chair covered in patterned cushions. On the nearby table, sandwiched beside miniature bars of soap and sachets of hand cream, lay a basket of condoms – I wouldn't be the first woman making decisions in this room. Should I confide in James about my daughter?

Back at our table, he had shoved his unfinished plate to one side and his breath reeked of garlic. My scallops tasted blander, more fatty – now they'd cooled.

'James, there's a reason why I'm here and can't leave. I know this is horrible for you, but we *had* ended our relationship. It's okay to phone me if–'

'Would you look after her?'

'Your mother?'

'You're a qualified nurse.'

'She doesn't know me... So, I'm good enough to nurse her, but not for you to introduce me to her as your girl-friend?' His anguished expression made me imagine how I'd feel if Dad were ill. Or Martin. 'Look, I'm sorry you've come all this way for nothing. There are agencies and I'm sure you can find someone suitable, if this is what your mother wants.'

Silence.

'I need to get back, James... Where are you staying?'

He was staring miserably out of the window and I felt sorry for him.

'I'll find you a hotel.'

The waiter approached our table, eyebrows raised at our half-eaten meals.

'My friend is ill,' I said. 'Could I have the bill, please?'

When we left the restaurant, I escorted James to a nearby hotel and booked him a small but functional room with a view of the bay. I promised to phone the following morning.

He scowled. 'Don't bother, Livvy.'

SILENCE EMANATED from the Chevalier house. The kitchen had been tidied and the tiled floor gleamed and smelled of pine. Empty worktops glistened with oil, a notice beneath them instructing, '*Ne touchez pas*. Don't touch.' Of course, Bertrand had taken the day off. When I popped my head round the sitting room door, he was lying on the sofa, reading *Le Monde*.

'Cerys?'

'She sleeps,' he said, without looking up.

Later, I lay awake, wondering if I'd been right not to tell

James the truth, if he was managing to sleep or worrying. He lunched with his mother every Sunday, took her to the theatre and concerts, and arranged holidays for the two of them. He'd be distraught when she died.

My mind switched to Paris, to the hospitals and universities I'd visit, the staff I'd speak to. Not until after midnight did my eyelids grow heavy.

At half past three I awoke to a weird noise. Initially I assumed it was a remnant of a dream, before realising the sound came from the landing. I slipped on my dressing gown and left the room.

Bertrand was rummaging in the walk-in cupboard, a grip bag and two suitcases by his feet. 'Cerys is going in labour. She must go to the hospital.'

'She's only thirty-three... thirty-four weeks.'

'She has pain.'

My stomach flipped. Cerys was supposed to give birth after my contract finished, not during it. But I must stay in the present. This was about her: her contractions, her labour.

'She won't need two suitcases... Have you called an ambulance?'

Bertrand seemed dazed. 'I will telephone now.'

In the master bedroom, I found Cerys half lying, half sitting on the bed, holding her stomach, groaning.

'Are you having contractions?'

'Yes. And my waters have broken. I was on my exercise bike earlier, see – I might have overdone it, they say that when you–'

'Bertrand's calling an ambulance... He seems terrified.'

She managed a smile. 'He's not so cool when it's family. Honestly, it's as if he's forgotten how to be a doctor when it's anything to do with me or the children. I told him if he didn't get a move on, he might have to deliver it himself. Gave him a fright.'

He appeared with a grip bag and suitcase. 'The ambulance will arrive soon.' He lifted a bundle of clothes from the floor.

'For God's sake, Bertie, the mess can wait,' she said. 'Make a flask of coffee for yourself.'

I helped her struggle into her oversized skirt and loose top, stopping every minute or so while she breathed her way through another contraction. I packed underclothes, pyjamas, toiletries. Finally, with me supporting her round the waist, we made our way downstairs.

'Don't worry about the children,' I said, when the ambulance arrived. 'Let me know how things are going.'

She nodded. 'Hopefully this will be quicker than the last two. Odette was a nightmare, in labour for forty-eight hours, I was. Oh, you'll have to phone Sandrine and explain. And ask her to let Christiane know, because she'll have to help out, and...'

Bertrand opened the door to the paramedics, who helped Cerys into a wheelchair and pushed it into the ambulance. He explained he would travel independently.

For a while after the ambulance left, I sat in the garden, staring at the full moon, inhaling the fresh, fragrant air. Then I remembered Paris.

There was no way I could go now.

13

Six years earlier

It's April and the pond is slate grey, around them, water dripping from trees and bushes. Someone has emptied the litter bin of its rubbish, and the words "Dave shagged Emma" are spray painted in purple on one side. Richie sits beside Olivia on the park bench, munching a sausage roll. Her sandwich remains in her bag. As a squirrel scurries across the grass and up a tree, his cocker spaniel strains at its leash.

'I can't leave Alice,' Richie says. 'It's not a perfect marriage, no, but I've made a commitment, you see.'

Which doesn't include monogamy.

'It's your decision if you want to keep the baby,' he adds. 'Provided the university doesn't know I'm involved.'

She chucks a stone into the water. 'Your bloody job...'

She despises herself for this. For reneging on her decision not to pressure him. He tugs the hairs under his watchstrap. 'If you were in my position–'

'Your position?'

'Yes, well, it hasn't been easy. You're aware I had to work

my way through university. You know that. You'd feel the same if it were you, I'm sure.'

'Richie, I can't get rid of my baby.'

He puts down his sausage roll and it slips from his lap to the grass, where the spaniel sniffs it, before turning away, shaking the wet from his ears. As she strokes the dog, it regards her with gooey brown eyes, making her long to bury her face in his silky hair.

Richie contemplates two ducks skimming over the pond, then chucks the sausage roll at the litter bin. It misses. He turns to her, expression distant. 'Who have you told?'

'You're doubting my discretion?'

He removes the sticky label from an apple, bites into it. His crunching grates on her – if only he'd stop eating.

'Didn't you bring anything?' he asks, mouth full of apple, its juice dribbling down his chin.

'They should make childcare more affordable.'

'I'll help financially – nursery, that sort of thing. Provided Alice doesn't–'

'I know.'

She thinks of the cottage he and his wife own in Cornwall, their timeshare in Sicily.

'How's the studying?'

She shrugs, wanting instead to grumble about back pain and the strange sensation of her body having been taken over. Wanting to know if he will be a father to their child. His voice has lost its softness.

It's drizzling again and the air smells of damp earth and flowering shrubs. He mumbles something about getting home, pats her shoulder. The spaniel looks at her mournfully.

The following morning, she ventures along the street of Richie's London home, scrutinises the terraced villa with its freshly painted beige door, its scallop-edged blinds. On hands and knees, a young woman is scrubbing the steps, the scratching of the brush rhythmic: one, two; one, two. When she pauses to draw from her cigarette, she drops it. '*Merde!* Shit!' she mutters, lips full, pouty. She retrieves the cigarette and straightens, breasts straining against her green housecoat.

Olivia steps sideways behind a tree as Richie's wife emerges and converses with the cleaner, pointing to the windows, before navigating the remaining steps and sliding into the taxi that's drawn to a halt. Alice's face is thinner, her expression more determined than Olivia remembers from the doctor's surgery.

Where is she going? A Harley Street clinic, perhaps? Considering IVF? Dealing with the polarised situations of his two women must be difficult for Richie. Nevertheless, while visualising him wanking into a container, his sperm being mixed with Alice's egg, a stronger image superimposes itself: him climaxing in the cleaner when his wife is at work.

Olivia slinks off to the tube station, sickened at having wasted time hanging around his home.

That afternoon, Martin drags her to the pub for orange juice, where, yet again, she ruminates on the pros and cons of keeping the baby. Not until she's finally stopped talking, does he mention an Australian woman he's met. She will love Zoë, he says.

Dad takes her to the zoo the following day. 'You're quiet,' he remarks.

'This is where I met Richie. In the restaurant when I was waitressing.'

'I had no idea... We can leave if it's too painful.'

She smiles unhappily. 'I can't avoid everything associated with him.' She'll never be able to obliterate him. Every time she looks at the baby/child/young adult's face, she'll be reminded of him.

When they reach the monkey house, she asks if Mum has accepted her pregnancy. Her father fans out his arms as if to say he's done his best.

She nods. 'How's school?'

He smiles wryly. 'I've refused another promotion. It would mean less teaching. Can't see myself getting embroiled in discussions over curriculum changes.'

'So, how did Mum... react?'

Silence.

She retrieves her camera from her bag. 'You haven't told her, have you? Isn't the misty light glorious?'

'No point going through the same old stuff, darling,' he says, reading the information about Diana monkeys.

'I'm opening a bank account for the baby,' he informs her while they peer at the polar bears. 'You can invest it if you'd rather – it could build into a sizeable amount before the child starts school.'

She selects a shutter speed, photographs him.

He slips an arm round her shoulder. 'This is between you and me: I've cashed in an annuity.'

They wander on, arms linked. His smile is the sweetest.

RICHIE ARRIVES LATE FOR DINNER, a stain on his blue chinos. He flops into a chair, switches on the television, watches the news for a moment before changing to golf, expression vacant. He wanders round the sitting room, examining plants for dryness.

When Olivia has served the meal, he returns to the

armchair with his plate, once more flicking from channel to channel. She remains at the table, flinching every time he changes programme, the meagre appetite she had, evaporated.

Building within is the longing for him to hold her. In the bathroom, she examines her changing shape in the mirror: the pendulous breasts and swelling stomach, its tummy button poorly concealed by layers of clothing. Her face seems puffy, moon-shaped. She dabs herself again with perfume.

When she returns, Richie is munching slowly. A necessary refuelling.

'Hi,' he says, as if he's just arrived. 'Aren't you eating, then?'

She kneels beside him, and although their relationship hasn't been physical for a while, places his hand on her breast. He recoils. Only then does she notice a wet patch on her sweatshirt – the start of the milk machine. Fleetingly she hates the baby who has commandeered her body, made her large and unappealing. She stares at the darkening sky.

He checks his watch. 'I need to go.'

'It's barely eight.'

'Yes, well, I'm off to a conference on Saturday and I haven't finished writing my Paper, you see.'

'Where?'

A pause. 'Florence.'

'I could come too. I love Italy.'

Time together will inject their relationship with energy. She'll wander by the banks of the Arno. Take arty photos.

'It's not a sensible idea, no.'

'I won't get in your way. Please... I'll visit the Uffizi, it's ages since I've been to a gallery, we'll have the evenings.'

He stares at her poster of Mykonos. 'There'll be conference dinners, meetings. You know how these things work.'

'I'll wait until you get back to the hotel. Besides, I don't mind eating alone and at least we could wake up together.... It'll be lovely.'

Silence.

The words force their way out. 'You're taking your wife, aren't you?'

'I've said I'm not, no, she's not going either.'

'Actually, Richie, you didn't say you weren't taking her.'

She ignores the inner voice telling her Alice is entitled to accompany her husband.

Especially after all she's been through.

His tone conveys weariness. 'Alice can't come. Work commitments.'

'You'd take her if she was free, you mean?'

An image of the French cleaner flashes before her.

'Yes, well she is my wife. It's possible, yes, she might have come too, provided she'd been free, but she isn't... I must get home now.'

His leaving hug is perfunctory. From the window she watches him exit the building, fumbling for his keys. He crosses the road, walks along the side street and opens the Saab door, without glancing back. His car slips into the traffic, heading north and home.

Home to his real life.

ON THE DAY Richie is flying to Florence, Olivia slumps over her muesli, wondering how to find out if his wife is going too. She hates herself for begrudging Alice anything. Outside, a dustcart clangs while it lifts and empties. Raised voices from next door indicate her neighbours are embroiled in their routine Saturday morning argument.

She grabs her jacket and leaves the flat.

At Victoria station, she reaches her train thirty seconds before the doors close, and sinks onto a seat with relief, before remembering her undignified mission. Her heart pounds at the announcement she's on the Gatwick Express.

At the airport, the departures board informs her that his flight to Florence is scheduled to leave in eighty minutes. She locates the check-in queue, the automatic check-in machines and the seated areas: no sign of him. He might already have gone through, of course. She should have got here earlier.

Tears are close – hormones.

'Can I help you?' asks a woman in a navy uniform. 'Do you have a flight to catch?'

'I'm fine, thanks,' she says, striding away, hoping to convey purpose. At Costa, she orders coffee. While she drinks it, her eyes remain peeled.

On the verge of abandoning her quest, she spots Richie in a dark suit, with another man, poring over a laptop. There's no sign of Alice. She lingers – his wife might be shopping. As for herself, she's desperate to pee. When she returns from the loo, he is chatting with his colleague. Then they lift their hand luggage and stand.

She watches, still half expecting a woman to appear. After all, having gone through those multiple miscarriages might have brought Richie and Alice closer. And a few days in a romantic city like Florence could rekindle their love. Even if they don't have much time together. She waits until he has gone through security, before she leaves the airport.

On the train back, she realises why he couldn't take her – his colleague might have known Alice. Idiot that she is, not to have worked this out. Her high is short-lived, however – he could have explained this to her, arranged for her to travel separately.

In London, head bowed against the heavy rain, she walks and walks, trying to think coherently about her future.

At the cul de sac, she searches for a chink of light in the sitting room curtains, hesitates before pressing the bell. The hall light appears, she hears Dorothy asking who it is.

'It's me, Olivia.'

Her aunt opens the door, gasps. 'You're soaking. Come in, lovie, come through to the sitting room.'

'Sorry it's so late.'

A smell of baking pervades the room as she wriggles out of her sodden clothes. Dorothy brings a towel for her hair, and a fleecy dressing gown. Appears minutes later with cocoa and thickly buttered treacle scones. Not until Olivia is seated and warming by the fire, does she notice the half-filled suitcases by the window, the chairs piled with clothes and books.

'Are you going on holiday?'

Her aunt rummages through the box of paint tubes and brushes on the table. 'I was going to phone you tomorrow. I've rented a villa in Gibraltar for three months. It will inspire my painting... I'll be back for the birth.'

Olivia helps herself to another scone. 'I'll miss you.'

'There's a spare bedroom in the villa. Come with me.'

'I couldn't, I mean...'

'Are you studying?'

She isn't, but she's still registered as a medical student, despite not having appeared at lectures for weeks now, reluctant to publicise her pregnancy.

Dorothy sits at the other side of the fireplace. 'Lovie, you are having the baby?'

She nods.

'Are you planning to return to university immediately afterwards?'

She shakes her head.

'Then explain to them what's happened and come with me. Just for a few weeks. It will be good for you to get away. I'll pay.'

It would mean no more Richie. Besides, would she be more purposeful in a strange country than she is in London?

'Are you still seeing Richie?'

'It's different now...'

Dorothy leans forward. 'Whatever the situation, pregnancy suits you. It's a marvellous sight, a woman with child. I would love to paint you.'

Olivia blinks back tears. 'Sometimes I hate myself for what I've done.'

A flicker of concern registers in Dorothy's eyes, then she says briskly, 'I leave on Friday. Think about it. Meanwhile, you'll stay here tonight. No arguments.'

In the spare bedroom, she remembers her aunt reading to her from the crimson armchair. Recalls various family crises during her formative years, the certainty she was always welcome here.

OLIVIA HEARS nothing from Richie on his return from Florence. In time, her yearning for him blunts – no man merits such longing. There'll be no more humiliating efforts to regain his love. She'll have the baby. Move on.

At active birth classes, she relaxes on foam mats in a

lofty room with corniced ceiling and full-length windows. While flutes warble overhead from a state-of-the-art music centre, and aromatic oils burn by the mantelpiece, she learns to breathe from the diaphragm and to exercise her pelvic floor. She participates in discussions about labour plans. Ponders the advantages of a pool birth. Smiles at the choices of music. For her, nothing less rousing than Wagner's *Tristan und Isolde* will accompany her baby's entry into the world. Furthermore, she'll accept pain relief but not an epidural. And definitely no stirrups.

The women are friendly, several of them single, but, unlike her, glad to be so. Sometimes they lunch together after class. The old timers detail their experiences of Caesarean sections, of forceps deliveries. Discussions abound on the merits of different pain relief and the quality of orgasms after childbirth, while they munch their organic salads and drink fruit smoothies. There's much laughter and, despite the predominance of wedding rings, a burgeoning sense of belonging.

Gone now are the three-hour siestas lying with a pillow under her knees, evenings slumped on the sofa watching tabloid telly. Gone, too, are any attempts to study. Instead, she attends a swimming class for pregnant women, buys wool to knit minuscule jumpers, and researches creams for reducing stretchmarks. She joins the National Childbirth Trust, strolls around the park, devours books on parenting.

Martin drenches her flat in pastel colours. Zoë, whom she already regards as a sister-in-law, encourages her with anecdotes of successful single parents. Dorothy sends a cheque for baby clothes.

It's been weeks since Olivia heard from Richie.

And then, one day, when she is six months pregnant, when she has accepted their affair is over, he phones.

14

After the ambulance left, I popped into the children's rooms, but they'd slept through the commotion. Back in bed, all I could think about was Paris and when I could rebook it. By the window lay my packed bag, my folder with lists and routes for universities and hospitals.

At six o'clock I went out to the garden, where the air smelled fresh, the grass still damp from Bertrand's twilight sprinkling. I lay on the hammock and eventually drifted off to sleep.

Later, while I prepared breakfast, the phone rang.

'Cerys has made a baby girl,' Bertrand announced. 'The doctors made a Caesarean section.'

'The baby's alright?'

'She is small but she is healthy also. We are calling her Frances.'

'Shall I bring the children in this morning?'

'*Mais bien sûr,* of course.'

I replaced the phone and inhaled deeply, before calling

Henri and Odette who immediately appeared from the garden.

'Was it *Maman*, Olivia? Has the baby been born?' Henri asked.

'You've got a sister – Frances.'

Odette jumped up and down. 'Now I have another girl to play with.'

Henri scowled and kicked the door.

'Stop it, Henri... What's wrong?'

'When's *Maman* coming home?'

'The baby was born early, so they'll keep her in hospital for a while to make sure she is okay. *Maman* will stay with her.'

He stared at the ground. 'Perhaps it will be a boy next time.'

For the first time, he let me hug him.

Later, my chest constricted as we walked through the outpatient department – past heavily pregnant women and bustling staff; past the florist's shop; past the gift shop displaying baby grows and balloons with congratulatory messages.

I should have been halfway to Paris by now.

My head swayed so I searched for a seat. Fortunately, I could see Bertrand approaching, and when the children spotted their father, they dashed up to him. He lifted Odette and swung her, ruffled Henri's hair. I said I'd join them in a few minutes.

Hovering outside the single room, I found myself pitched back to the last time I'd been in a hospital, peering into my aunt's room before she died. Fleetingly it was Dorothy I saw, her dying face and limp body. Then, like a radio tuning in, I returned to the present: Cerys sitting in bed unwrapping Odette's gift; both children gazing uncertainly at their mother; Bertrand by the window.

'Good, you're here,' she said, when I opened the door. Despite her pale and tired appearance, she conveyed the inner glow and happiness of a newly delivered mother. A strength of joy which would compensate for broken nights and twenty-four-hour service.

'Were you there when the baby was born, *Papa*?' Henri asked.

Bertrand nodded proudly.

Odette glanced around the room. 'Where *is* the baby?'

'She's in a special room at the moment, *cariad*, love, because she was born early,' Cerys said. 'You can see her later – examining her, they are, at the moment.'

Bertrand stretched his arms, yawned. 'I will find the coffee. *Allez,* come on, Odette, Henri. *Maman* wishes to talk to Olivia.'

'It's okay...' I began, even as he guided them from the room.

'Let them go,' Cerys said. 'Dying to have a woman-to-woman chat, I am. So dramatic it was, the ambulance whizzing along the road to hospital. Of course I was expecting a bit of hard graft in labour.'

I braced myself for the most intimate details. Where were her friends?

'When I arrived,' she said, 'they monitored the baby and told me they needed to deliver her immediately. Didn't want a section, see. But there was no choice, her heart rate was dropping, so they whisked me off to theatre...'

Her account of the birth continued, the sound far away, like distant winds. From the open window I could hear traffic, church bells.

'Olivia? Are you listening?'

I leant towards her, forced myself to feign interest, forced myself not to think back to my experience of giving birth.

'Then they gave me a local anaesthetic and I felt a poking around in my stomach and finally they produced this little baby. It always seems so easy but it isn't. It's not like taking a cake out of an oven. It's a big operation. There are risks. I'll be sore for a while but they've given me painkillers – euphoric they make me feel... Are you all right?'

I reached for my inhaler, puffed the medicine into my mouth. It wasn't enough. 'It's hot in here, I need air. Sorry.'

The beauty of the hospital grounds intensified my anguish as I slumped, head in hands. All sense of time and place deserted me, a gamut of emotions ricocheting round my head. After a while, I sensed someone beside me.

'Olivia!' Laurent said.

I glanced up. 'What are you doing here?'

'I had a meeting with a colleague. What is wrong?'

'It brought it all back... giving birth, I mean.'

He sat down beside me and I leant against him, words haemorrhaging out. When finished, I pulled away, mortified by such outpourings to a man I'd met three times. 'I was going to Paris today, I had the tickets booked, and now it'll be even more difficult.'

'Olivia, this was several years ago that Richie was working in Paris. Perhaps he has moved away. I think that you must look also in other places.'

'I've spent hours on websites.'

'Perhaps it would be better to visit the hospitals and the universities on the Côte D'Azur. Websites are not always current. You can then show the photos. Also, if Richie has changed his name, you can look at the notice boards and ask questions to people.'

'It could take forever.'

'I have a few days of holiday. I will be happy to drive you. I know the area and it will be more pleasant for you in the car rather than the motorbike.'

'You're so kind.'

His expression was serious. 'One day I will explain to you the reason.'

I got to my feet. 'I should return to the ward. They'll be wondering where I am.'

'I have made some copies of your photographs,' he told me as we walked back to the hospital. 'With the beard and without the beard. It is the same with the moustache. I have sent the photos to my colleagues in Lyon and in Marseille.'

At the ward entrance, I hugged him. 'Thank you for everything.'

Back in Cerys's room again, I managed to smile.

'I'm dying to show you Frances,' she said. 'Normally only immediate family are allowed in the unit, but because you'll be helping me with her, I can take you along.'

The special baby care unit swarmed with gowned figures who monitored ventilators and machines recording heart rates. Staff made notes on clipboards and reassured anxious parents.

Lying in an incubator was a white bundle with a tuft of dark hair peeping out from her knitted hat. A nasogastric tube fed her formula milk. I studied the red face, the fluttering hands. As memories assailed me, it was all I could do not to turn around and leave. If I hadn't reacted so badly to the epidural, I could have witnessed my own baby girl's fight to survive, perhaps given my son the will to survive. I clutched my necklace and focused on the sunlight streaming through the window.

My daughter was alive, and I might find her.

'You must leave now,' a nurse said. 'We are receiving two
more babies.'

Cerys barely acknowledged my departure.

Later, I took Henri and Odette to the cinema, acqui-
escing to demands for popcorn and coca cola and lurid pink
chewy sweets. I hung out washing, darned a rip in Odette's
swimming suit and made lasagne. Once the children were
in bed, nevertheless, the house quiet while Bertrand visited
Cerys, I found myself trembling. If only he would return
and I could go running.

When I looked in on Odette, I noticed a line of dolls and
teddies along one side of her room. Henri's room contained
a mass of bobbing white balloons with "Frances" painted on
them in pink.

I didn't even know my daughter's name.

THE FOLLOWING AFTERNOON, I drove Odette to Beaulieu to
visit a friend from her dancing class. When we arrived, the
mother invited me to stay for coffee and cakes while the
children played.

I hesitated, having planned to visit several clinics to
show Richie's photos.

'Do stay,' Lynn urged. 'I bought lots of chocolate cakes
and I'll end up eating them myself – they're too rich for the
children and my husband doesn't have a sweet tooth.'

I followed the small fair-haired woman into the sitting
room, a large sunny space with picture windows, and every
surface covered with photos. The doorbell rang and she left
the room, her expensive perfume wafting through the air.
While she was away, I studied those photos, its subjects in

traditional poses, everyone smiling, no heads turned away, no one blinking or looking bored.

From the hall I could hear English voices. She called out, prompting a tapping sound as a child ran downstairs. Two young voices dominated, then faded after the children had gone upstairs.

Moments later, Lynn reappeared. 'That was Michelle, my younger daughter's friend. Her mother couldn't stay, so it's you and me to tackle those cakes.' She rolled her eyes in mock concern.

We discussed ex-pat life, how easy it can be to surround yourself with English speakers. She knew people who, after eight years, barely spoke any French, used British doctors and plumbers, and rarely socialised with non-native English speakers.

'Such arrogance, such superiority,' Lynn said. 'I suspect they're only here for the climate. They certainly have little interest in French culture. They mock their customs. When Tony and I moved here, we immersed ourselves in French immediately.'

'So, are most of your friends French?'

'Fortunately, yes. Except for Alice – who thinks exactly like us and has spent thousands on French classes.'

'Alice?'

'Michelle's mother.'

The room was swirling. Alice... British... Mother of a little girl.

'I'll turn up the air conditioning,' Lynn said. 'Sorry, I should have realised you're not accustomed to French summers.'

'How old is Josette?'

She adjusted a switch, then paused on her way to the

door. 'Newly six... I'll see that the girls are okay upstairs, then I'll make more coffee. Help yourself to another cake.'

I didn't want more coffee or cake. I needed to regain my composure, to think coherently. In such an expat area, there could be loads of British women named Alice, with five or six-year-old daughters. Besides, I didn't even know Alice's surname. There was no reason to think that this was Richie's wife and the child upstairs was my daughter. Yet the possibility that she might be, cause my heart to pound.

Seconds after Lynn returned, her phone rang, she mouthed "sorry" to me, opened the French window and stepped into the garden.

Poised on the edge of my chair, I considered rushing upstairs to find Michelle, see if I could learn anything, even just her surname. Phone to her ear, Lynn was pacing the garden, shaking her head, sighing.

My mobile rang – Bertrand informing me he'd collect Odette after picking up Henri from football. I cut him off, needing to concoct a convincing reason for taking her home myself. If I got nowhere in learning about Michelle's identity, I had to stay until a parent – Richie? Alice? – collected her.

Lynn reappeared, stared at me for a moment as if wondering why I was there, then remembered the coffee and went into the kitchen. When she brought through the coffee pot, I asked for directions to the bathroom, hoping it was upstairs, so that I'd have a chance to speak to Michelle.

'I'll show you,' she said, taking me into the hall, pointing to a door at the end of the corridor. 'The wash-hand basin is in the room next door. A nuisance really. Tony is always saying he'll remove the wall, make it into one room, but I'll believe it when it happens.'

'Your phone's rung twice,' she told me when I returned.

Shit! I hadn't switched it off properly. When it rang again, I pressed the "off" button, while pretending to talk to the caller. My hostess seemed miles away.

On the pretext of checking Odette was wearing sun cream, I wandered into the garden. The girls were sitting under a plane tree, seeming older than seven as they conversed in French.

'Don't Josette and Michelle want to play outside with you?' I asked them.

'Michelle is allergic to strong sunlight,' Delphine said. 'And she forgot to bring her proper clothes.'

I hesitated, wondering how to extract further information about the child who could be my daughter. 'Do you know what Michelle's second name is?'

Delphine shook her head.

'Is she British?'

'I don't know. Ask Mummy.'

Disconsolate, I returned to the house.

'There you are,' Lynn said, her voice brighter.

'When are you expecting Michelle's mother or father?'

She regarded me curiously. 'Around five.'

'I could drive her home, save them the bother,' I said to allay suspicion, and, hoping it sounded like general conversation, asked, 'Did you and Michelle's parents move here around the same time?'

She took another cake. 'No, the Williams have only been here for about three years.'

The name fitted, of course, also the timing, and my heart leaped, but before I could think of an acceptable way of asking more about Michelle's parents, Lynn added, 'It wouldn't surprise me if they returned home soon. Alice's mother isn't well, and she doesn't like being so far from her.'

'You can get to the UK in hours – if you fly,' I pointed out unnecessarily.

She blinked at me, her preoccupied expression returned. 'They're from Sydney – but you'd never know it from their accents.'

She continued proffering cakes, described the French wine tasting club she and Tony belonged to, the English-French language exchange she facilitated, the pros and cons of French schools. Drained from having my hopes reduced to rubble once more, I only managed the occasional comment.

That evening, I ran even faster along the beach. In the distance, a water-skier zigzagged across the wake as a golden ball of sun descended. My spirits lifted.

WHEN I ARRIVED at the maternity unit two days later, Cerys's room smelled like a florist's shop, an extra trolley having been acquired for the flowers. Far from appearing radiant, however, she was in tears.

'The baby has a hole in her heart,' she said. 'She needs a chest x-ray and a cardiograph.'

I glanced at the empty crib.

Recalling my learning from medical school, I chose my words carefully. 'This is quite common. There's a high chance it'll heal by itself. And even if it doesn't, a simple operation would fix it.'

'Too young to have an operation, she is,' she wailed.

'Cerys, lots of adults have holes in their hearts and they're completely healthy. There's nothing to worry about.'

'I can't stop thinking about a tiny white coffin with her body in it.'

'Why don't you phone Bertrand?'

'Get me the new *Elle* from the hospital shop, would you? It'll distract me until I have the results... You hear such terrible stories.'

'Wouldn't they let you be with her while they did the tests?'

'What if she dies? What if her heart just stops? She's so tiny.'

I leant forward, took her hand. 'Speak to Bertrand. He's a doctor, he can–'

'He's not a paediatrician. Get the magazine, before it sells out.'

When I returned, she smiled at me. 'Bertrand agrees with you, there's no need to worry. Will you stay until they have the results?'

I put away her clean clothes, refilled vases and located her cosmetics bag. I retrieved "congratulations" cards that had drifted to the floor, rearranged them on the locker top. Lastly, I bundled together soiled nightdresses and shoved them in my rucksack.

When the doctor appeared, I made to leave but Cerys grabbed my hand. 'Stay.'

'Both the x-ray and cardiographs are normal, Madame Chevalier,' he said. 'The hole in the heart will probably mend spontaneously. If not, we can perform a routine operation. Your daughter will be fine.'

Her eyes filled with tears and she clasped his arm. 'Thank you, thank you. How reassuring to speak to an English doctor.'

He smiled and left.

Minutes later, a midwife appeared with Frances. Cerys stretched out her arms and held her baby close.

Rather than return straight home, I strolled along the

waterfront in Villefranche, restored to peace by boat life: the adjusting of sails; flapping and tinkling flags; the slopping of water and aroma of cooking from galleys. How lovely it would be to head out to sea.

Memories surfaced. In a reckless moment, Richie had once arranged to borrow a friend's boat and I'd been giddy at the prospect of a weekend together. Then, assuming Richie was taking his wife, the chum and his girlfriend had suggested accompanying him. He'd cancelled.

On impulse, I stopped now at a café, ordered a Caesar salad and glass of wine. Several men entering and leaving the restaurant glanced lingeringly at me.

I was more than a nanny.

After putting the children to bed that evening, I was too tired to jog. Instead, I lay on the hammock in the back garden. My challenge was to resist being tugged down. Somehow I'd negotiate time off, rearrange Paris.

When I returned to my bedroom, my laptop screensaver of waves dispensed its calming effect. Then I noticed my sandals had been moved from under the table, and my chair was at an angle. Henri and Odette wouldn't interfere with my things. Which left Bertrand. I opened "history", to see my websites of London psychiatrists, from searching for Dr Barak's number, and the doctors' sections of *Pages Jaunes*, Yellow Pages. Bertrand and his bloody nosiness. How dare he snoop around!

I set a password for my computer.

THREE DAYS LATER, I paced my room, waiting for Laurent to collect me. It felt like a big event, our driving east along the coast to visit hospitals and universities. And if we got nowhere today, he'd promised, another day we'd try further west – Cannes, Toulon and Marseille.

'Have you planned the route?' he asked, when we left the Chevalier home.

I scrutinised my list: Menton first, no university there, but two hospitals and some clinics. Then Antibes – again no university, but hospitals. Despite having worked out a logical order for visiting each hospital, I knew we'd be hard pushed to achieve all this in one day.

At his suggestion, we avoided the choked up *moyenne corniche* to Menton, instead driving higher.

'What's that?' I asked, as we passed an ancient village perched on a rock, with magnificent villas sloping down the hillside.

'It is called Eze,' he said. 'It is the real Côte D'Azur. There are the ruins of a 12th century castle.'

'Sounds idyllic.'

'The views over to Cap Jean Ferrat are wonderful. If I were an artist, I would live there. I would paint tranquil courtyards and quiet squares.'

When we viewed Monte Carlo from above, my bubble burst – concrete buildings, glass towers, a waterfront with large cruise liners belching out tourists. It would have been a delightful place once, and I could understand affluent Brits spending their winter months here, developing a routine of morning strolls, gentle afternoons on the beach, elegant dining in the evenings, a modicum of gambling, perhaps.

At Roquebrune-Cap-Martin, we followed the coastal route to Menton. Approaching the old town felt like a homecoming, with its pantile roofs, palm trees, and marina, its graceful old hotels lining the beach. Despite low cloud partially obscuring the mountains, the colours were rich.

Suddenly I wished I wasn't required to summon the energy to present Richie's photos to indifferent hospital staff and pester them for information. It would be lovely to simply sightsee.

Like a mind-reader, Laurent said, 'One day we will visit here to enjoy the city. Every February there is the Lemon Festival. There is always a different theme. Many bands play and the local people decorate the Casino Gardens.'

While driving along Menton's Avenue de Verdun, we heard a wail of ambulance and police sirens. The traffic crawled to a halt, more sirens sounded.

He frowned. 'I think there has been an accident. The driving here is crazy.'

I observed my surroundings – elegant salmon coloured apartment blocks with bay windows and wrought iron balconies, some with cream awnings; shaded parks with fountains and sculptures; and the ubiquitous tall palm trees. To the right, however, loomed two high-rise apartment blocks, painted in a garish orange and turquoise zigzag effect. I imagined the wrath of neighbouring residents when they lost their mountain views. Pondered the insensitivity of town planners who permitted modern monstrosities to be built so close to traditional houses.

My eyes were stinging. 'I can smell hydrogen sulphide.'

He closed the windows. 'Perhaps there has been a gas explosion.'

It took thirty minutes to edge along the avenue de Verdun. When we turned left onto rue Antoine Peglion, this was even slower, and soon we drew to a halt once more. In the distance we could see the Centre Hospitalier La Palmosa and ambulances pulling in and out. Overhead, two helicopters circled.

'This is the main hospital for emergencies in the area,'

he said, fiddling with the radio until he found a news broadcast.

'There has been a gas explosion in an apartment block to the east of the city. The hospital will be busy.'

Of course it would: patients with smoke inhalation, burns, broken bones and abrasions. In particular, the radiology department would be in overdrive, x-raying lungs, scanning head injuries.

'Should we give this one a miss?' I asked.

He switched on the radio again. The presenter gabbled away, but I understood one sentence, delivered more slowly and repeated: only those with serious injuries should use the emergency department of the Palmosa today.

'Perhaps we should try one of the clinics,' I suggested.

'Let us continue to the hospital and see what will happen.'

There were no vacant spaces in the hospital car park so we drove round the immediate vicinity. Vehicles were parked inches from each other, front wheels on pavements. When we eventually found a space, it took fifteen minutes to walk to the hospital gates. There, a cluster of journalists bombarded us. '*Avez–vous été témoin de l'explosion*? Did you witness the explosion?'

'*On vient d'arriver à Menton*. We have just arrived in Menton,' Laurent explained.

Spotting a few patients leaving the main entrance, the journalists rushed off. Laurent then struck up a conversation with another man, learning that the apartment block had collapsed, damaging neighbouring shops.

I wrestled with my conscience, before saying, 'Let's find radiology – if Richie's there, we might glimpse him. We don't need to speak to him, not today.'

Laurent hesitated then followed me into accident and

emergency where we navigated our way past trolleys of patients with shards of glass and metal protruding from their bodies, with burns to faces and torso, with broken limbs. There was a quota of walking wounded, dabbing bleeding faces, clutching injured arms. Staff scooted about, assessing the urgency for treatment.

I turned to Laurent, 'We should leave.'

At the hospital entrance, we dodged past journalists still hoping for stories from survivors. The smell of rotten eggs lingered in the air as we returned to the car, stopping on the way for a baguette and espresso. We then drove to the *Centre de Ré-education Cardio-Respiratoire.* There, we checked a board of staff photographs, but it didn't included Richie's, and the receptionist recognised neither my images of him nor his name.

Laurent was now coughing and seemed tired.

'Let's call it a day,' I said.

He nodded. 'I am catching a cold and cough. I have run into steam.'

I laughed. 'Out of steam, you mean.'

We drove out of Menton to the intermittent wail of ambulance sirens conveying more victims to the Palmosa. With relief, we heard a radio presenter pronounce the initial conclusion that the explosion had been accidental and no terrorist involvement was suspected.

Hours later, lying in bed, my reflections turned from disappointment at today's lack of progress, to what must be happening now at the Palmosa: the patients who hadn't survived; those badly injured; bereaved relatives. I thought about the staff exhausted from doing double shifts, and those called in on precious days off.

Mostly I thought about how life can change in an instant. Like mine had, six months earlier.

FOUR DAYS LATER, while I was putting away the children's clean washing, Henri rushed over to his bedroom window.

'Olivia, they're here. *Maman*'s here,' he said, pushing past me to run downstairs.

'At least your room is tidy, Odette,' I said. 'Let's go and see and Frances.'

She hung back, so I bent down, clasped her hands. 'Tell me what's wrong.'

'Will *Maman* love me now there's another girl?'

'I promise you she will, sweetheart. It doesn't matter how many children you have, you don't stop loving one because another has arrived.'

Still Odette lingered.

'Come with me,' I said, leading her to her bedroom where I lifted a doll wearing a lacy dress. 'When you got Claudine for your birthday, did you stop loving the other dolls?'

She shook her head. 'I love them all the same.'

'This is how it will be with *Maman* and *Papa*. You'll see. Come on, *Maman* will be wondering where you are.'

She slipped her hand into mine.

DURING THE NEXT week or two, visitors came and went. Frances fed incessantly so I prepared nourishing snacks for Cerys, observing how she ignored her own needs. Planning unusual offerings – soft goat's cheese and fresh figs served on nut bread, baked peppers filled with smoked fish and walnuts – provided a welcome distraction.

I now felt disconnected. Discomfort with Bertrand was

the norm but feeling separate from Cerys and the children was new. Up to a point, daytimes took care of themselves, Odette and Henri keeping me busy. Not so the evenings, Cerys and Frances in their cocooned world of feeding, changing, singing to sleep; Bertrand, Odette and Henri comprising another unit. These days, Bertrand was returning earlier to eat with the children, before playing with them in the garden or taking them cycling. Several times on departing for my French class or Cap Ferrat, I'd seen them dancing in the sitting room, Bertrand teaching jiving steps, encouraging Odette to practise for her next class. Despite the fact that his presence allowed me more free time, the enthusiasm I had for my usual activities had lessened.

Running helped, but immediately afterwards, the loneliness returned. If only I could get to Paris. If only I could sleep through the night without such awful dreams.

I was slipping off the map.

ix years earlier

S   Despite the radiator next to her, Olivia shivers in the pub. It doesn't seem like June, sleety rain pounding off the window.

'Yes, well how are you?' Richie asks, his voice slightly hoarse.

'Better than you by the sound of it.'

He sips his whisky, glances at his watch. His eyes scan the room, as if checking for anyone he knows.

'How are you?' he asks again. 'How is the baby? Do you know yet if it's a boy or girl?'

She shakes her head. 'I haven't had a scan. It kicks a lot, it's kicking now.'

He smiles. 'Can I touch?'

While guiding his hand on her abdomen, she experiences desire, his musky smell ever present.

He leans forward. 'I wanted to talk... I'll get the drinks, back in a tick.'

She watches him navigate his way to the bar, relieved that her presence at the airport remains her secret. That she didn't accompany him to Florence. He needed time to miss her. Them.

'Fancy something to eat?' he returns to ask.

She nods. His aura seems different. Understandable though, given the circumstances. Why has she always been so negative? He'll support them, and when the baby's older, she'll resume her studies. With his salary, nursery fees will be a doddle, and Mum might even babysit, especially if it helps Olivia qualify as a doctor. By then, of course, they'll be married, ultra-respectable. Their age difference isn't uncommon.

He appears with the drinks, a filled roll for her.

'Not hungry?' she asks. 'This isn't like you... I suppose it's your cold.'

She laughs. He doesn't.

She bites into the wholemeal roll, savouring the chicken mayonnaise. His eyes are strained and she understands – the deadly cocktail of a cold and stress. Poor Richie: while she's been suffering, so has he. Life at home must be fraught. Or perhaps he has already left Alice. How admirable not to have come straight to her.

He tosses back his whisky, Adam's apple bulging as he swallows. He tugs the hairs under his watchstrap. It's not like him to be so nervous. Should she make it easier for him, take the initiative? But this would be like opening a present before her birthday. Eventually he puts down the whisky glass he's been clutching.

Richie lifts her hand, fingers the jade ring she always wears. 'Such a fabulous stone.'

When he releases her hand, she resists the urge to lean over and hug him. There'll be time enough later. As he delves into his pocket, she wonders if he can hear her heart thudding. This is so romantic, not classically, what with the rain rapping against the window and the bracket lamps already on at three o'clock, but, hey ho.

He produces a hanky, blows his nose.

'Sorry. I can't shake off this sniffle, you see.'

He needs peppermint tea or perhaps elderflower. With added catnip, for fever.

And St John's Wort for angst.

He lifts her hand again. His is clammy.

'Yes, well, I wanted to talk to you,' he begins.

She smiles. He averts his eyes, drops her hand.

His voice is slow, deliberate. 'Alice has found out.'

A wave of compassion floods her. Alice will lose so much.

'You are aware,' he continues, 'last time she miscarried, she was told she can't carry a baby full term... can't have children. This has been such a sadness, for her, for us.'

A pause while he selects his next words. He wants to be sensitive, of course, not rush straight from Alice's pain to their happiness.

She reaches out, touches his arm. 'I know,' she says.

He withdraws his arm. 'You, well, you are obviously not in a position to raise a child on your own. It's not an ideal situation, no, but–'

'It *would* be easier with two parents,' she admits, trying to contain her smile.

Richie nods.

All he has needed is time. Life is about timing. Adjusting to change. And he'll be a great father, despite his additional years.

Like a driver struggling to change gear, he shifts his tone up. 'And so we have a suggestion, you see.'

'We?'

'Yes. Please hear me out. We – Alice and I – would like to bring up the baby ourselves, we would really love to do this.'

This can't be right – who wrote this script? She waits, allowing him the chance to rephrase, to say what he intended to say. He waits too, searching her face, an unambiguous gravity to his expression.

'You want... you want to adopt my baby, you mean?'

'*Our* baby.'

She knocks over her glass.

'I can't... how could you... how could you even think of such a thing? For God's sake... I can't believe you're serious.'

'It's pragmatic.'

'Callous more like.'

'It's not a conventional situation, no. It may sound strange, but if you think about it... Provided the child doesn't know the truth, I don't see why things shouldn't work out.'

'How did your wife find out?'

He hesitates. 'She was aware of there being another woman. I told you she turned a blind eye. But when she found out you were pregnant...'

'So, your wife finds out and you agree you'll raise the baby together, like I never existed?'

'Well, no. It wasn't so straightforward. You don't need to be aware of the details. I'm just making a suggestion about to how to get out of this mess, you see.'

'Mess? This isn't a student problem you have to sort. This is about a baby. Besides, *you* pursued me. You... I thought you were going to suggest we give our relationship a go, that you'd decided to... I thought you'd decided you wanted a family with me.'

'I'm sorry, yes, I am truly sorry you hoped this would happen, but it was never an option, you know that. You have always been aware I wouldn't leave my wife.'

She squeezes her swollen feet into her shoes, lifts her jacket and stumbles off.

'Wait,' he calls. 'Come back, please. Please.'

She returns to her seat, stares at her hands. The finger bearing Dorothy's ring is puffy. She hadn't noticed this when Richie admired the jade stone.

'Finish your roll,' he says. 'You must eat.'

The rain is now torrential, cars pulling into the roadside. To her left, a bulb from one of the lamps has gone and there are worn patches on the orange carpet. And she'd considered this place romantic...

'When Alice discovered you were pregnant,' he says, 'she insisted I leave and–'

'Where did you go?'

'Does it matter?'

'Where did you *go*?'

'The golf club. I stayed at my golf club.'

'You didn't think of contacting me? Obviously not. How did she find out?'

'I'm just trying to keep to the essential details.'

'How considerate.'

He averts his head. 'She found the number of a clinic in my pocket.'

'A temination clinic, I assume.'

'Just let me tell you what happened.'

She lifts her phone, dials a taxi company. He grabs the phone.

'Two days later, Alice contacted me. Her terms were that if we agreed to raise the child, we could stay together, provided I didn't see you again.'

'And this was acceptable?'

'Well, there's more to it, you see.'

He clenches his hands, the hands that have given her

such pleasure. They seem smaller.

'She threatened to report me to the faculty. And I might not lose my job, I suppose, but it would jeopardise any promotion. So you see, I had no choice... I can promise the baby will be greatly loved. And it will have everything. Everything.'

'Except its natural mother... It's not like buying a sofa.'

He flushes. 'Well, no, I'm not implying that.'

She stares at her doughy hands. He won't notice them now. It's the baby he wants.

'Olivia, I can understand this is a shock. And you don't need to let me know now.'

'That's all right then, that's brilliant... What, you're giving me a day, a week?' She stares out of the window. The rain has eased off, traffic is moving again.

The barman announces a customer's steak pie and chips is ready.

Richie leans forward. 'She's desperate for children, you see. Before you and I got together, we were considering adoption and it's possible, yes, that we'd have gone down that route, but our marriage was shaky and it would have been hard to convince adoption agencies that our relationship was strong enough to–'

'I've heard enough,' she says, rising.

'I'll drive you.'

'I'll get a taxi.'

'It'll cost a fortune from here. Let me drive you – please.'

If she lets him take her home, he'll have time to reconsider. But he won't change his mind – Alice is too strong for him. She imagines Mum's disgust, her withering comments.

The words slip out. 'And then?'

'You'll have to let us know your decision.'

The "us" stings. Yet she hears herself ask, 'And you and me?'

He turns away.

'You don't want to see me again? Of course not. Why would you? I mean, it's not like I was ever important to you.'

Silence.

'So, this is it?'

His nod is barely perceptible.

She leaves. Lingers by the pub entrance, willing him to appear, to admit he needs her.

IN THE OUTPATIENT department of the maternity unit, Olivia searches for other women without partners. There's one by the door. Then a man appears, sits beside the woman, kisses her neck. As Richie did in the early days. She examines her oedematous fingers, knowing that had she, in a moment of madness, agreed there and then to him and Alice raising her baby, he'd have grilled her about her pregnancy. If only he'd now pop his head round the door, having miraculously tracked down her appointment. Eyes welling with tears, he'd view the scan and rewrite his script of that awful afternoon in the pub.

She averts her eyes from the lovey-dovey couple. Scans the waiting room. Its pastel green and pink walls are bedecked with posters of breastfeeding women, bearing slogans, "Breast is best" and "Give your baby the best chance in life". The featured mothers have shiny hair and glowing skin enhanced by subtle make-up. They look rested, their designer babies having permitted them an unbroken eight hours of sleep. She visualises a poster of a pale-faced woman with baggy eyes, mohawk hairstyle and nose ring, struggling with a disgruntled baby.

The strains of Abba's *One Man, One Woman* drift round the room. It's a while before Olivia realises she, too, is singing,

'*One man, one woman, one life to live together,*

One chance to take that never comes back again. You and me, to the end.'

'*You and me to the end,*' she repeats, this time silently. 'Oh Ritchie...'

She remembers Anni-Frid Lyngstad, whose daughter was killed in a car accident.

Surviving your child, the greatest grief of all.

After filling another plastic cup with water, she studies a poster listing the health benefits of drinking water. H_2O, such a simple molecular structure, but the panacea for all ills. Except heartache. She strokes her rapidly growing abdomen. Twists the silver band she's placed on her wedding finger.

'How is it going?' a nurse asks.

She finishes her fourth carton of water. 'My bladder is full.'

The nurse smiles. 'Not long until you are called.'

Several minutes later she hears a voice, 'Olivia Bowden.'

In the treatment room, the radiographer introduces herself, explains the procedure, and asks Olivia to lie on the couch. Heart thudding, she rolls down her skirt and shoves up her sweatshirt to expose her stomach. What if something horrible shows on the screen?

'This will be cold,' the radiographer says, applying gel to her abdomen. 'This is your first scan?'

Her bladder will burst open any minute.

The radiographer directs the probe. 'It won't take long.'

It had better not. How uncool it would be to flood the room. She wonders if this often happens.

The radiographer is now homing in on the screen. 'There's one heartbeat and there's the other one.'

'What?'

'You're having twins. Everything seems fine.'

She lies there. 'I didn't know. Is it... are they... What are they? I mean, are they boys or girls?'

'Are you sure you want to know?'

'I am. Yes.'

The radiographer pauses before answering, 'One of each. Mothercare have a sale of double strollers at the moment.'

Olivia's eyes spike with tears while she reassembles her clothes. 'Can I have a photo of the scan?'

The radiographer smiles. 'Of course, but we ask for a donation.'

Dazed, Olivia slips a two-pound coin into the box at reception, collects her photo and stares at it in the visitors' loo. On the way home, she buys a large bunch of freesias.

IN HER KITCHEN, she pores over the photo of the scan. It resembles two little otters. She prods her stomach, searching for four legs. Wonders why, despite knowing that female twins are more likely to conceive twins, she's never entertained this possibility. Do twins communicate with each other in the womb? Did she and Martin? She imagines one saying to the other, 'You kick, then I will.'

On the kitchen table, Richie's envelope lies unopened.

Shortly before midnight, she opens it. The grey textured paper bears his elegant, navy script. '*I received your letter,*' he writes. *'Please reconsider. I promise that Alice and I will give the child a happy life, the best that money can buy. He/she will want for nothing.'*

She imagines Alice coaching her husband while he scribes.

For a moment, the feeling of leverage not unpleasant, she considers offering them one of the babies in exchange for Richie's presence in her life. A win-win situation. She and Alice get to be mothers, they share Richie. Of course this is a ridiculous idea. She's been reading too many Simone de Beauvoir novels.

After shredding the letter, she bins it, then slides the photo into a plastic cover and inserts it in a pocket of her purse. Later, she slips out of bed, retrieves the photo and gazes again at the otters, wondering how she could have contemplated – even momentarily – parting with one of them. With a lump in her throat, she kisses the photo.

She dreams of being in the desert with Richie. He's carrying one baby on his back, she another on her front. It's hot and they've run out of water.

'This way,' he says with a sweep of his arm. 'There's a well near here. We should make it before dark.'

As they tramp off into the falling sun, the baby in her arms cries and Richie turns round.

'I'll catch up with you,' she says, unbuttoning her blouse.

'We must keep going – a sandstorm could blow up,' he says. 'There's a shelter near the well.'

Agitated about the increasing distance between them, she stumbles on. When she reaches the water hole, two turbaned figures spring out and grab the baby from its papoose. Richie shrugs, continues walking.

Her body is saturated in sweat when she wakes.

As a ribbon of light streaks the sky, she flings belongings

in a bag, finds her passport and pauses by the front door. Already a bird is in song. She drops her bag, retrieves the photo from the bedroom floor and places it in the inside pocket of her jacket. After locking the front door, she feels for the outline of the photo.

16

'Fabrice and Antoinette are early,' Cerys said, scampering into the kitchen, Frances in her arms, a stain from regurgitated milk on the shoulder of her brown blouse. 'Did you find clean towels for the spare room, Olivia? Why isn't Bertrand back from the supermarket? I hate it when people arrive early.'

While the adults chatted in the garden and Odette and Henri played in the swimming pool, one gripe dominated my thoughts: with two extra people to look after the children, I could have been in Paris, searching for Richie and my daughter.

Just before I went off duty that evening, Antoinette suggested we walk down to Villefranche. Bertrand, Fabrice and Henri were settled into the World Cup and Cerys planned an early night once she'd fed Frances. Apart from intermittent cheering from bars, the streets were quiet as we descended the corniche.

'I hate football,' Antoinette admitted. 'Such a story! Fabrice has watched every match. I do not care if Brazil wins.'

The sun was dropping towards the horizon when we reached the harbour. A hint of lavender and the salty tang of seawater pervaded the air.

In Place Amelia Pollonnais, I said, 'I love coming here, 'specially after running. I imagine how it must have been before tourists came in their hordes. I picture myself on one of these balconies or walking along a narrow alleyway for bread. I visit the Sunday markets – I never buy anything.'

'I also love to visit the markets... Have you made any progress with your search for your daughter?'

I filled her in about what had happened since we last met.

'But there is more troubling you, I think.'

Antoinette wore a low-necked purple maxi dress and dangly orchid-shaped earrings, an outfit that complimented her grey eyes and softened her features. She could be barely forty-five, hardly a different generation, but this evening I regarded her as a benign mother.

'It's so difficult, with the baby, I mean. I feel as if I'm sinking into a black hole.'

'Why not return to London to see your therapist? You have so much pain.'

'I was ready to go to Paris when Cerys went into labour... I can't ask her now for time off to go there.'

Antoinette hesitated. 'I think it would not be wise to go to Paris at the moment. You are vulnerable. You should visit your home. I can stay longer with the family. I will speak with Cerys.'

~

By the time the plane descended through layers of cloud, the light and vibrancy of the Mediterranean seemed distant.

At Heathrow, the ubiquitous easily understood conversations felt intrusive, accustomed as I'd become to being surrounded by unfamiliar tongues. Nevertheless, when I spotted Dad in the arrivals lounge, emotion surged and I rushed over to him.

'It's lovely to see you, darling,' he said.

'I'm glad it's you. I was hoping it would be. Could we get a drink before we leave? We could say the flight was late – it was a bit.'

'Better not. Your mother's in the car. She's... having a difficult day.'

'Because I'm back, you mean?'

'She got a letter from Mr Minto – he's asked her to... to reconsider her challenge. The GP vouched for Dorothy's state of mind when she dictated the letter.'

'Is she likely to back down?'

Dad didn't reply but when we reached the exit, he turned abruptly. 'Sod it, a quick coffee.'

'Text her to say the luggage has been delayed.'

When we received our coffees, I plunged straight in. 'I haven't been straight with you about why I went to France – it wasn't for a long holiday.'

I explained about Dorothy's letter and my search for Richie, about not having confided this until now to avoid problems for him with Mum. How I hoped he'd understand. 'So, you're a grandfather... Say something, anything.'

His face was an emotional palette: astonishment, joy, concern, bewilderment, his Adam's apple working furiously. Once or twice he opened his mouth then closed it again. I awaited signs of hurt, disappointment, anger even, but saw none. My eyes brimmed with tears for him, for what having a granddaughter would mean. It was so easy to imagine him with her, teaching her to swim, reading her books about animals, calming her simply by his presence.

Aware of the shortness of time, the preciousness of every moment, I continued, 'I don't know why I didn't think of this before, but I'm wondering if Dorothy discussed this with William, if she told him... if he knows anything which might give me a clue about Richie, where he might be. She wrote the letter not long before she died – perhaps she forgot to add something important... Are you alright?'

Dad blinked hard. 'Considering I've found out I'm a grandfather, I suppose I am.'

'You do think I'm doing the right thing, don't you?'

'Yes, yes. Heavens, this *is* a lot to take in... I assume you don't want your mother to know.'

'Part of me thinks she should. The other part...'

He glanced at his watch.

'I know, we should get going.'

He lifted my bag, placed his free hand on my arm. 'Don't say anything about the Will, darling, if you don't mind.'

Observing his fatigued eyes, I imagined life at home: Mum's gripe about the Will, and her general discontent, supported by an ever-growing repository of grievances. Might having a grandchild soften her? Eventually?

'At least you got your luggage,' Mum said, when we pulled out of the car park, provoking in me guilt about the true reason for our delay, a yearning to tell her the truth, without risking repercussions for Dad. 'I've made sweet and sour pork and it doesn't keep well in the oven.'

As the car sped along the motorway, past muted greys and greens beneath an un-textured white sky, I zipped my jacket, wondering if I'd packed a jumper.

'Your father thinks we should go for white but I'd prefer buttermilk,' Mum was saying. 'Olivia, are you listening? I was telling you we're repainting the outside window frames at the back of the house.'

Her conversation continued, me lapsing in and out of concentration. Now Dad knew the truth, I didn't feel so alone. After a while, the smooth glide of the car made me drowsy and I eventually woke when he pulled into the drive.

Mum rushed to the kitchen to rescue the pork. Dad poured himself a large whisky. Having detected nothing new to admire in the sitting room, I rabbited on about how lovely it was being home again. In truth, I longed for my flat. Even though having tenants covered the mortgage.

'I can't believe I've been gone six weeks,' I remarked after lunch, while filling the sink with water.

Mum added detergent to the dishwasher. 'Hmm, anyone would think you'd lived there for years, the way you went on at lunch – France this and France that... Leave the baking tray to the end.'

'I hoped you'd be interested. Besides, you've always loved France. Especially the south coast.'

'It depends on the circumstances.'

'Believe me, I have an important reason for doing what I'm doing.'

I watched her wrapping cling film round dishes of rice and broccoli, spooning lemon meringue pie into a plastic container.

Talking to her was like navigating cobbles in stilettos.

'We've been busy here, too. Getting William settled in the care home and deciding what to do about their house. He's adamant it's not to be sold. He knows perfectly well that he couldn't manage there on his own.'

'You can understand why he'd be hacked off about selling his home.'

She pursed her upper lip. 'You're parroting your father.

No one understands I'm the one who'll be landed with all the work of renting it out. It'll have to be completely redecorated, of course, and the carpets need replacing.'

Now she was labelling *Tupperware* containers. 'I'll put these in the freezer.'

Listening to her flat-heeled shoes tapping downstairs to the basement, I recalled our childhood game of speculating on what she would retrieve from the freezer: mint flavoured ice cream, mulligatawny soup, Dorothy's famous chocolate fudge cake. If we guessed correctly and it was a cake or pudding, Mum would give Martin and me a helping when it defrosted.

In those days her footsteps were lighter.

I took my luggage up to my old room, then tracked her down in the conservatory, watched her dusting and misting the cheese plants. Her lips were moving, though her words were inaudible. She was definitely talking to her plants, and in her enthusiasm, her voice grew louder. 'Another new leaf, well done yucca. Cheese plant, are you listening? It's time you produced a new leaf. See what you can do. I'll be checking.'

Instinctively, I stepped back and tiptoed through to the sitting room. A moment later she appeared. 'Oh, there you are. There's a new garden centre I thought we might visit.'

'Actually, I've an appointment at three.'

'I suppose you'll be out running afterwards. I hope we'll see something of you while you're home.'

I glimpsed sadness in her expression. Then it vanished.

Too drained to reply, I drifted back to the kitchen – to the tidy worktops; the pansies compliantly flowering on the windowsill; the cork board with a WRVS rota, and notes to phone the window cleaner and dentist; the calendar of

English gardens with the last Saturday in August ringed in red for a Brahms *Requiem* recital.

Closing my eyes, I summoned another kitchen: an oak table strewn with pens, receipts and limbless soldiers; a window ledge crammed with yoghurt cartons of thyme and basil; cupboards displaying the children's art work; the broken flagstone where Henri had dropped a frying pan; an obdurate spider's web that Odette talked to.

'It's Dr Barak, the appointment,' I said, when Mum appeared to refill the watering can.

'You're not ill again, I hope. You didn't eat much lunch.'

A FRIDAY AFTERNOON vibe emanated from the waiting room, its silence broken only by clicking of computer keys from an adjacent office and the occasional drip from the water fountain. Surrounding the tiled fireplace, a jungle of umbrella plants, ferns and vines achieved its intended soothing effect, enhanced by the fragrance of rose wafting from three red candles in the fireplace. On either side of the window, pine bookcases overflowed with academic texts – the logic of the female mind, theories of depression, understanding death – and popular psychology paperbacks.

As usual, I felt ambivalent about my session with Dr Barak. Although I trusted him and would feel calmer afterwards, the opening up, the thinking required during those sixty minutes was invariably harrowing. I likened the psychotherapeutic technique to cleaning leeks: a flushing out of dirt from layers of green and white leaf, whilst maintaining the vegetable's integrity. Or the skilled excision and irrigation of an infected wound. The pain would remain, but blunted, more manageable, the accompanying weeping, cathartic.

'Where would you like to start?' he asked, after calling me through.

I summarised my time in France, cringing at an early display of tears.

'I'm tired, and I wake unrefreshed... I dread getting out of bed. And I'm finding it increasingly difficult being with Cerys and the baby.'

'Tell me about this.'

'I get... panicky. And jealous...'

'Jealous.'

'She gets to do all the things I couldn't do with my babies. There's a way she holds her – with the baby's head snuggled into her shoulder. Like they're welded together. Cerys normally rabbits on the whole time – I stop listening. But when she's with the baby, I mean, she's different, her expression's... it's like she's at peace, despite the fact she's up feeding her half the night.'

He crossed his legs. 'It sounds as if it's hard watching her do the things you weren't able to do. It's hard to see her enjoying her baby.'

'If I believed I'd get my little girl back... if I believed I'd have another chance, then I wouldn't find it so difficult... despite the fact I'd have lost those early years. I mean, she'd still be young enough to really need me. I want this.'

'You need to be a mother, to have a child dependent on you.'

I now regretted having arranged the appointment for my first day home. Tired from my early departure, from absorbing Mum's negativity and Dad's anxiety, I was already running close to empty.

'What's the baby's name?' Dr Barak asked.

'Why?'

'You talk about her as "the baby", not giving her a name. I wonder if this is because it makes her existence less real for you. As if she's not a real person.' He passed me the paper hanky box and I grabbed a tissue.

'They call it "flesh time", you know? The holding of the baby next to your skin. It's a unique experience – the relationship with a new baby. And I didn't have it... She'll be almost six.'

I stopped, wondering if he had children, and if he didn't, if this was painful for him. An issue he'd had to address during the mandatory analysis required of trainee psychotherapists.

'This is a big thing for you. An important thing,' he said. 'The nurturing, the dependence of a child on its mother.'

'Wouldn't it be for all women?'

'What do *you* think?'

'I don't know... My closest friend, Roz, is in no rush for children. But people I was at school with – most of them longed to become parents, and most of them have.'

'Is there something about wanting to be like other people, like your friends?'

The need to belong had never occurred to me before. Perhaps this explained my closeness to Roz.

I was now crying so much I could barely speak. 'It's about knowing I could have had this, if I'd... behaved differently.'

He poured me a glass of water. I sipped it, regained control.

'You were diagnosed as experiencing a negative reaction to the diamorphine. One which was at least partly responsible for your leaving the hospital in the way you did. Yet you still blame only yourself for your actions.'

I was silent for a moment, before telling him about the aborted trip to Paris.

'I'm hearing anger in you, towards Cerys,' he said.

Suddenly I wanted the session to be finished. To go to the movies and be comforted with a bag of liquorice toffees. Ten minutes left.

'It wasn't Cerys' fault. It was bad timing. A week later, three days even...'

I described the effect of my lack of progress, the worry my eating disorder would return. Dr Barak made the occasional observation and suggested calming techniques. When I mentioned my attempts to meditate, he nodded approvingly. The session ended with an agreement that because our therapist/client relationship was established, we could have phone sessions while I remained in France.

WHEN I ARRIVED at the care home, I found my uncle in the sitting room, clutching a crumpled newspaper while peering at the motor racing on the large flat screen television. Residents (many asleep) slumped in vinyl chairs: women in synthetic dresses; men in checked shirts, and beige trousers. On noticing me, William beamed, and I managed a smile.

'I've brought ginger biscuits,' I said, kissing him, relieved to sniff his familiar Old Spice aftershave. 'Do you still like them?'

'It's lovely to see you, dearie. Have you left France?'

'Only for a long weekend. Have you settled in here?'

He looked as tall as ever, but his face had thinned considerably.

'We play backgammon in the evenings. Helps pass the

time. And they do relaxation and exercise with us. There's a residents' meeting every week. I complained about the gristly meat in the steak pie.'

'Are you happy?' I asked, a stupid question when he was so recently widowed. Perhaps when I found my child, she would add another dimension to his life.

His attention was now focused on the door, and I turned to see Mum sweeping across the room. Despite her enigmatic expression, the thickly coated lipstick revealed much: the worse her mood, the more she applied.

'Hallo William,' she said.

He didn't answer, his hands shook and a pulse in his throat throbbed. When the trembling increased, I signalled to a care assistant, recalling his distress at Mum's presence when Dorothy was dying.

The care assistant appeared, studied my mother. 'I'm fairly new here: I don't think we've met.'

'I'm Mrs Bowden, William's sister-in-law.'

'You're Nora... Could I have a word, please?' she said, taking Mum aside. For several minutes she remonstrated with Mum, then Mum left the room.

The assistant reappeared. 'Nora has gone now, William, and we'll make sure she doesn't visit again. Are you alright?'

He blinked furiously then yawned.

I talked about France for a while. Although he asked a few questions, he didn't fully recover his composure, blinking often, struggling to open the biscuits.

'I'll see you again before I return to France,' I promised, when I left.

As I paused at the door, another resident was shuffling over to him, clutching a zimmer. He smiled at her and pointed to a chair. My weariness lifted: perhaps this was the best place for him.

JAMES WAS ALREADY SEATED when I arrived at the restaurant the following day.

That morning, Dad had driven Mum and me to the Docklands Garden Centre to buy bulbs and a new bird feeder, after which we'd had coffee and flapjacks. Superficially, at least, the atmosphere had been calm. My mother should have volunteered in a Botanical garden or garden centre as anything connected with horticulture made her happy.

Fingers crossed, her benign mood would last until I returned to France. After the excursion, my parents dropped me off on their way to an organ recital at Dad's church, and during the ten minutes' walk to the restaurant, I felt the most relaxed I'd been since leaving Villefranche.

'You're looking well, Livvy,' James said.

'Surprising, given that I'm staying at my old home...' I broke off, unaccustomed to discussing my family dynamics with him.

Noticing the waiter hovering, I scrutinised the menu. Expensive.

'How's your mother?' I asked, when we'd ordered.

'Not good.'

His hair needed cutting, and there was congealed blood on his chin from a shaving nick. I wanted to hug him but displaying affection publicly would embarrass him. Besides, he might misinterpret my gesture.

I filled our glasses with water. 'I'm sorry. Is she at home?'

'She refuses to go into hospital. I'm trying to find a nurse for her. I don't suppose you'd reconsider...'

'I'm only here for a visit.'

'I don't understand why being in France is so important.'

'James, when we first met, you made it clear you weren't interested in my past, despite knowing something traumatic had happened. What I'm doing in France is connected with this. You didn't want to know then, so–'

'Things change,' he said, rubbing his eyes. 'I'm sure there's been a cat in here and I forgot to take my antihistamine this morning... Well, are you going to tell me your big secret?'

'If you're sure you want to know... Brace yourself – okay, I'm... I have a child. A daughter. She's five.'

He knocked his knife to the floor. He tugged at his sleeve. He gazed at something fascinating on the carpet.

'Were you married?' he asked eventually, avoiding eye contact. 'Are you? Have I been... in a relationship with a married woman?'

I laughed at his horrified expression. 'No.'

'Where is your... daughter?'

I explained about Dorothy's letter and my resolve to find Richie. Throughout, James listened silently, expression distant as he waited for me to finish my sordid story.

The waiter brought our food. I ate my veal escalope, James poked at his meal, the smell of his sole catapulting me back to Place Amelie Pollonnais at dusk – the alleys from where I would peer into restaurant basement kitchens and watch the fish frying.

We attempted to discuss other things, but his sentences petered out and eventually he stood. 'I need to get back to the office. I'll settle the bill.'

I wondered if we'd ever meet again.

Ignoring the waiter's stony expression, I finished James' glass of Chardonnay.

~

LATER THAT DAY, I lingered at the entrance of the care home lounge. Dead flowers had been replaced, and afternoon sunshine streamed through the spotless bay window. There weren't many residents there and I couldn't see William.

A carer directed me to my uncle's room, where I found him resting on his bed. When he saw me, he beckoned me with a bony finger.

'Have you found your baby yet, dearie?'

My pulse quickened. 'You *know* about her?'

'Dottie told me after the row she had with your mother. It was a terrible row. I never saw her so angry. It was shortly before she had her stroke.'

'What did they row about?'

He fiddled with his frayed shirt cuff. 'Her face was red when she got home. She drank a large glass of sherry. Then she had another one. Her face got even redder.'

'What did they fight about?'

'She was shaking. She couldn't eat her dinner. They give us Guinness here, if we can't eat. Dottie and I sometimes drank Guinness after we left Gib.'

'Uncle William, I need to know. What did Mum and Aunt Dorothy row about?'

'You shouldn't have done that, Nora,' he said, hands trembling.

'It's Olivia.'

A nurse came in with a plastic container of pills and a polystyrene cup of water.

'Time for your medicine, William.'

He swallowed the pills, his faded blue eyes blazing.

'It was wrong of you, Nora. You tell Olivia I want to see her.'

The nurse regarded me sympathetically. 'His periods of

lucidity vary. At any minute his concentration and memory can go.'

I shrugged into my jacket and said goodbye to him. Perhaps there'd be time for a final visit before returning to France.

'Come back again,' the nurse said, wheeling the medicine trolley round, dispensing completed. 'Late morning is normally when he's at his best.'

'How is he, I mean, in general?'

'Quite calm, as a rule. But he talks about a baby and a row with Nora. He becomes agitated when he mentions her... We haven't been able to find out what this means.'

'Nora is my mother, and something happened between her and Dorothy – her sister and William's late wife.'

'This is helpful. If it's okay with you, I'll pass this on to the team psychologist.'

'Could you email me if William does say anything more about a baby? Anything that makes sense, I mean. Here's my card.'

While jogging later on, the conversation with William kept surfacing. I'd ask Mum about her argument with Dorothy, but it would be difficult – if she didn't want to talk, she wouldn't.

'How's William?' Dad asked at dinner.

I shrugged. 'I could talk to him at first then he became confused. He thought I was Mum.'

'He's in the early stages of dementia,' Mum said. 'It's the best place for him. Olivia, fetch the parmesan from the fridge, please.'

'He told me you and Dorothy had a terrible row, not long before she died.'

'You're supposed to be fetching the parmesan.'

In the kitchen, I retrieved the cheese. The sun had cast a glorious misty light on the rose bushes, and only the need to find out about Mum and Dorothy's row, drove me back to the dining room.

'What was the row about?' I asked my mother.

'It was a private matter.'

'William said he'd never seen her so angry... He asked me if I'd found my baby. Was it to do with this?'

Mum turned a deathly white and a pulse twitched on her cheek. Fleetingly I felt sorry for her, not having known about my daughter's existence until now. Wishing I'd broken it to her more gently.

She recovered her composure a moment later. 'Nothing can be achieved by talking about it. It was a long time ago.'

Something in me snapped. 'Mum, did Dorothy talk to you about my baby? Did you know something? If you won't tell me, I'll see William again.'

The cheek twitching increased and my mother spoke quietly. 'Now surely you're not going to upset an elderly man?'

Dad leaned forward. 'Olivia has a right to know.'

'I will ask William if you won't talk to me,' I said.

Mum wore her self-righteous expression. 'I did what I believed was best at the time.'

My chest thudded. 'Did what? What *are* you talking about?'

Dad shoved his plate aside. 'I'd like to know what this is about, Nora.'

She lifted her fork. 'Is neither of you going to eat your lasagne?'

I gagged at the sight and smell of glistening cheese, and in a voice drained of energy, asked again, 'What did you do?'

She pursed her upper lip and replaced her fork. 'The hospital wrote to us.'

I clutched my stomach. 'The hospital in Morocco?'

'I didn't know anything about a letter,' Dad said. 'What did it say?'

The room swayed, my breathing constricted. I gripped the sides of my chair.

Mum's eyes were focussed on the sideboard. 'They were trying to get in touch with Olivia.'

'Why?' I managed to ask before my throat swelled shut.

'To...to let you know that one of the babies had survived.'

17

I reached for my inhaler.

Dad clutched his head and his voice seemed to emerge from deep down. 'Jesus Christ, Nora, how could you conceal this?'

'You know perfectly well Olivia couldn't have brought up a baby on her own. She had a career ahead of her. As you'll realise, I've had my comeuppance, being written out of Dorothy's Will. A frightful way to be treated by one's sister.'

'We could have helped Olivia with the baby,' Dad said. 'I could have worked part time, you could have helped.... Lots of grandparents do this.'

Dad's quietly expressed anger was more potent than shouting. He, it seemed, was almost more outraged by my mother's behaviour than I was. And it was a moment before the thought occurred to me.

'Did you know Richie had my baby, Mum?'

Silence.

I heard my raised voice: 'Did you know Richie had my child? Dad, make her tell me... she must tell me, please. She must tell me everything.'

Mum lifted her head, sniffed. 'The hospital wrote to us... your father. They didn't know how to contact you and his name was on your passport as the next of kin. I opened the letter. I managed to contact Richie and he said he'd go to Morocco to collect the baby.'

'And what about me?'

I slumped back in my chair. All those wasted years...

'We didn't know where you were,' she told me, voice steady. 'I hoped you'd return to London, become a doctor, have a future.'

'So, you had no intention of telling me this when I returned to London. Obviously not. God, you're sick, you know that? Twisted, sick–'

'Olivia, enough,' Dad said without conviction.

Someone was standing, shouting, 'You believed you had the right to let this happen to my child... you had the right to make such a momentous decision that Richie would bring her up, that I'd have nothing to do with her?'

Mum raised her chin. 'This is all in the past.'

'Oh, really? You have divine wisdom, do you?'

I wanted to slap her self-righteous face. To rip off the necklace, scatter its faded pearls across the floor.

'How did Dorothy become involved?' Dad asked.

Mum hesitated. 'She found out about the letter.'

He leant forward. 'How? Did you simply tell her?'

'We argued... it came out. She contacted the hospital in Tangiers.'

Mum walked over to the window, frowned at a skate-boarder falling off his board. 'They spoke in French. It was a bad line... but she understood that Richie had collected the baby.'

I searched my mother's face for a glimmer of emotion – regret, guilt.

'And me, didn't they want to know, didn't I bloody count for anything?'

'According to Dorothy, he told the hospital you were too ill to travel. They assumed you were his wife.'

I clenched my damp hands. It seemed like a lifetime, those months of knowing my daughter existed. Even imagining Dorothy not having rowed with Mum, not discovering the truth, frightened me. Reminding me that as a child, I'd lie in bed, wondering how it would be if the world had never been created, I'd never been born.

'I can't believe you didn't tell me. I could never do such a thing.' I reached for the inhaler again. 'You saw me at The Priory, when things were bad, when I couldn't eat, how bereft... how... Even if you'd told me then...'

Dad's eyes appeared dead, he couldn't even look at my mother. 'How could you, Nora?'

She pursed her lips 'I can't imagine how Olivia thought she would have coped as a single mother. It would have meant the end of a respectable existence.'

'It's outrageous that you made such a decision. Outrageous.'

'I'm not saying I would do it again, but I was only thinking of Olivia.'

'Of course you were,' I said.

Silence, then she left. I heard her ascending the stairs, my parents' bedroom door clicking shut.

My father's face had paled, and he raised a helpless hand.

❧

As I COLLAPSED onto the park bench, a bank of murky clouds heralded heavy rain and within minutes it was driz-

zling. Nearby, picnickers packed up and tennis players
conferred. A mother called to her son, who was tugging a
toy yacht on the pond. Despite the rain now dropping in
unrelenting sheets, I remained seated, watching the bedrag-
gled ducks. My mouth tasted of bile and my head throbbed.

Just my luck having a fucked-up mother.

A day after the revelation, the shock of my mother's
deception had blunted. Reluctantly, I'd reclaimed some
responsibility for my initial loss - I couldn't justifiably blame
it all on an adverse reaction to the pain relief. If I'd stayed in
the Moroccan hospital or been brave enough to return there
to collect my passport, I would have left with a baby girl.
Bereaved of my son, of course, but still a mother.

Even so, I couldn't forgive Mum for concealing the fact
my daughter was alive, for contacting Richie, as if I had
died. She and Dad could have collected the baby. Instead,
she'd given Richie what he and Alice wanted.

At home, my mother was trimming oasis, inserting the
green, crumbly block into a vase. She then picked up her
red secateurs to trim some flowers, the snapping noise harsh
on my ears. I watched her install a yellow chrysanthemum
in the centre, then one on either side. After adding orange
roses and sprigs of silvery grey foliage, she stood back to
judge the effect. Constrained by oasis, the flowers resembled
soldiers standing to attention. I pictured Cerys ramming
geraniums into a crooked jug Henri had made in pottery
class.

I stood to leave the room. Dad had left the house mid-
morning and hadn't returned, and the thought of being on
my own with my mother any longer was repugnant.

'Dinner's nearly ready,' she said.

'I'm not hungry.'

'I've made one of your favourite dishes.'

'I *am* trying to find my child, you know. This is why I went to France. Dorothy wanted me to, that's why she wrote to me before she died.'

As I rushed from the room, I heard the key in the front door. Dad was back.

In the garden, I leant against the wall of the house, ignoring water dripping from the Virginia creeper onto my shoulder, shivering despite the August evening. Through the open window, I heard my father say, 'You've only yourself to blame,' a rare hardness to his words.

Then Mum's reply, 'Don't use such a tone with me. I'm the one who made the sacrifices.'

'Sacrifices? Oh yes... Well, you won't have to make these anymore.'

'What do you mean? What *are* you talking about, Ronald?'

I crept closer to the sitting room window. My father, elbows on knees, pressed hands forming a steeple, preparing to deliver a speech. My mother's long fingers twitched in the lap of her cotton skirt. As I lingered, she reached for her specs on the coffee table and toppled off the sofa. A few seconds elapsed before he rose.

'It's my ankle,' she said. 'You'd better call an ambulance.'

'I'll drive you to hospital.'

'I can't possibly walk to the car. Help me onto the sofa.'

I watched him half lift, half support her, then I went in. She lay on the sofa, expression steely.

'Ambulance, Ronald. But explain it's not an emergency.'

After he made the call, she remained silent, clenched lips the sole indication of pain. I imagined her thinking the accident could be advantageous, restore her to where she'd been with her husband of more than three decades.

Dad stood by the window, head bowed, hands clasped. I wanted to hug him.

Mum scanned the room. 'Ronald, tidy the coffee table, and take the glasses through to the kitchen.'

'Jesus Christ, Nora, it's an ambulance we're waiting for, not a photographer.'

'Just do it. I think they're here.'

He removed the glasses, wiped the table with his hanky.

The paramedics examined Mum's ankle, and within a short time had transferred her to a wheelchair.

'Either of you want to come with us?' one of them asked.

'We'll follow in the car,' Dad said eventually.

I hovered at the front door until the ambulance left. Across the street a net curtain twitched in the fading light.

Dad reappeared, expression inscrutable, 'We should eat, I suppose.'

'What did you mean when you said that Mum wouldn't have to put up with any more sacrifices? I heard you from the garden.'

'Haven't we been through enough these last few days?'

I followed him through to the kitchen. 'I'll be back in France soon, and I don't know when I'll see you again.'

'I really shouldn't be talking to you before I've spoken with your mother... Oh sod it, I have a friend, Louise, we've become close.' He stopped, gauging my reaction. 'I always told myself I wouldn't leave a marriage, but after this... this revelation...'

'How long have you... known each other... been together?'

Dad smiled. 'Long enough...'

'Tell me about her. What does she do?'

'That's enough information for now. Please don't mention this to Martin yet.'

'I want you to be happy,' I said, hugging him. 'You've tolerated so much. It's your time now.'

The phone went, he answered, listened for a moment. 'It's probably a sprained ankle... Yes, thank you... It was good of you to call, we'll let you know.'

'Mrs Barker,' he told me, pouring himself a whisky. 'Want one?'

I shook my head. 'I'll support you, whatever you choose to do.'

'Thank you, darling. It seems strange to seek approval of a new relationship from one's daughter. I'll speak to your mother when the moment is right, but my first priority is to help you find your child.'

We returned to the sitting room, me with tea and a packet of Jaffa cakes, Dad with his whisky bottle and glass. I switched on a lamp and the gas fire. He drew the sitting room curtains, but when he tugged the cord, a fold of curtain slipped from its ring.

'I've always hated these curtains. Oh, sod it,' he declared, pulling at the curtain until it landed on the floor.

We laughed like children.

'If I do find my little girl, I don't know if I'll have any legal claim,' I said when we recovered.

'I am so sorry, Olivia, truly sorry. I've been a useless father – too busy protecting myself – but I'll do anything I can. If we manage to track down your daughter – my grand-daughter, I'll support you in court.'

'You can't be a character reference. You're my father.'

'But I can tell them you knew nothing of your child's existence. There's nothing like the love for a child, and you and Martin have kept me going. I want you to experience such love. You're young, you might have other children. But

the thought of you being apart from your little girl tears
me up.'

I squeezed his hand, my throat aching from unshed
tears.

'Olivia, there's something you should know. When your
mother was in labour, she went into heart failure. At one
point it seemed like I might have to choose between saving
her or you and Martin. I decided on you two... I believed it
would break her heart if she lost you.' Dad paused, swal-
lowing hard. 'When she found out, it affected her
profoundly. She felt I didn't love her enough... This didn't
help our relationship, and then, as you know, she had the
ongoing disappointment of my lack of meteoric rise up the
education system.'

'I didn't know about her problems in labour.'

'It left her with a weakened heart. I'm telling you this so
that you can understand her better. And perhaps understand me, too. I'm not naturally confrontational, but one of
the reasons I have held back was worry about her health.'

I shook my head. 'Yeah, but it doesn't excuse what she
did.'

At eleven o'clock, Mum phoned to announce she could
be collected. After Dad had left, I raided the sitting room
cupboard for magazines. As I lifted a copy of *Homes and
Gardens*, I noticed a turquoise box containing a faded white
photo album tied with pink and blue ribbons. It was a
journal that had begun on the day of Mum's pregnancy
confirmation.

"I am eight weeks pregnant," she had written in royal
blue ink. A weekly progress record followed. Week sixteen:
"I felt both babies kick at the same time. Ronald wondered
how I knew it was both of them but I was certain. The
nausea has gone and I am so happy."

A layer of discoloured tissue paper protected each page. Her plastic hospital identity bracelet was there, and several cards of congratulations. There were photos of Martin and me at two days old, large-headed with wispy hair; at three months, in Dad's arms, his expression conveying both pride and bewilderment, his mouth open as if to say, "I can't hold both of them at once".

I moved the remains of a fly from the album's spine. Now a comment in green ink, "Olivia smiled at me today, at three and a half weeks. She was sitting in the armchair wearing her green hat with the penguins. I'd been up half the night and sat down for a moment. When I looked up, she was smiling at me. Suddenly my tiredness lifted. Later Rosemary and I went to a concert at the Albert Hall to hear Rachmaninov's Piano Concerto No. 3 but all I wanted was to go home in case I missed another smile."

Also included were a menu plan for our introductory solid foods, hair snippings, and a note of our first words: appu (apple), boo (book), carbon (cardigan). In a polythene pocket I could see our baby teeth, individually wrapped in tiny polythene bags. When I read a comment referring to the end of primary four, tears spiked my eyes, "Twins above average in ability and well-behaved and popular. I am so proud of my little poppets. Ronald and I had booked a table at Whyte's but we cancelled. Instead we had mince with mashed potatoes and ice cream at home."

Halfway through our tenth year, the album ended with a photograph of Martin and me at a beach in Cornwall. We were sitting in a yellow inflatable dinghy, wearing red sunhats, our arms caked in sand.

After returning the album to the cupboard, I lay on the sofa, ensconced in the travel rug that smelled faintly of grass. Twenty minutes later, the key turning in the front door woke me and slowly I roused myself from a cloud of sleep.

With her right ankle strapped and a stick helping her bear weight, Mum appeared smaller, older.

'I'll make you a sandwich,' Dad said as she lowered herself into an armchair. I jumped up. 'I'll get coffee.'

In the sitting room, I awaited interrogation about the abandoned curtain on the floor, complaints about the gloom, the crusts on the sandwich. Instead, clutching her stick, Mum rose from the armchair, declared she had no appetite and was going to bed. I listened to her as she hobbled up the stairs.

A CRISPNESS in the air and an occasional fluttering leaf, signalled the early arrival of autumn, as Roz and I meandered along Oxford Street the following morning.

'Do you really think your father will leave your mother?' she asked.

'He's considering it... I want him to be happy.'

'Let's try in here. Emma was wearing a lovely dress the other day – I think she got it here... I hope it works out with your father and Louise. And when you finally meet the right man, he'll either be like your father or the exact opposite.'

'Yeah, right.'

I put on my jacket – it would be double the temperature in Nice.

Roz nodded. 'It's to do with your childhood experience. Your father is the first man in your life, in a way. You've seen how he's under your mother's influence. Either you'll choose someone one passive like him and you'll dominate, like Nora does, or you'll go for a man who can stand up to you. It's all subconscious, you realise, when you fancy a guy.'

'Where do you dig up all this psychobabble?'

Her expression softened. 'When do you think you'll get to Paris?'

'When Cerys'll give me time off again. Soon, I hope. I could have gone this weekend, but I felt too vulnerable.'

'If you knew several weeks in advance, I could meet you there. Help you search. Richie could have changed his name, by the way.'

'I know. Thanks for the offer of coming over, I'll let you know... Isn't this a gorgeous colour? Pity they don't have it in my size.'

'Any developments with Laurent?' Roz asked, trawling through a rack of dresses, deft hands rapidly assessing the merits of the garments. I suppressed my irritation.

Roz clicked her teeth. 'Let me guess. The problem is he's available, and you prefer men who can't commit. All those relationship nomads you've hankered after – Tom, Mark, Bill... And James wasn't much better–'

'For God's sake, we're here to shop, not to analyse me.'

She examined a lacy top with loose threads galore. 'Let's move on, this is tacky stuff.'

My thoughts reverted to breakfast: Dad's silence and Mum's one-sided conversation about replacing the cracked kitchen sink, as if the shocking disclosure of two days before had never taken place. She'd been seated at the kitchen table, stick by her side, a psychological and physical support.

Dad obviously hadn't told her about Louise.

Roz and I continued to comb Oxford Street in search of a party outfit for her. We laughed while she wriggled into tight dresses and I tried on hats and high-heeled shoes I'd never wear. We indulged in coffee and chocolate cake at Starbucks. At 12:30 pm, we parted company and I rushed home to skype Martin.

CERYS'S CAFÉ was situated in a small square in the Old Town of Nice, nestled between a handmade paper shop and a butcher's. Opposite was a 17th century church whose bells chimed every fifteen minutes, and in between, a park framed by plane trees provided a shady place for elderly men to play boules. She'd bought the building for a knock-down price as it needed a huge amount of work, much of which Bertrand and a friend had managed to do.

I smiled when I stepped inside to walls of coral wash, and mature palms resting in corners. By the window were rattan tables and chairs for sit-in customers. A wooden rack displayed porcelain mugs, bars of soap and muslin sachets of herbs, and there was a strong smell of coffee and lavender.

In my pocket was Mr Minto's recent letter informing me my inheritance was safe. Financial autonomy at last.

Despite the busyness, Cerys chatted at length with regulars, even while breastfeeding Frances. Customers were patient when I didn't understand their orders and I relished my change of role, wishing it was for more than one day.

After the lunchtime rush, Laurent appeared. He seemed different today, his hazel eyes brighter, his hair longer.

'Bertrand said to me that you are here. The next weekend I will go to a European conference about cancer in Paris. There will be radiologists attending. You must come, too.'

'I've hardly been back.'

'It is one day only. You can take the train in the night and return the next evening. It is at the Sorbonne. You can be my psychology student.'

PEOPLE WERE ENTERING the Sorbonne Nouvelle in droves while I paced the Parisian pavement three days later. As I checked for missed texts, a taxi pulled up and a flustered figure emerged.

'*Desolé*, sorry,' Laurent said. 'There was a *manifestation,* a strike, near to my hotel and the traffic was bad. It is not Paris if there is not a *manifestation*... I have a badge for you.'

I inspected the badge – BOWDEN, Olivia, *étudiante de la psychologie*, psychology student. 'What if anyone talks to me in French?'

'When people come to talk with me, you can make an excuse to leave. But you must avoid the registration table.'

I lingered while he registered. When he rejoined me, I grabbed the professional conference pack and scanned the list of delegates – no mention of Richie. As I studied the programme, my heart sank: there were more than four venues. The plenary sessions were being held in this room, but in between, other rooms had been allocated for parallel sessions. At least lunch would be served in the university refectory. This might be my best chance of spotting Richie – if he was here.

'What is wrong?' Laurent asked.

'I'd forgotten there might be more than one venue. The university refectory is probably the easiest place to check. At lunchtime, I mean, apart from the main room.'

He was struggling to attach his name badge, cursing as the pin drew blood from his thumb. 'It is possible that some delegates will go to a restaurant at lunchtime. It is also possible that some people attend for this morning, or for the afternoon only. It will be difficult but we must try... Come, the conference is starting. Stay calm.'

We entered a large room with a platform at the front where four panellists were in discussion behind a table. He indicated we move to the back as there was more chance of spotting Richie. I watched as chairs filled, participants studied the programme, donned headphones. When the chairperson spoke into the microphone, an air of expectation filled the room. At the far end, translators, encased in glass-fronted cubicles, gave the "thumbs up" sign.

At coffee time, two men approached Laurent, glancing at me. I smiled at them, then slipped away. In the foyer, I circulated amongst tables bedecked with posters, leaflets and treatment protocols, yearning to see one face. Then I rushed to the building where coffee was being served, and scrutinised delegates engaged in serious conversations.

Laurent was waiting for me in the main room when I returned. 'What do you wish to do about the parallel sessions?'

My heart lurched. 'I can't participate in something like that. I'll just have to hang around as people come and go.' Again I checked the map of the Sorbonne Nouvelle.

'Session B has the most attendants. Session A is nearby. I suggest that you wait around these rooms for people to enter. I am attending Session C.'

For 90 minutes, I divided my time between the two rooms, initially noting people joining the sessions, then peering in to check again. There must have been at least 100 delegates in each room. Assessing who was there should have been easy, but each room had two entrances, and there were comings and goings as participants answered calls, arrived late and left early. Through lead paned windows at the other side of the wide corridor, I heard the intermittent beeping of gliding trams and the rumble of a pneumatic drill. Part of me wished I was out there, having a normal day.

When the conference broke for lunch, I scurried between the two exits of each session room, as attendees left. Still no sign of Richie. I then met up with Laurent at the refectory building, where we lingered by the buffet table.

'Some people have gone to a restaurant,' he told me. 'I think also that some delegates will now return to work.'

Despondent, I returned to the main room shortly before two. New delegates searched the room for familiar faces. Afternoon presenters conferred with the translators. Richie might yet appear.

After three presentations, it was time for coffee. Again, I searched for him. Finally, in the main building once more, we listened to two further presentations, then the chair announced a panel discussion. A heated debate began about the role of complementary therapies in cancer treatment and I yawned. Employees darted about, shoving wireless microphones into eager hands while questions were asked and duly answered. The chairman invited one last question. A man rose to speak.

I turned to Laurent. 'It's him, it's Richie. Oh God...'

'Stay calm.'

A panel member answered Richie's question and the chairperson seemed poised to deliver his closing remarks. I bundled my conference pack into my bag, glanced at Laurent, hoping he was ready to leave. Then I looked over to Richie's seat – he'd disappeared.

'*Merci pour votre attention, bon weekend.* Thank you for

your attention, have a good weekend,' the chairman concluded.

I leaped to my feet, squeezed past dillydallying delegates.

When I reached the aisle, a voice boomed in my ear, 'Olivia!'

'Helen!'

'So you *did* qualify as a doctor.'

I peered over her shoulder, searching for Richie.

'I'm a senior registrar now,' she said. 'In radiology. There's another delegate here you'll know – Dr Williams, the hunky Richie...'

'I don't mean to be rude, but–'

'Quick coffee or drink? It would be *lovely* to exchange news.' She laughed. 'It's so strange seeing him, especially now he's–'

'I must go.'

She shoved a business card into my hand. 'Hot date? *Do* get in touch.'

I dashed into the foyer. Participants clustered by the exhibition stalls, none of them familiar. Hovering outside the men's toilets, I signalled to Laurent to join me.

'See if he's in there. He's wearing a green shirt. He's tall. Keep him talking if you see him. I'm going outside – he might be waiting for a taxi. Quick Laurent!'

It was raining heavily. Taxis honked at pedestrians weaving through traffic to cross the boulevard, women lingered in the doorway of the nearby hotel, a porter retrieved an elderly couple's suitcases from a taxi boot. No Richie. I rushed back into the foyer where I found Laurent, now waiting outside the men's toilets. He shook his head.

'At least you have seen him,' he said. 'It is progress.'

'Not if I don't know where he was going. He could have

booked a taxi to the airport, to a station – where do we start?'

My hand flew to my mouth. Helen might have been able to tell me where Richie was living or working. In my haste to find him, I'd choked her off. I rushed around the main conference area again, this time searching for her. Then, having retrieved her business card, I dialled her mobile number, to hear a continuous tone.

In the foyer a group of men huddled by an exhibition board.

'I heard them talk about radiotherapy,' Laurent said.

'Ask if they know him.'

He returned a moment later. 'They told me that some of the radiologists will go to a café in Montparnasse. If we take a taxi, we will arrive by five. *Allons!* Come on!'

The heavy rain continued while our taxi squished its way along thoroughfares, blasting its horn randomly at traffic. Shoppers sheltered under waterlogged awnings; people crowded onto concertina buses; resigned grocers rescued crates of sodden bananas and courgettes. Two and a half hours until my train back to Nice.

When the taxi arrived in Montparnasse, I leapt out, in the process dropping my open backpack, its contents scattering over the pavement. I rammed them back in and sheltered in the café doorway while Laurent settled the fare.

'What do I say to Richie?'

'You must be discreet, Olivia. You must ask if you can arrange to meet together.'

The café was packed, its ornately paned windows covered in condensation. In the corner, a group of men and women were eating crêpes and drinking from carafes of wine. Richie wasn't one of them.

'I will ask if they know Richie,' Laurent said.

I checked other areas of the wood-panelled room, scrutinising several groups of people.

When he found me, he said, 'They work in Paris. One of them recognised the photo – it resembles a doctor that she met this afternoon. She thinks that he will go to the airport after.'

'And she definitely recognised the photo?'

He nodded. 'It appears that Richie Williams has a new name. He now calls himself Dr Vernay. The woman could not remember his other name.'

My heart thudded. 'That's a huge step forward. Where was he flying to?'

'She was not certain. She thinks it was in the south of France – perhaps Marseille.'

'Come on. We can get a taxi.'

'Olivia, Orly and Charles de Gaulle, they both have more than thirty airlines. We do not know where he is flying to, or what airline he will use.'

'You go to one, I'll go to the other. We can keep in touch. Please!'

'*D'accord*, okay. I think it is best if you go to Orly. It is the airport for flights to many parts of France. Orly Ouest.'

ix years earlier

S Dorothy is inspecting an easel in the garden when Olivia arrives in Gibraltar. Her aunt wipes her hands on her smock and stands back to study her.

'Tell me you didn't fly here.'

'I'm only twenty-seven weeks... This is lovely,' Olivia says, gazing at the house, at its red pantile roof, the iron grillwork on the windows, the purple bougainvillea scaling its walls. 'So peaceful.'

'A lucky find. Close enough to the old town, far enough away from those ugly hotel complexes. Let me show you round. Your room's ready.'

'*My* room?'

'*Your* room.'

She smiles on seeing the white plaster walls and terra-cotta floor tiles; the wrought iron bedstead with its green and orange striped cover. In the living room, her eye focuses on another easel: an impressionistic oil painting of the Rock looming over the town beneath. Tubes of oil paints, paintbrushes and stained cloths litter the floor. The room smells of paint thinner and cigarettes.

Dorothy nods in satisfaction. 'This is an inspiring place for an artist. Stay as long as you like – I won't smoke inside... Your parents do know you're here?'

Olivia turns away.

'I'll phone your mother. Now, rest. I'll wake you for dinner, then we'll talk.'

After several lazy days, Olivia shops for loose ankle length skirts and tunic tops which minimise her bump, leather sandals to accommodate her swollen feet. Comfortable now, she wanders the narrow lanes of the old town, visits the Moorish Castle, and, of course, the Rock. Dorothy often accompanies her on these morning walks. In the afternoon, she tends to be busy. But seldom at home.

'Where do you disappear to?' Olivia asks one day.

'Here and there.'

Olivia spends her afternoons on a lounger in the garden, usually dozing off in the warmth, to the sight of drifting butterflies and the occasional plaintive cry of a gull. When she wakens, she's always pleased to find she's still here.

'We're having a guest for dinner,' Dorothy announces, a week into her visit.

'I'm glad you've made friends,' Olivia says, dropping the dishtowel, placing her hands on her abdomen to locate the kicks. 'Will I be a problem?'

Dorothy hesitates. 'He'll assume you are married.'

She processes the fact that the friend is male. As a child, she'd often asked why Aunt Dorothy wasn't married, and been told that she'd had her chances.

'I could go out. I don't want to make things awkward.'

'You won't, lovie. But I would like help preparing the meal.'

'I assume he's retired.'

'Ex-navy. William lived with his sister then she died a few years ago. He's found it difficult being on his own again.'

'How did you meet?'

Her aunt can converse in the strangest of situations, projecting a persona to which people of all ages and circumstances respond.

Dorothy rummages for shopping bags. 'A story for another time. Come on, I'm taking you to the public market. It's a great place for shopping.'

At seven o'clock, the doorbell rings. Olivia inspects herself in the wall length mirror, smiling at the flattering effect of her red and gold maxi dress against her tanned skin. She sniffs the rose scented beads she bought in the market, drapes them round her neck.

Pausing by the front door, she observes Dorothy and William in the garden. He is tall and slim, with an impressive crop of white hair, and eyes that, even from this distance, appear brilliantly blue. He seems about seventy – older than her aunt.

Dorothy serves dinner outside, the aroma of lamb blending with jasmine-scented candles. William listens attentively, a sweetness to his smile, an aura of gentleness. When prompted, he talks about his chess club, reminisces with Dorothy about exhibitions they have visited. He offers to show Olivia the military quarters where he was based.

At ten o'clock, she bids them goodnight, leaving her aunt in full flow about a teaching disaster she'd experienced in Zimbabwe. From her room, Olivia hears flamenco, castanets and clapping. Experiences the strongest urge to drink wine – which she resisted at dinner – and dance. To display her bump, celebrate her femininity, her ability to conceive and carry twins. As her eyelids grow heavy, she thinks of Alice.

THE FOLLOWING MORNING, Olivia wakens to a clattering. It's barely nine – Dorothy normally sleeps later. In the kitchen her aunt is buttering rolls.

'I'm making a picnic. I thought you'd like to visit the Alameda Botanical Gardens then take the cable car to the top of the rock.'

'How are you?' Dorothy asks when they leave the cottage.

It has rained overnight, the smell of earth and eucalyptus sweet.

She shrugs. 'Tired, but I'd expect to be.'

'You never mention Richie.' Dorothy stops walking. 'Does he know you're having twins?'

She shakes her head. Will she ever reach a stage of surviving one day without thinking of him?

'It's impossible to understand the pain of the childless,' Dorothy says.

Could her aunt be talking from personal experience? In Alice's situation, might Olivia herself have behaved similarly?

'It would make things easier for you if you learn to forgive him, lovie. Anger is a drain, and you'll need all your energy for bringing up twins.'

'I'm sure Mum will come round eventually. Dad'll do what he can.'

Dorothy squeezes her arm. 'You'll have me, too. Not that I know anything about babies. I was never entrusted with you and Martin until you were at least four.'

Clouds are giving way to another glorious morning, and a squawking gull whisks her back to childhood holidays in Cornwall: rock pool fishing with cane poled nets; the sensation of warm sand in canvas shoes; hopping from foot to foot, willing Dad to give her the chocolate flake from his ice cream.

'So, you and William,' she says, when they reach the Gardens.

Dorothy's eyes sparkle. 'As you rightly guess, we're more than friends.'

'How much more? Did you know him before you came here?'

'Sort of.' Dorothy bends to examine a hibiscus bush. 'It's a lovely idea, don't you think? Commissioning the gardens to give soldiers a relaxing place to go when they were off duty. It was the idea of the British Governor. Around 1815, I think.'

'Dorothy!'

'Oh, very well. I answered an ad in a Military Dating Agency. We wrote to each other, then I decided to visit, meet him.'

She stares at her aunt's bottle-aided light brown hair and the brown eyes that frequently twinkle with pleasure or mischief. In earlier days, she would have been more stunning than Nora.

'He advertised? I wouldn't have thought he was the type.'

'A friend did, on his behalf. He was mortified when he found out.'

She inhales the clean, cool air, the whiff of pine, a florally smell from a bush she can't identify. 'Does Mum know?'

Dorothy reels back in horror. 'You mustn't tell her how we met. It's yet one more thing for her to disapprove of in me.'

'There've been others?'

'Of course. My little flutters in the casinos of Monaco, for a start. Oh, what happy days... Dressing up, drinking champagne. I was lucky, mind you, and sensible. And disciplined. I always knew when to stop. But I made a fortune and your mother has never forgiven me.'

'Wow... good for you.'

Dorothy laughs. 'William was quite taken aback when I told him... We've talked about marriage. Personally, I'd be happy to live with him, but he's old-fashioned.'

They cross the wooden bridge over the African flowerbeds, pass the stone pines, the wild olive trees, and the dragon trees with their thin, spiky leaves. Dorothy points out various flowers. Mentions the trees she loved in Zimbabwe. Olivia appreciates the delicate petals, vivid colours. The smell of leaves and seeds.

Pregnancy, she thinks, this heightened awareness.

The next day, Olivia is in the garden when Dorothy returns from an outing. Her aunt sinks on to the lounger, pours a glass of homemade lemonade and sighs contentedly.

'William's had a marvellous idea. We – and this includes you – are taking a trip to Tangiers. We're going to do the Artists' Tour.'

'Artists' Tour?'

'You must know that Tangiers is known for writers and artists – Matisse, Tennessee Williams, the Rolling Stones... William suggested we visit the famous Grand Café de Paris and the Café de France. We'll watch the sun set from the terrace of the Hafa Café like famous people have done. I hope you'll be up for it.'

She visualises teeming souks: their exotic spices, saffron and lime coloured fabrics, scuttling chickens and tethered goats. She can smell chicken couscous and aromatic ice cream, hear wailing instruments and haggling voices.

'He insists you come, too, lovie. So, no arguments. We leave on Saturday and return the following Wednesday. He's booked us into a classy hotel with a rooftop garden and a lovely view of the sea. You can rest when you need to. The rooms are air-conditioned so you'll be comfortable.'

FROM THE TANGIERS COASTAL ROAD, Olivia gazes onto a sandy beach, appreciating the sunshine and sea breeze. She's glad she came. That she wasn't deterred by the risk of a rough crossing from Gibraltar. That she heeded Dorothy's insistence to go ahead, instead of waiting until William recovered from his stomach bug. And she is complying with her aunt's request to text her every day to let her know she's okay.

While she rests against a rock, staring at the hazy line dividing sea from sky, a car stops and a fair-skinned woman emerges.

'There's a storm coming. You can't stay out here. It's not safe. Come with us.'

Around her, dirt and sand particles are being lifted into the air.

In the car, the woman checks the windows are tightly shut, hands Olivia a mask.

'I'm Fiona. This is Paul... Didn't the hotel warn you this morning about the Chergui winds, the sandstorms they bring?'

'I left early.'

'We should be able to outrun it,' Paul says.

Through the back window all she can see is the dust cloud rolling towards them.

Her chest constricts, her heart races.

'Are you asthmatic?' Fiona asks, looking round.

She nods, reaching for her inhaler.

'I'll turn up the air conditioning.'

Moments later, she is gripped by stomach pain. While waiting for it to pass, she feels her waters break. Then another pain.

She's only thirty-one weeks.

Fiona turns round again. 'Are you all right?'

'I'm in labour, it's too soon...'

'We'll take you to the hospital.'

She thinks of the flamingo patterned kimono Dorothy gave her, the relaxation music on her iPod. 'I need to get my things from the hotel.'

'No time for that, I'm sorry.'

On arrival at the hospital, she can barely see the building for sand and dust. Fiona and Paul help her in, Fiona waiting until a nurse has settled her into a wheelchair.

PAIN, terrible pains, sweating, vomiting. Thunder rumbles and wind roars. The lights go out, are replaced by dimmer ones and a chugging diesel engine. Hours arrive and depart. A blur of drifting between shallow sleep and blunt, all-consuming pains. Figures appear and disappear, their voices muted, footsteps subdued.

As dawn breaks, Olivia wakes to the roar of the sand-storm through heavy shutters. A doctor examines her, draws up a shot of diamorphine. The pain fades and she sinks into a sleep from which she surfaces sporadically, vaguely conscious of a nurse's presence.

'You are okay, it is not long now,' the nurse says,

squeezing her hand. 'We call the babies who are being born here during a sandstorm, "Chergui's Children". Did you know this?'

Pulled into a deeper slumber. Dreams of floating above the clouds, of gazing down on fields of cows and sheep, on wheat and corn waving in the wind. Dreams of daylight surrendering to darkness, being surrounded by stars and moonlight. Relief at observing, detached, having escaped the normality of life on earth.

The morphine wears off and she wakens. The nurse has gone. The contractions are gathering momentum. She attempts to walk, but fatigue pulls her back to the bed. The room is hot, the ceiling fan switched off to conserve energy. She stares at the white walls, at the chunks of chipped plaster.

The nurse reappears. 'Can I examine you?' she asks, donning latex gloves. 'It is not long now,' her soft voice reassures. 'The babies are moving. We take you now to the delivery suite.'

Dim lights, hazy faces, mutterings in Arabic, in French. People coming and going. 'No epidural,' someone says, and she lacks energy to say she's changed her mind. A mask is attached to her face and someone explains how to use it. It doesn't work and they apply another one. Claustrophobic, she resists it.

'The gas and air help, if you let them,' a male voice reasons.

The sensation of being boxed in remains, but she is too woozy to protest. All she wants is to sink once more into sleep, where she drifted in the sky, distanced from everything. Safe.

A figure appears, his skin lighter, his head bald. A whispered conference takes place before he introduces himself as the consultant obstetrician. Her fogginess lifts. Why is a doctor needed? There must be a problem. A midwife puts her legs in stirrups, reminds her to breathe her way through the pain. She struggles to free her legs.

'Keep your energy to pushing,' the doctor says. 'Push. This is good... Push again. Now stop. Don't push. Concentrate to breathing.'

She's doing great, she tells herself. Martin would think so, Roz would think so. Everyone would be pleased if they knew how hard she was pushing. Except her mother. Mum wouldn't think she was doing well with this pushing business. Mum would have pushed harder when she and Martin were born. She would have got it right. Mum got everything right. Except the love.

She hadn't got the love bit right and this was the problem.

A machine beeps, another huddle of whispering... '*Les frequencies cardiaques sont en baisse.* The heartbeats are dropping,' says a woman in scrubs. The doctor washes his hands and arms, is shrugged into a theatre gown.

He smiles at her, dark eyes hypnotising. 'Push now, a big push, come on, we must deliver these babies. Three more pushes.'

'*Les frequencies cardiaques sont encore en baisse.* The heartbeats are still dropping,' a voice says.

She hears the word "forceps". A trolley is brought nearer, its instruments gleaming against the white enamel tray.

'No, I don't want forceps.'

The doctor glances at the wall and she notices a cross. Is he praying?

Her eyes focus on the cross. 'I don't want forceps.' If she keeps watching the cross, they'll listen to her.

A nurse pats her arm. 'A big push, *encore,* again – big push.'

Her body is splitting, she's soiling the bed with her pushing. She will die. This is why the doctor studied the cross – he knew before she did.

A quick conferring. 'There is not enough time. We must use forceps.'

She doesn't want her babies pulled out with tongs, all the work from Active Birth classes rendered useless. She groans in pain.

'We need more light. Now.'

A nurse appears with two torches.

Someone inserts a catheter, explaining that an empty bladder will give the babies more space to arrive.

'We must give you a spinal anaesthetic,' the doctor says.

They cover her legs with a green sheet.

He takes her hand. 'This should work quickly. Please try to relax.'

In minutes, her lower half is numb.

'You must now push hard every time there is a contraction,' the doctor says.

She does, aware of a simultaneous tugging action. There's a hazy sensation of one baby arriving, then the second. After that, a blur.

She awakes to solemn faces.

The obstetrician takes her hand. 'Both of your babies are in intensive care. The girl has better health than the boy. I am sorry. We will do everything that is possible.'

Rough justice. She doesn't deserve to be a mother. She never did.

She should have got married dressed like a meringue, taken out a mortgage on a three-bedroomed home and not conceived until her husband earned enough to support a family. If she'd done so, this wouldn't be happening now. Instead, she'd have given birth in a London teaching hospital, her husband and midwife encouraging her to breathe deeply and push, the babies slipping out like notes from a cash dispenser.

'I want to see them,' she says.

A nurse wheels her to the baby unit where's there's a commotion around two incubators. Tubes, machines, monitors, so much equipment surrounding such little beds. All those green gowned figures and her in a white robe. She should be in green too, then she'd belong. Could participate. A woman rushes into the room, bumping her wheelchair, apologising. Figures huddle over the incubators, adjusting this, checking that. She glimpses two little heads in white caps, two red wrinkled faces. Observes a figure shrugging.

'Don't stop, for God's sake, please don't stop,' she whispers.

The snoring and hissing sounds of ventilators increase and increase. It's all she can hear, this roaring noise. She tries to call out, but no words emerge. 'Please don't stop,' she mouths. 'Please.'

The action by the incubators slows down. There's no urgency.

They know. She knows.

Quietly she wheels herself back to the room she was in, dresses and grabs her money belt. Ignoring the pain, she limps past reception, awaiting sounds of running feet, a nurse calling her name.

After leaving the hospital, she walks through mounds of dust, then hails a taxi. All around her, road-sweeper machines are pushing heaps of sand and debris off the main roads. It's like a scene from a disaster movie.

The taxi reaches the ochre alleyways of the medina, its jumble of Moorish and colonial architecture. Within minutes, she is surrounded by a kaleidoscopic blur of colour and movement, immersed in unfamiliar smells. Stall keepers are removing dust from their products. The air smells clogged. Overhead, the sky is a dusty pale blue.

All those signs of everyday life, and two dead babies. She wanders, dream-like, breasts heavy with colostrum, redundant, like the rest of her.

19

I fastened my seatbelt and leant back against the taxi seat, '*Orly aéroport, s'il vous plaît*, Orly airport, please.' The rain showed no sign of easing while we sped along the busy street. I glanced at my watch – two hours until my train. As I inhaled deeply, the taxi halted behind a river of cars. The cab driver was mouthing, '*Une manifestation,* a demonstration.'

I dialled Laurent's number. 'Where are you? I'm stuck in a traffic jam. A bus driver demonstration. Hang on, we're moving again.'

The taxi edged forward. Horns blasted, the driver scratched his head and muttered. Five minutes passed, then another five. Already the meter read twenty euros. I craned my head out of the window, wishing Laurent was with me as he'd know what to do. Suddenly the driver turned right and shot along a narrow street. After navigating a labyrinth of pot-holed alleys, we emerged onto a thoroughfare and accelerated. Then a further traffic jam. Another ten minutes lost.

At Orly Ouest, I rushed through the main entrance and scrutinised the departures board. A flight to Bordeaux leaving in thirty minutes, a delayed one to Nantes, a KLM flight to Amsterdam with no departure gate showing – so many possibilities.

Oh God! Laurent didn't have Richie's photo, he wouldn't know how to recognise him. I dialled Laurent's number, only to see the "low battery" message appear on the screen, so I darted about until I found an unused power socket and plugged in my phone.

'I didn't give you back the photo, you won't be able to recognise him–'

'Relax yourself, Olivia. I have a copy of the one that you gave me before.'

Hordes of passengers swarmed around. Sweat trickled down my face and my stomach felt hollow with hunger as I rushed around the automatic check-in machines. Flights to Marseille and Lugano, to Geneva, Barcelona, Dijon. Nearby, a baby wailed. A woman collapsed, prompting a flurry of activity. A PA announced the last call for a flight to Brussels, thunder reverberated round the sky and a child screamed.

I examined the queues of passengers needing to check in luggage. No sign of Richie. Then I noticed a tall, green-shirted man at an information desk. Heart pounding, I approached him but as he turned to speak to the woman next to him, I realised it wasn't Richie. A lump lodged in my throat as I trudged away. Even if he had been here, he'd probably be through security by now.

I wouldn't find him this evening.

It was half past six, too late to catch my train and I was too exhausted to contemplate another overnight journey. My head ached and the smell of discarded food in a waste bin taunted me. When I spotted a vacant power socket, I plugged in again and dialled Laurent's number. 'I can't find Richie.'

'It is the same also for me. I am sorry.'

'There's nothing more we can do this evening... I need to find a hotel, I presume you have one... We could go for dinner, if you'd like.'

'I am sorry, but in fact I have a rendezvous with a friend. I hope that you will find a hotel easily. *N'abandonnez pas.* Don't give up. I will phone you when I return to Nice next week.'

Reluctantly, I switched off my phone, wishing he'd invited me to join them for dinner, or was it a date? How little I knew about him, who and what defined him, our meetings, our conversations always focusing on my needs, my moods. Perhaps I should take him out for dinner in Nice, have one rendezvous where discussing Richie and my daughter was off limits.

FROM MY HOTEL ROOM PHONE, I could hear Frances bawling.

'I've said I'm sorry, Cerys,' I reiterated. 'I mean, I thought I'd left enough time to get to the station.'

I sank onto the bed, punching the bolster pillow to make it more comfy.

'Bad timing, this is, Olivia. First your week in London and now this. I'm struggling as it is, I am.'

'Bertrand is around and–'

'Bertrand!'

'Look, I'll get the first train tomorrow. I'll be back by three. I won't take Tuesday off.'

Cerys' voice slipped into a whine. 'You've no idea how tiring it is being a parent.'

I rang off, sighed. With Dorothy's money, did I need this job, the constraints it imposed?

But I couldn't quit. It was one thing relishing the prospect of more time to myself, another not having a structure to my day. Besides, if I found Richie and faced legal proceedings for access to my daughter, a recent reference for childcare would support my case.

I'd try Helen again – perhaps I'd misdialled earlier. The business card wasn't in my bag, though, nor in my conference pack or the damp pockets of my jacket.

In different circumstances, I would have enjoyed my luxurious accommodation: the king size bed and heavy burgundy bedspread; the mahogany table with its leather container of writing paper; the list of laundering prices – *chemise* 5€, robe 9€; the bathroom, with its soft green Egyptian towels and basket of complimentary Clarins toiletries.

I imagined the ambience of the dining room – chandeliers and embossed linen napkins, table centres of real flowers; solemn waiters in white jackets, undertaking their duties quietly and efficiently, expecting their patrons to behave with decorum. In my head, I heard unobtrusive piano music, the quiet clink of heavy antique cutlery, an occasional muffled pop of a champagne cork and the muted hum of conversation.

There'd be no raucous laughter from the kitchen, no near-miss collisions at the swing doors, and certainly no misunderstandings over menu orders. Tips would be generous but not ostentatious, acknowledged as appropriate by the waiter with a discreet incline of the head and no change of facial expression.

After helping myself to a packet of biscuits and a sparkling water from the mini bar, I stepped onto the balcony. In the distance, the iron latticed Eiffel Tower loomed. Nearer by were streets of neoclassical Parisian

apartments with their sloping slate roofs and ornate carv-
ings, their wrought iron balconies and floor-to-ceiling
windows. Closer still, in the row opposite the hotel, gentle
light from bracket lamps revealed cosy sitting room
tableaux as the sky darkened.

All I wanted now was to locate a bistro, and afterwards
sink onto the meticulously ironed sheets, drift into oblivion.

Later, I remembered the conference delegates' list – it
would contain Helen's details. And Richie's, under his
assumed name. I sprang out of bed, retrieved the conference
folder from an outside pocket of my backpack, but the lists
inside the sodden cardboard cover were indecipherable.
Laurent would have his copy – I'd ask him to check it. The
prospect of significant progress rekindled my appetite, so I
raided the mini bar for more biscuits and Kit Kats. I wolfed
down the miniature bottle of red wine. Then I demolished
the complimentary bowl of grapes and oranges.

'WHAT DO YOU THINK?' Cerys asked.

I raised my head from tidying away Henri's Lego.
Draped against my employer was a black dress featuring a
low neck and straight pleated skirt – impossible to visualise
her in.

'Black is an elegant colour, but–'

'I'll try it on. Back in a jiffy.'

When she returned, I was reaching under the fridge for
stray pieces of Lego. I straightened and inspected her.

She pulled in her stomach. 'Appropriate for a dinner
party? Of course, I know it's not a great colour for me, but
apart from that what do you think? I didn't want to buy a
size forty- two. I've got time to lose a bit of weight, if I do an

hour on the bike every day... It's the café, it is. Too much temptation. What do you think?'

'I think you'd have to lose quite a lot... When are you going out?'

'Didn't I tell you? We've all been invited to the Bruhmans for dinner on Friday to thank us for having Philippe. Her husband will be back. He's been lecturing in Florence and Paris. Just think – no cooking or dishes for one evening. I'll ask Henri what he thinks of my dress.'

Several minutes later she reappeared, mouth downturned. 'Well, because you and Henri both disapprove of my new dress, perhaps I should find another outfit. I'll need your advice on colours, and we should do it now while Frances is asleep. Leave the tidying.'

I dragged my feet up to her bedroom and plonked myself on the rocking chair. Fingers crossed, this wouldn't take long. My eyes were strained from the previous night's mammoth search of social networking sites, for any mention of Helen, or Richie, under his new name.

ON THE MORNING of the Bruhman dinner, Odette ran into the kitchen while I was clearing away the breakfast. '*Maman* wants you.'

'What am I to do?' Cerys wailed when I knocked on the bedroom door. 'It's awful, it is.'

The black dress seemed even tighter than before, some of the pleats flattened to accommodate her girth.

She pulled and tugged at the bodice. 'You should have told me it didn't flatter me.'

'I did... indicate–'

'You should have been firmer.' She twisted and teased

herself out of the dress. 'Maybe I could let it out. Do you think I could?'

I examined the seams. 'There isn't enough material.'

'This is a disaster. I did so want to make an impression.'

I suppressed my irritation – I was becoming twitchy about the evening, wanting to see Philippe, not wanting to see Véronique. Cerys could appear in a whisky barrel, for all I cared. Noting her dark-ringed eyes, however, I said, 'Would you like me to phone the shop in Nice, see if they have the bigger size? I could nip in on the moped, collect it for you?'

'The next size up would be too big.'

Frances yelped and I made for the door. 'I'll get milk from the freezer.'

'No!' Cerys called after me. 'I'll feed her. In fact, I'll get her to feed as much as possible today. It might help my weight.'

Half an hour later, when leaving for the beach with the children, I heard a whirring sound from the exercise bike. When we returned, again there was the same noise from her bedroom.

At six-thirty, I nodded approvingly in front of the mirror. The cap sleeves of my green dress enhanced my tanned arms, and the flouncy skirt made me feel sexy. As I adjusted the neckline to reveal a hint of cleavage, I imagined Mum's reaction. "Well, if you want to attract *that* sort of attention..." I applied glossy lipstick and a second coat of mascara, now wondering at my efforts. It was dinner with "smug marrieds", not a speed dating event. Would anyone notice, let alone appreciate my endeavours?

Odette burst into my room. 'Aren't you ready yet? This is my second-best dress. *Maman* said I could wear it tonight, and she found a new velvet ribbon for my hair. I love velvet.'

I bent to kiss her. 'You look gorgeous, sweetheart.'

'Olivia, Olivia, it's time to go,' Henri called from the hall.

'Tell them I'll be there in a moment, Odette.'

'I want to watch you put on your earrings.'

'Another time, darling. Go and tell them I'll be ready soon.'

My phone rang as I lifted my bag. Finally – it had to be Laurent.

'I checked the delegates' list,' he said. 'Richie is listed as Dr P. Vernay, but there is no other information. I did find the contact details for Helen. Do you have a pen and some paper?'

After ringing off, I wanted to phone Helen immediately, see what information she had about Richie's whereabouts, but I heard Henri calling my name again. The call could have to wait until tomorrow.

At the top of the stairs I halted, viewing the Chevalier family like a theatre cameo: Bertrand pacing the hall; Henri standing, one leg twisted round the other, fiddling with a gadget; Odette, seated underneath the coat stand, reading a book; Frances asleep in her carry tot.

Just then I heard the familiar whirring noise – surely Cerys couldn't be cycling now, for God's sake? As I navigated the stairs in my heels, Bertrand was tearing his hands through his hair. Then he noticed me, his eye lingering on my dress.

Minutes later, a flushed Cerys appeared in the black dress, the orange Pashmina scarf round her shoulders not large enough to conceal bulges. Bertrand grabbed the car keys from the rack and Odette ran into the kitchen to say goodbye to the spider's web.

During the short drive to the Bruhman home, Cerys fidgeted in the front seat, unusually silent. Seated behind me, Henri and Odette argued about which were more dangerous – tigers or sharks. Beside me, Frances slept, pudgy fingers clutching a rattle. Poor Cerys... Doubtless, Véronique would look stunning. Doubtless, Bertrand would notice.

AT THE BRUHMAN'S front door, I became jittery. Not only did I dislike Véronique, but her husband might be equally unlikeable. As a car blasted its horn, I looked round to see what was happening. When I turned back, the others had entered the house and a bespectacled man waited for me to join them.

My stomach lurched.

20

Six years earlier

At her Tangiers hotel, Olivia slips into a deep sleep. When she wakens, she phones Dorothy, explains what's happened, and persuades her against coming over to collect her. After ringing off, she justifies not having told her aunt the full story. That she left before the end.

She finds a clinic where she waits in a queue to have her wound checked. No one questions her about why she's not in hospital.

Next day, she travels by bus to Marrakech, spends the night in a hostel, where, fortunately, she is given a two-bedded room to herself. She wakens early the following morning, and for hours trails round narrow, crowded streets, wiping off sweat and flapping away flies. Late afternoon, she stumbles across a sign, "Mimosa, *chambres à louer*, rooms to rent," and for a paltry sum is offered a first floor room overlooking a courtyard framed by palms. The room is clean and furnished with a mattress, table and chair, a two ring electric hob and a washstand with bowl. A worn rug partially covers the stone floor.

'Your passport, please?' requests Jean Luc, the small chubby French landlord.

Her hand flies to her mouth. In her haste to leave hospital, she's forgotten her passport and camera, both of which were lodged in the security office on her arrival. 'I don't have it... I was in hospital. I mean, I forgot to take it when I left.'

He notices her distended stomach. Gives her a form to complete.

The relief is overwhelming – she'll contact the hospital when she feels stronger. For the moment, all she craves is sleep. Her wound throbs and she feels hot and shivery. In her room, she sinks onto the mattress, pulls the cotton bedspread over her.

WOMEN'S MUTED VOICES. Soothing creams applied to her vagina, beakers of thick liquid placed to her lips. Mournful singing in alien tongues and the Muezzin call to prayer. These are what she registers during those early weeks. She sleeps, she aches. She tells the time by the changing light, by the noise or silence in the building.

One morning she wakes with a normal temperature and less throbbing from her wound. In the communal ladies' bathroom, the cracked mirror reflects a thinner face, but her eyes seem normal, as if nothing extraordinary has happened. When she returns to her room, a plate of bread and brown cheese is outside the door. Her eyes spike with tears at the unexpected kindness.

'I am looking for work,' she tells Jean Luc.

He scrunches his hair. '*Eh bien,* well, there is a leather factory near here. Shall I ask them?'

'I don't know if I'm strong enough to work in a factory...' She breaks off, aware of not having thought this through.

Half an hour later, he knocks on her door. 'I have an idea. You teach English to my children. Jamal is seven and Biba is nine. I cannot afford to pay you much, but it will be enough for your rent and to buy food. Perhaps one and half hours each day?'

'Aren't they at school?'

'You can teach them when they return home.'

Later that day, he introduces her to Biba and Jamal. They have liquid eyes, impish smiles and an infectious enthusiasm. She agrees to begin the following week and plans her first lesson that evening.

Before long, she adjusts to her new existence. Its pace and simplicity suit her – no trains to rush for, shops to catch, family tensions to circumvent. A routine develops. Morning visits to the souk for fruit, goat's cheese and fish; preparing her English lesson. A post lunch siesta until Jamal and Biba return from school. After class, an evening walk in a public garden, or around the red city walls, now aflame in the setting sun. The structure to her day anchors her.

She texts Martin, Dad and Dorothy regularly.

One afternoon, there are two more children at Jean Luc's home.

'Their parents wish that they learn English, they will pay you,' he says. 'You can use a bigger room.'

Within a week, her class has expanded to ten. She derives comfort from her pupils' earnest dark eyes and high-pitched chattering voices. Welcomes their kisses in the way a starving person welcomes food.

Residents cook in the courtyard, and her neighbour, a

dark-skinned, elderly woman, shows her how to bake the chewy Kesra bread. Sometimes there are impromptu parties with dancing and lamb tagine and wine. She surveys the scene from her upper floor room, charmed by the fairy lights decorating the palm trees, the raita pipes and the drums, the tunic-clad people who drift into the courtyard, swaying instinctively to the music. Frequently she is invited to join them. Moved by their desire to include her, occasionally she agrees, finds herself responding to their music, drinking their rough wine. Mostly, though, she remains in her room, weeping until she fears she will drown.

'I'm glad you phoned today,' her aunt says one Saturday morning early in November. 'When are you returning to Gibraltar? Nora called and accused me of being irresponsible, letting you go to Tangiers on your own.'

'That's not fair, blaming you.'

'Perhaps not. Anyhow, I'm going back to London with William. We're getting married – registry office, no fuss. I wish you'd travel with us.'

'I'm not ready to leave yet.'

Unable to summon enough courage to even contact the hospital, let alone return to it, she reports her "lost" passport to the police. Informs the British Honorary Consulate and applies for an emergency travel document. At least she now has the choice of leaving the sanctuary of Mimosa.

Stronger now, in the mornings she dons her hijab and visits the heart of the city. Although hot, the garment protects her from contemptuous but lusty gazes. At the famous Jemaa el-Fna square, she is hypnotised by snake charmers, acrobatic feats. Perplexed by tenacious water sellers and fortune-tellers. Enchanted by the haunting music of pipers, the distant snow-capped Atlas mountains. After her class, as darkness falls, she returns to the square to watch it convert to an open-air restaurant for the thronging crowds, tempted by spicy vegetable stews, thick harira soup, almond and honey pastries. Swaying gaslights enhance the atmosphere. The spirits of the mountains reach out. When tiredness kicks in, she takes a horse and cart back to Mimosa, often with tears streaming down her face. Such emotion is cathartic, enabling her to sleep.

Occasionally at the weekend she takes the bus into the mountains, travelling along narrow snake-like roads, through Berber villages and terraces of vegetables, wheat and barley. Dark-haired, tanned, dressed in baggy trousers and loose-fitting long-sleeved tops, she escapes excessive attention. And there's always her hijab for additional cover-up. She watches goat herders guiding their animals. Eats from bottomless pots of vegetable stew. Enjoys moments of oblivion.

Eventually she'll have to go home, but she'll know when the time has arrived.

ONE DAY in the Menara Gardens, Olivia notices a man perched on the wall surrounding the artificial lake. Dressed in the kaftan-like gandora, he's in his fifties, and Western. When she emerges from the pink pavilion, he is still there so she approaches the wall. Immediately she understands why he has chosen this spot. It's mid-November and the mountains are enveloped in snow. The pavilion is framed by olive groves and giant date palms, its green tiled, pyramid-shaped roof sparkling in the winter sun.

'What a glorious view,' she says. 'Before I came here, I never understood why people made such a thing about Marrakech. Now I understand.'

He doesn't reply.

When she turns to leave, he speaks, 'Sultan Abd al-Rahman used to stay here in the 1870s. I love the roof... I've tried to paint it.'

She studies him, his blue/grey eyes and weather-beaten skin, and revises his age – early forties, like Richie.

'I'm Seth,' he says.

'Olivia. How long have you been here?'

'Five years, give or take. And you – is this a holiday or a self-imposed exile, too?'

She gulps. 'Self-imposed exile, I suppose.'

They sit there, their shared status forging companionship. As the sun sets and pink light steals over the snowy mountains, he talks, his soft Canadian accent beguiling. 'After my wife left me, I came here. I couldn't have stayed in Toronto, or even elsewhere in Canada.'

He stops. Cattle egrets shimmer past, white plumages vivid against the darkening sky.

'Why Morocco?' she asks.

Initially he doesn't reply, then while she thinking of how to return the conversation to something more low-key, he speaks. 'Because nothing here reminds me of her... Because everything I love about the country she would hate.' He turns away, staring in the direction of the pavilion. 'When I see something beautiful, I don't have to wish I could share it with her... It took a while for me to realise this. That being in Morocco could work for me in a way that other countries couldn't.'

'And you?' he asks after a while. 'You smile and laugh, but all I see is sadness.'

He remains silent while she talks, her story spilling out with painful detail.

'You must have been in hospital during the sandstorm – the Chergui winds, *Chergui's Children*.'

They agree to meet again the following day. Talking has been purgative, and she expects to sleep properly that night. Instead she paces her room.

She wakes around midday, wonders where she is. Several moments elapse before she remembers.

'I want you to see something,' Seth says, when they meet at the city walls.

He takes her to a convent on the outskirts of Marrakech, shows her gardens with women tending vegetables. Points out the chapel. 'Nuns must pray for three hours a day.'

She shakes her head. 'I'm not religious. How could I understand such a life?' Then she laughs: it's great having a new friend.

He sits on a bench. 'Many Western women come here, avoiding their pain. Experience shows that they are unable to devote their lives to God while they are in turmoil. They are requested to leave the convent for six months and then return if they still want to use their lives in this way.... The thing is, few return.'

While talking, he searches her face. When she starts sobbing, he places a hand on her shoulder. Eventually he stands, glances over to the mountains. 'I suspect you are running away from your pain, Olivia. Travelling, escaping, will prevent you from recovering fully.'

When she says nothing, he continues, 'You may not be religious, but you do have a belief system, a higher self.... You do, really.'

She laughs. 'You've lost me here.'

'It's the part that guides people through difficult situations.'

'I certainly can't have one,' she says, laughing again.

'Otherwise I ... I wouldn't have run away from the hospital, I would have stayed... found the courage.'

'Have you heard of Deepak Chopra?' he asks as they retrace their steps. 'Dr Chopra is a Hindu and he's written about the higher self. I'll lend you one of his books.'

Seth slips an arm round her shoulder and she feels his strength. Experiences desire. He continues talking, using unfamiliar words such as mindfulness, channelling, higher intelligence. His eyes convey passion, but not for her.

They won't become lovers.

Her class is due to begin in two hours' time and she has yet to prepare the lesson. Ten minutes into her walk back to Mimosa, she enters a park and finds a shady spot. When rested, however, she can't remember which direction to take – despite having been here many times. She tries to relax. It's a while before she recognises a building diagonally opposite her.

Seth shows her parts of Marrakech she might otherwise not have discovered. The 16th century Saadian Tombs, the tanneries, the Jewish quarter of the city. He converses knowledgeably about these places, interspersing facts with anecdotes and philosophy. She loses herself in his words.

One day she waits for him at the park but he doesn't appear and she finds herself crying uncontrollably. When he eventually arrives, she flings herself into his arms.

'I didn't think you'd turn up. I reckoned you'd dumped me – not that we were an item. I thought – I don't know.'

He pulls out of the embrace, takes her hands. 'Olivia, has it occurred to you that you might be suffering from post-natal condition?'

She laughs, then tears appear again.

'You were a medical student, you know the symptoms: mood swings, confusion, difficulty sleeping. You're laughing one moment, weeping the next... Go home, I'll pay for your flight.'

'I could go by bus.'

'Honey, you're not fit enough for a complicated journey. You must get home soon, get treatment.'

She spends several days ruminating over his advice. Weighing up the pros and cons of staying longer in Morocco.

The evening before her flight, Seth appears at Mimosa. Hands her a rope of sandalwood beads. 'Safe journey.'

'I don't even know your address,' she says, but already he is walking away.

Early the following morning – five months after arriving in Morocco – she perches on the wall outside Mimosa, watching the sunrise. Clutching his beads, she bids a silent farewell to the city in which she has taken refuge. Listens one last time to the first calls for prayer. While on the crowded bus to the airport, she searches for him.

21

Cerys hesitated before extending her arm. 'You must be Pascal. I'm Cerys, and this is Bertrand, Henri, Odette and Frances.'

The man stood aside to let them pass.

'Come on, Olivia!' Henri called.

I stepped into the house, aware of a floating sensation, a ringing in my ears. It was definitely Richie.

'This is Olivia – our nanny,' Cerys said to the man who now called himself Pascal.

He stared at me.

She frowned. 'It is tonight, isn't it? The invitation to dinner?'

'Yes, yes, it is. It is. I... please go through to the sitting room. Do you want to have the baby with you? Or in one of the bedrooms? We have a... a monitor.'

'A bedroom will be fine. You *were* expecting us?'

'Oh yes, yes. It's along here... the sitting room.'

An elderly woman in a navy dress appeared, conferred with Richie and took Frances's carry tot.

As the Chevalier family made their way into the sitting room, he grabbed my arm. 'Don't say anything, please, I'll–'

Clara ran downstairs, jumping the last three steps. '*Philippe te demande. Il pleure.* Philippe wants you. He's crying.'

Richie bounded upstairs. I lowered myself into a chair in the hall. What was he doing here? Where was my little girl? Where was Alice? I found my inhaler and waited for the medication to take effect.

Clutching the banister, I heaved myself off the chair, went into the sitting room and whispered to Cerys, 'Can I speak to you in private?'

Eyes alight with curiosity, she scuttled after me into the hall. 'Why are you being so secretive?'

'Pascal, is he Véronique's husband?'

'Isn't it obvious?'

The sound of footsteps on the stairs interrupted our conversation. Richie scrutinised us before entering the sitting room.

'Véronique calls herself "Bruhman", right?'

Cerys blinked. 'Might be her maiden name, or it could be her first husband's name.'

I checked we weren't being overheard. 'Do you know Pascal?'

'No. I hardly even know Véronique. She's a friend of Antoinette's sister. Why all these questions? Honestly... Can we please go back to the others?'

I followed her into the sitting room, praying she wouldn't mention our conversation.

Richie handed Bertrand a glass of wine. 'Rosé or red, Cerys?'

'Either. It's such fun being out to dinner. It's ages since we've done this, isn't it Bertie?'

'Bertrand,' he said.

Richie caught my eye, 'Olivia?'

'Red.'

Surely he didn't expect me to acquiesce to this charade? I gripped the glass and stood by the window. When he excused himself, I made to follow him.

'The room's lovely, isn't it?' Cerys said. 'Olivia?'

I turned round. Nodded.

She frowned. 'Where are you going?'

'To check on Frances.'

Bertrand pointed to the baby monitor. 'We will hear her if she will cry.'

'I'll see she's okay.'

At the door I collided with Richie who was brandishing another corkscrew. The metal spiral grazed my hand, so I found a bathroom, waited for the blood to congeal and washed it off. Despite my attempts to breathe deeply, my heart wouldn't stop thumping. What I must do was endure dinner, then catch him on his own. I allowed myself a few more minutes before returning to the sitting room.

In an effort to regain a semblance of calm, I studied the room: its cream leather seating and watermelon walls, the oak parquet floor with its silk Persian rugs, the antique walnut sideboard, desk and coffee table. Most impressive was a Steinway grand that would overwhelm most sitting rooms.

Bertrand, in a dark green jacket and white shirt, was seated at one end of the sofa, Renée, in a low-cut yellow dress, at the other. Installed between Bertrand and Renée, Cerys beamed and prattled on about the beautiful room and how lovely it was to be out to dinner, from time to time glancing down at her tight dress, rearranging her shawl.

Richie's face had thinned, his cheekbones now more

clearly defined. Brown thin-rimmed spectacles framed dark, clear eyes, and his straight fair hair showed no sign of receding. Gone was the moustache he'd sported at the station in Nice. Tailored trousers replaced baggy cords and his blue linen shirt displayed the Ralph Lauren logo.

I used my inhaler again, conscious of this halting the conversation, remembering how in such situations he would hold me, murmur reassurance. Vintage Richie.

When Véronique entered the room, Bertrand gasped. The knee-length aubergine satin dress displayed her contours to perfection, and her dark hair, fashioned into a roll at her bare nape, shone. Silver pendant earrings reflected the colour of her dress and her olive skin glowed. I flinched at the familiar perfume filling the air. Richie had presented me with *Paloma Picasso* after we first made love. *Cut, cut...*

'*Bienvenue*, welcome,' Véronique said. 'This is a beautiful night. I hope that my husband is being hospitable. Has he offered to you a second drink?'

I sighed. No rush to serve dinner. This was France, though, and when we finally did eat, the meal would probably last for hours. At least Richie couldn't slip away.

'What a lovely dress, Véronique,' Cerys said. 'From Paris? Milan?'

'I made it,' Véronique replied, smiling at Richie.

Fifteen minutes later, she stood. 'Now to eat.'

While walking along the corridor, I feared my legs would buckle. '*Entrez, s'il vous plaît*. Please, come in,' she said.

The dining room displayed a glorious mix of dark French-polished furniture and coral and hunter green tableware. Piano music played discreetly. My throat filled with bile.

I must speak to Richie now.

'Just as well the children are eating in the kitchen,' Cerys whispered. 'Can't imagine them in the sitting room, spilling food on those wonderful Persian rugs. Or in here...'

I lifted a forkful of ratatouille to my dry mouth, blushing when the food dropped onto my plate, spattering tomato sauce on the tablecloth. Raising my head, I noticed Richie watching me, removing his gaze when Véronique suggested another bottle of *Côte du Lubéron*. After sipping some water, I managed a mouthful of courgette and aubergine.

A discourse on housing policy, led by an animated Véronique, was followed by a heated debate about Sarkozy's time in office, moving seamlessly to a Hungarian trip the Bruhmans had planned. Much of this conversation was conducted in French. Throughout, Bertrand positioned his body towards the French woman, oblivious to the hand Cerys would tentatively place on his arm.

As Marie-Beatrice cleared away plates, I noticed Véronique's loving look bestowed on Richie, his strained response. Pleading a headache, I left the dining room and made my way outside, where I was able to think more coherently. If it proved impossible to speak to him this evening, I'd write a business-like letter asking what had happened to our daughter. Deep in thought, I jumped at a tap on my shoulder.

'Are you all right?' Cerys asked. 'You missed the most wonderful Banon goat cheese. It's so nice having a grown-up meal for a change, it is. We're about to have crème brulée. Bertrand will be in raptures. Better than sex, he says... Come on.'

Back at the table, I studied the plate of crème brûlée in front of me, its garnish of mint and slivers of strawberry.

When I heard the coffee percolator's contented chugging, my heart raced. An opportunity might be approaching.

'I show you my art,' Véronique said to Cerys, after we finished coffee.

Cerys giggled. 'I'm a Philistine about art.'

Véronique stared at her daughter. 'Viens, Renée.'

Marie-Beatrice appeared with a tray, removing crystal glasses and crumbs of Banon cheese.

Noticing Bertrand frowning at me, I stood, resigned to complying with the custom of leaving the men to discuss topics too erudite for women.

Then he rose from the table. 'In the car I have the cigars.'

Surreptitiously, I opened my bag and dropped it so that its contents spilled out. When he left the room, I knelt to gather my belongings, heart thumping.

My breathing was shallow when I sat down again – Bertrand would return soon, this might be my one chance. I snuck a look at Richie as he poured more coffee. His neck was blotchy and a vein on his forehead pulsed. I then studied Marie-Beatrice as she gathered lily petals from the sideboard. Would it be safe to talk? Did she understand English?

As she left the dining room, I heard Véronique and Cerys's voices, the sound of the front door opening.

'Bertie, you must see this painting, you must,' Cerys said, her voice high.

Tugging my necklace, I waited to see if Véronique would reclaim her husband. Cerys was eulogising over the latest acquisition.

'*Chéri, ça va*? Darling, are you okay?' our hostess asked from the doorway, throwing me a puzzled look.

Richie cleared his throat twice before replying: '*Oui, ça va bien*. Yes, everything is fine.'

'Véronique, do come and explain the paintings to Bertie,' Cerys called.

Once his wife was out of earshot, Richie leant forward. 'Thanks for not saying anything.'

'Where's... where's my daughter?'

Tugging the hairs under his watchstrap, he said. 'She didn't make it. She only lived for about two hours.'

'But I found out... my aunt told me she'd survived, she was–'

'Well, no–'

'*There* you are, Pascal,' Renée said, entering the room, followed by Philippe in his pyjamas, clutching his toy monkey.

'*Papa*, *Papa*, will you read me a story?'

'Renée will read to you tonight,' Richie said, scooping the child into his arms.

'I want *you* to do it, *Papa*.'

'Tomorrow night, darling.'

'Promise?'

Véronique called from the door. '*Viens, chéri*! Come on, darling!'

Richie, Renée and Philippe left the room.

I remained at the table. I didn't have a child, I wasn't a mother. Dorothy had misunderstood the hospital conversation... I wanted to rush down to the sea and wail. All this hoping and now nothing. But the hospital had written to my parents, saying one of the babies had survived. None of this made sense.'

Richie reappeared. 'Meet me at the harbour in Villefranche tomorrow – four o'clock.'

Véronique called again. '*Pascal, viens*! Pascal, come!'

A clamour now inhabited my head, a buzz of deep voices that faded as a child's voice demanded attention: *I want you to do it, Papa.*

Philippe: running over to Richie, their obvious bond; Véronique's distant manner with him.

He was nearly six. Could Dorothy have misheard the gender of the surviving child? Could he be my son?

I waited until my head quietened. Then I rose, gripped the back of the chair to steady myself, and made my way to the sitting room where the others had congregated. There, I perched on the edge of my chair, praying for another private moment with Richie, the chance to ask him one question. We drank more coffee, Véronique circulated Belgian chocolates. Richie and Bertrand discussed heart surgery developments and Cerys rambled on about Persian rugs and art and how she might take up painting when the children were older.

When not required in conversation, Richie's gaze focused on the carriage clock on the mantelpiece. Several times I absented myself, hovering in the hall in case he appeared. I considered finding Philippe but didn't trust my self-control.

Before we left, I lingered by the sitting room door, still hoping for a moment to catch Richie on his own. But Véronique remained by his side.

On the return drive, one question dominated my thoughts: was Philippe mine?

~

'YOU SEEM ROUGH,' Cerys remarked at breakfast the following morning.

As she stretched her chubby arms, her blouse rode up, revealing a row of neat stitches from the Caesarean.

I remembered how I'd narrowly avoided having one. Wondered, yet again, if the forceps delivery had been responsible for the poor condition in which my babies were born. *Cut.*

'Cerys, do you know how long Pascal and Véronique have been married?'

She buttered another croissant. 'Honestly, you're obsessed with them, you are, their marriage, their... Can we change the subject, please? What are you doing on your day off?'

'Laurent's taking me to Grasse, there's a market.'

She raised her eyebrows. 'You two becoming an item then?'

'Not you, too.'

'You *are* in a strange mood. Think I'll go back to bed while Frances is asleep. She was cranky last night, kept me awake for ages, she did. First, I must phone Véronique, thank her.'

While Cerys waited for her call to be answered, I watched the children playing in the paddling pool, Odette squealing in delight as Henri soaked her with water. I turned away. How much notice would be required if I terminated my employment early? It was one thing working with children when I still believed I could find my child. Quite another, being amongst them, knowing I wasn't a mother.

If Philippe *wasn't* my son, continuing here would be unbearable.

'It's Cerys. Thank you for a lovely evening... We must have you here for dinner, soon... Yes, yes he did... Try not to worry, the weather's fine, not a hint of wind around... Bye now.'

'Cerys, what's wrong?'

'Pascal is sailing this afternoon. Véronique gets twitchy. Righto, I must go before Frances wakes and demands more milk.' Cerys peered out of the kitchen window. 'Why are they in the paddling pool? They know Bertrand's taking them fishing. Henri's getting quite good, Bertrand says he's a natural.'

By the time Laurent collected me, I was desperate to be away from Cerys, who, despite her intention of napping, had emptied out the utility room cupboards, consulting me on what she should discard, deliberating on each opinion I offered.

'It's hard to believe,' I said, when Laurent turned west, heading out of Nice. 'I mean, I've had five months of believing that I had a little girl, you know? And now I've found out that I don't, but I might have a son... I tried to phone you last night.'

'I am sorry that we were not able to speak. You must have been shocked.'

I summarised the evening: my realisation that Philippe might be my son, my frustration over not being able to ask Richie.

'We've arranged to meet this afternoon. I'm so nervous.'

As the red and orange tiled roofs of Grasse rose to greet us, I felt lightheaded and this sensation increased while we strolled through the crowded market. Everywhere, I could hear children's musical voices. The need for Philippe to be mine increased with each passing hour.

At lunchtime, we found a quiet spot overlooking a swathe of lavender. A heady fragrance permeated the airless day, the distant purple mountains were hazy.

'Do you have feelings for Richie now?' Laurent asked, offering me a pastry.

'I can't forgive him for what he's done, the deception... Have you ever lost someone?'

He viewed the mountains. 'Once before.'

'What went wrong? If you don't mind me asking.'

'We planned to marry, but it did not happen.'

He turned away, but not before I registered the bleakness in his eyes.

'Do you know what you will say to Richie?' he asked, opening a flask of coffee, reaching for the polystyrene cups.

'Have you heard of Eve Arnold, the photographer? When her baby died at birth, she went round photographing newborn babies to exorcise her grief... Richie told me our daughter died the day she was born, two hours after her birth. Oh Laurent, when he told me this, I–'

'It is possible that he is lying. Perhaps the child is with Alice and she has asked that he keeps this as a secret.'

'It's such a strange situation – I mean, part of me is grieving for having lost my daughter, and yet I might have a son. When Dorothy phoned the hospital, she thought they said "*fille*", daughter, when they could have said "*fils*", son. It would be easy enough to mishear.'

'You may be right,' Laurent said, glancing at his watch. 'We must leave now.'

ON THE HOMEWARD DRIVE, the overcast sky made me despondent and I barely spoke. This afternoon's meeting with Riche would be one of the most important events of my life. What if he told me Philippe wasn't mine? What if he was mine but Richie didn't want me having access to him? And there was Alice. Did she now share custody of Philippe? Or could Laurent have been right when he suggested that perhaps Alice did have custody of the little girl?

'I'm sorry I've been lousy company,' I said when Laurent dropped me off. 'I'll call you later. Wish me luck.'

As I opened the front door, Cerys scuttled downstairs. 'Thank goodness you're back. We have to take Henri to hospital, see. Can you stay with Odette and Frances?'

'What's wrong with him?'

'Severe vomiting and diarrhoea. Began when they were fishing, it did. Oh no, there's Frances – take expressed milk from the freezer. I have to pack.'

Bertrand carried a rough-looking Henri to the car and laid him across the back seats. Seconds later, the boy was vomiting into a plastic bowl, Bertrand supporting his head.

Cerys appeared, clutching her overnight bag. 'We'll phone once we know what's what. Once they've got him rehydrated. I've no idea when we'll be back. I'll stay if they keep him in overnight.'

While defrosting milk for the baby, my mind kicked into overdrive. How could I get in touch with Richie? I felt sorry for Henri, of course, but what terrible timing.

'Is Henri going to die?' Odette asked, while I fed Frances.

'No. He's got a bug, that's all.'

She wrinkled her nose. 'He was sick in the bedroom. All over the floor. It's yellow and it smells yucky–'

'I'll sort it.'

'I'm hungry. *Maman* couldn't make me lunch 'cos of Henri.'

'Take a cereal bar, Odette. I'll make you a toastie when I've fed Frances.'

When the baby was finally satisfied, I laid her in the cot. Then I filled a bucket with hot soapy water and tackled the mess on Henri's bedroom floor. By the time I'd

finished, it was twenty minutes to four. In the family
address book I found the Bruhman number and dialled it.
Fingers crossed, Richie hadn't left and Véronique wouldn't
answer.

'*Est–ce que je peux parler à Pascal?* Can I speak to Pascal?'

'*Il n'est pas là, desolée.* He isn't here, sorry,' Marie-Beatrice
said.

Before I could request his mobile number, I heard
Véronique's voice in the background, and hung up.

I made a toastie and paced the kitchen while Odette ate.
Would Richie wait for me or assume I wouldn't appear? I
had to see him today. My hand flew to my mouth: with
Cerys's car I could be there in ten minutes.

'Get your shoes, Odette. We're going to Villefranche.'

'Why?'

'I'll explain later.'

'I haven't finished my lunch, have I spider?'

Ignoring her startled expression, I grabbed the toastie,
shoved it into a bag. 'Take it with you.'

'Are we going by bus?'

'We'll take *Maman*'s car.'

'It's gone. They took Henri to the hospital in it.'

Of course. 'Then we'll take *Papa*'s.'

But it wasn't insured for me to drive.

Five minutes past four. I rummaged in a drawer for the
bus timetable – the Saturday service to Villefranche ran
half-hourly and we'd just missed a bus. Fleetingly I considered zipping down to the harbour on Laurent's moped,
dismissed the idea. If Cerys discovered I'd left Odette and
Frances on their own, even briefly, she'd go apeshit. And
rightly so.

It was raining now, the sea choppy. Perhaps Richie
would abandon his sailing this afternoon. Arrange another

time to meet. But how... If only we'd exchanged mobile numbers.

When the phone rang, I jumped.

'Olivia?' Cerys's voice sounded relieved. 'Henri's better. They've given him medicine for the vomiting and diarrhoea, and they're rehydrating him. He's asleep, now. So relieved, I am. We should be able to bring him home this evening. Can you hang on 'til we're back?'

A beeping sound went. Richie might be trying to get through.

'Okay, I'll see you then. That's great about Henri.'

'I got such a fright,' she continued. 'The vomiting was awful, it was. And the diarrhoea poured out of him, it did. Poor love.'

The beeping sounded again.

'I'd better go,' I said, ringing off.

When the phone rang a moment later, I grabbed it. 'Richie?'

'We got cut off,' Cerys said. 'Would you cook? We probably won't be back until after seven and–'

'I'll cook. See you later.'

Once more I waited by the phone. After ten minutes, I tried the Bruhman number again.

No reply. I glanced at the clock and decided to go for the next bus – Richie might still be there, tinkering with his boat.

Odette ran into the kitchen. 'Frances has done a poopy... Can I pick some flowers in the garden? *Maman* said I could, if I asked you first.'

I cursed and collapsed onto a chair. By the time I'd changed the baby's nappy and strapped her into her carry tot, the bus would have left. Richie and I simply weren't fated to meet this afternoon. Nevertheless, I tried the

Bruhman number repeatedly. Twice Véronique answered and I hung up, three times the frosty Marie-Beatrice lifted the phone.

At seven o'clock, I had just sat down at the kitchen table to write to him, when Cerys's car drew to a halt outside the front door. Bertrand appeared a moment later, his arm supporting Henri.

'How are you, Henri?' I asked.

He shrugged. 'Okay, I guess.'

'I'll put him to bed, come on Henri,' Cerys said, staring at the cooker.

I jumped up. 'I was about to prepare a meal.'

'Bertie, get three large pizzas from the freezer... Thanks for staying around today, Olivia.'

Fifteen minutes later, the phone rang. I heard Cerys answer, exclaim. Bertrand then took over, speaking in rapid French. I went downstairs and halted by the kitchen door. Head in hands, Cerys wept at the table.

'What's wrong, Cerys?'

'I can't believe it, I can't, and we had such a lovely evening... It's too awful...'

'What is it?'

Bertrand placed a mug of tea in front of her, added milk and sugar.

'It's Pascal – and he'd hardly been home again,' she said eventually. 'And I told Véronique not to worry, I thought she–'

My heart thudded. 'What's happened to him?'

'It was a sailing accident.'

'Is he in hospital?'

She raised her red-rimmed eyes. 'He's dead.'

ix years earlier

Already the heat, flies and Muezzin calls of Morocco seem dreamlike in the grey dampness of a London January. Olivia wonders if her babies sensed her dismay when she discovered her pregnancy. If they died for fear she wouldn't love them, protect them. She's read that if not cuddled, infants lose the will to live. Furthermore, if a foetus can appreciate music, be nurtured by the mother's conversation, surely it can detect ambivalence, can die of heartbreak?

She paces the flat during the day. Unable to sleep, at night she roams the streets or watches B movies. One minute she is laughing, the next, crying uncontrollably.

'Jeez, Liv, you wanted the babies, you were only unsure at the beginning,' Martin reminds her. 'It wasn't your fault. Stop beating yourself up.'

One evening, she flicks the remote control – a programme on IVF, a soap with themes around young children, a boy actor's rise to stardom. The news broadcasts stories about parents' heartache at the disappearance of their twelve-year-old daughter; about an award to a leukaemia survivor who inspires other children with similar conditions.

Remembering Seth's advice, she consults with Dr Wilton who agrees she is experiencing mild postpartum psychosis and prescribes lithium to stabilise her moods. After four weeks, her mood swings lose their intensity. But the weight piles on, so, confident she can manage withdrawal of medication on her own, she gradually reduces the dose of lithium.

'What's happened to you?' Roz asks one February morning on Primrose Hill. 'Are you starving yourself or what?'

'Just trying to get to a reasonable weight. Can we walk more quickly, please?'

'How much have you lost? Are you overdoing it at the gym? How often are you going?' Roz sits on a bench, pulls Olivia down beside her. The wood feels rough under her thighs.

Moisture from the grass seeps through her worn trainers and the wind buffets her flimsy jacket. Roz tightens her scarf. 'We studied this at med school, don't you remember?'

'Remember what, for God's sake?'

'Do I have to spell it out?'

Olivia walks on. Roz catches her up. 'Liv, are you making yourself vomit?'

'I need to go now. Dental appointment.'

The gym is mobbed with lunchtime members, so she reorders her fixed weight exercises to avoid waiting for machines. She finishes her programme, repeats it, and swims sixty lengths.

At the flat she eats a bowl of soup and two oatcakes. Bloated afterwards, she makes herself sick in the bathroom. What relief.... After brushing her teeth twice, she inspects herself again in the mirror – her stomach is flatter.

From her sitting room window, she gazes at the wet streets and the eerie light from street lamps. She stares at her photos of the market place in Marrakech and the Toubkal National Park, feeling the heat on her shoulders, tasting the spiced goat stew.

Martin appears the next day. 'You look awful, Liv... Have you eaten today?'

'If *you're* hungry, take something from the fridge.'

She watches him rummage through her low-fat yoghurts and salad greens.

'We're going to the pub,' he says, finding her jacket, dragging her out of the flat.

She lets him order her a ham salad. Tolerates his observation, while he tucks into steak pie. 'Mum's upset you haven't been in touch.'

She tugs her necklace. 'I can't face her.'

'At least see Dad. He's worried.'

'I'll speak to him, Marti. I promise. I have to go now – I want to run before it gets dark.'

Three days later, he reappears at her flat with Dr Wilton. Too weary to hold out, she admits she needs help.

A GREY ROOM with floral prints, and lead paned windows giving onto fields and distant hills.

Pills in plastic containers. Orange-coated women mopping floors and ramming flowers into green-tinged vases. She is monitored around meal times, but occasionally, when the ward is short-staffed, she manages to dispose of her food. More often, though, she has to eat, with no opportunity afterwards for making herself sick.

She shuffles around airy corridors in dressing gown and woolly socks. 'Cigarette?' a woman offers.

She shakes her head.

'Too posh for us, aren't you?' another patient says.

How could they understand? How could anyone really understand? She caresses her stomach, as if by so doing, she can restore the foetuses.

A psychotherapist meets with her, a middle-aged man with dark eyes and gold-rimmed spectacles. Dr Barak tolerates her initial silence, then listens while she skirts round the issues, comparing her life in Morocco with that in London.

In time she reveals her thoughts about her body, about control. Descriptions spill out: her labour, the fight to save her babies. Richie.

A dietitian visits, the antithesis of their brusque nutrition lecturer at med school. Rachel has long fair hair, wears tweedy trousers and rough fabric shirts with cloth-covered buttons. She smells of *Chanel 19* perfume.

'When did your attitude to food change?' Rachel asks.

Olivia describes its gradual onset, the exhilaration when she first vomited.

Rachel nods. 'Do you think there's a connection between what happened to your babies and what is happening to your body?'

Olivia's eyes brim with tears.

They discuss possible links between her unconscious desire to starve herself and leaving her twins before they actually died. Her belief of being unworthy to eat. The need to forgive herself for her actions.

'What do you think about your weight now?' Rachel asks.

She hesitates. 'I know I'm too thin, but I don't want to become fat again.'

'How about planning a regime for you? I can visit every day, help you decide what you'll eat the following one. You can weigh yourself twice a week, then if you're worried about weight going on too quickly, you can cut back. You'll be the person in control.'

'I don't want calories smuggled into my food,' she says. 'Or extra protein.'

'Nothing will be added, I give you my word. What you must remember is that the work you're doing with Dr Barak is equally important to the work you do with me.'

Nurses produce magazines and puzzle books that she sweeps aside. Occupational therapists offer clay, oil paints and other tools for expressing emotion. How can she paint a void? Sculpt a vacuum? Nevertheless, when the music therapist tempts her with drums, balalaikas and woodwind instruments, she experiments with sounds and rhythms.

She continues to respond to Dr Barak. Grows to trust and like Rachel, who consults with her daily.

Dorothy visits one day. 'You poor pet, how are you? I will never forgive myself for letting you go to Tangiers on your own.'

'It's not your fault, what happened.'

Dorothy hands her a bag and Olivia smiles on seeing the pink blouse.

'How long are you likely to be here for?' her aunt asks

'They're pleased with me... but it's one thing being here where I have support, another living on my own.'

Dorothy strokes her arm. 'You're welcome to stay with

me any time. William and I are now married. So respectable, I can hardly believe it.'

'I'm glad you have him.'

She talks about Marrakech and Seth, her reasons for returning to London. Dorothy describes the wedding.

'William would like to see you, lovie, if you're up to it. Perhaps next visit?' Dorothy says, embracing her before leaving.

That evening, Olivia anticipates dinner with less apprehension – stew with broccoli and two scoops of mashed potato (no added butter). It's been almost two weeks since she made herself sick, her breasts have grown, and the fine raised hairs on her arms are disappearing. These improvements she notes in the diary that Dr Barak suggested she keep.

Three days later, her mother visits on her own for the first time She is wearing her uniform striped shirt and brass buttoned cardigan, and her red lipstick seems more lurid than usual.

'I've written to the Faculty,' her mother says, while tidying her locker. 'To see if you can resume again in the autumn.'

'Resume what?'

'Medical school, of course. I only want what's best for you, Olivia. I think you'd make a good doctor.'

Medical school, she thinks, picking at her hands. How can she heal others when she can't even look after herself?

'Finishing your studies will be the best thing for you,' her mother says when she leaves.

Staff dispense afternoon tea. After eating her scone with low fat spread, she hovers over the bathroom wash-hand basin, one voice telling her to vomit, another, not to let Mum's visit sabotage her progress. The healthy voice having won, she goes to the music room where she devises a tickly rhythm on the drums. When she feels calmer, she returns to her room.

She dreams of being lost in a souk in Marrakech, hearing the Muezzin call to prayer and being unable to reach the mosque. The Sunday bells of the local church waken her.

After breakfast, she vomits in the bathroom.

'Tell me about your relationship with your mother,' Dr Barak says that afternoon.

She picks at her knuckles. 'If it hadn't been for her, I probably wouldn't have gone to Gibraltar to stay with Dorothy and then I wouldn't have gone to Tangiers... I might have carried my babies to term. Who knows?'

'Do you blame her for what happened?'

She describes her childhood – the impact of Mum's frustration over Dad's lack of ambition; the thwarting of her mother's own career aspirations; how she lives life through her children.

Dr Barak leans forward. 'Would you rather she didn't visit?'

'You can hardly stop her... I can't ask her to stay away, can I?'

'Any visitor who has a negative impact on your progress should stay away. I'll phone her, with your permission.'

She thanks him for his support. His validation.

'I believe in you, Olivia,' he says, when she leaves the room.

Friends visit, their stays limited by buses to catch, essays to finish. She discovers the rarity of real mates. Explains this to Hilary, who plans to specialise in mental health, who can hold Olivia's gaze, who doesn't suggest playing table tennis or other avoidance activities.

She continues charting her progress: reduced anxiety about gaining weight; pleasure from the azaleas in bud; her drumming, and the enormous bunches of freesias Martin brings. She talks to other patients with eating disorders.

Dorothy and William take her for afternoon tea. While scanning the oak panelled hotel lounge, she wonders if the other guests can detect she's from The Priory, but no one seems to be paying her any attention. She manages to eat two sandwiches and a piece of cake without counting calories in her head, and when William suggests they go to a Turner exhibition, a sensation of normality returns.

ON A SUNNY SPRING AFTERNOON, Martin collects her from The Priory, stopping on the way home at Waitrose for her to stock up on food. Back at her flat, he informs the health centre about her return home, while she makes coffee.

'What would I do without my twin?' she says, when she hugs him goodbye.

Roz and Zoë visit, as do Dorothy and William. The days become easier, so she approaches medical school and arranges to repeat the year. She spends the summer months temping for banks, legal offices and insurance companies. Despite the mind-numbing work, she welcomes a reason to get up in the morning, a structure to her day.

During the autumn term, she struggles in to lectures, scrapes by on lab work and attempts to mug up with textbooks. She is relieved to learn that Richie has left the university.

'How's university going?' Dr Barak asks at an outpatient appointment.

'I'm hanging in there,' she says. 'But I'm... an outsider. I used to enjoy being in the pub with other students, but I find their conversation superficial, you know? It's hard to connect with them... I mean, I understand their stresses, but after what I've been through...'

'Everything else seems trivial?'

An ambulance siren drowns her reply. She tries again. 'I don't want my loss to... to define me, but it does.'

He leans forward. 'And where do you see yourself in five years' time?'

She blinks. 'What a question...'

'Can you visualise yourself being a doctor?'

She tugs at a cushion tassel. 'Perhaps this is why I haven't been able to arrange a placement for next year. I don't know if I want the responsibility.... My mother is desperate for me to become a doctor.'

They discuss the importance of Olivia assuming her own identity.

By Christmas she has withdrawn from medical school. She spends hours rehearsing how to tell her mother – anticipating responses, counter-arguments. Aware of her ongoing vulnerability. Despite the therapy, the support from friends and Martin. Eventually she blurts it out during a family Sunday lunch.

Her mother stops serving, tongs gripping a Yorkshire pudding. 'You're making a mistake.'

` 'It's Olivia's decision,' Dad says.

She inspects her plate: the viscous gravy, the slightly burnt roast potatoes.

When Mum clears away, Dad puts his hand over his plate. 'I haven't finished yet.'

Her mother stomps out of the dining room. Through the serving hatch they hear the scraping of a scouring pad on pots.

'I'll talk to her,' he says.

'It's not right for me,' she tells him. 'I don't think it ever was, it was what she wanted. I mean, it's not like it's the only respectable career.'

'You can work in a fish factory if you want, darling, provided you're happy.'

'I wondered about returning to nursing – when I'm ready.'

A YEAR after returning from Morocco, Olivia meets Martin and Zoë for a pub meal. Before Olivia's removed her coat, Zoë says, 'Anya's bought an old mansion in Hertfordshire. She's opening a rehab centre for young people recovering from accidents. I'm transferring there, it'll be great physio experience. She's got vacancies for nurses.'

Olivia tugs her necklace. 'I don't know if I'm ready for this.'

Zoë passes her an envelope. 'Anya is keen to meet you. There's an application form – if you're interested.'

'What does she know about me?'

'She knows you've been through a rough time,' Martin says. 'Zoë didn't go into details.'

At home, Olivia lights some apple-scented candles, locates her sandalwood beads, and sits cross-legged on the rug by the fire, practising a meditation Seth taught her in Marrakech. She wonders if he ever thinks about her.

The following week she meets Anya, a tall, charismatic Swedish woman with short fair hair and intelligent blue eyes. Early fifties, she reckons.

'I'm recovering from an eating disorder,' she admits,

after Anya has described the job. 'I'm much better than I was, you know, but...'

'You could work part-time, see how it goes.'

'Why me? I mean, aren't you worried about taking a risk?'

Anya smiles disarmingly and states her belief that the more life experience people have acquired, the better equipped they are to understand and support others. The patients Olivia will be caring for face huge challenges and she needs staff with empathy.

'Would you be able to provide an up-to-date reference?'

'I still see my psychotherapist – I'm sure he would give me one.'

'Provided the reference is okay, I'd be happy for you to join our team.'

She begins working part-time at The Grange. The staff work ethic is strong, and she appreciates Anya's holistic approach to health, her consultative management style, and her meticulous organisation. As for the old stone building, its green and dusky pink decor, the yuccas and Kentish palms, bestow on her a wonderful sense of calm, which helps balance the harrowing conditions she encounters in patients.

Within several shifts, she realises the wisdom of her decision – the job less intellectually demanding than medicine, its opportunities to immerse herself in caring for her patients. Time permitting, she participates in patient activities: Pilates, Ashtanga yoga, aromatherapy. When the other physio is busy, she assists Zoë, relieved to be friends with Martin's girlfriend, rather than regard her as a rival.

Eighteen months on from her bereavement, the pain is blunting. Each week she visits the local cemetery, prays for forgiveness for abandoning her twins, her Chergui's Children.

In the middle of autumn, Anya hosts a party for the pioneers and staff of The Grange. There, she introduces Olivia to the lawyer involved in purchasing the building, James Chatterton: a nondescript looking man with a prematurely receding hairline, posh voice and wearing a drab grey shirt. Olivia dismisses him as stuffy until they discover a shared love of jiving.

Several months later, after The Grange Christmas party, a bunch of them continue on to a Ceroc club in south London, where James wriggles and spins in demoniac fashion.

Bewitched, she accepts his tentative invitation to dinner.

23

That evening, Richie's accident made local headlines. When his boat capsized, a couple fishing off nearby rocks had rescued him and bound his injured head with a scarf until the ambulance arrived. Despite receiving treatment from the paramedics, however, he'd been pronounced dead on arrival at hospital. The weather forecaster warned of strong, gusting winds over the following days, advising caution when driving, and avoiding unnecessary boat trips.

Eventually a tearful Cerys switched off the television and announced she would take a bath. Bertrand disappeared to his study. Incapable of coherent thought, I remained on the sofa, a sleeping Frances in my arms. I wanted to phone Martin or Dad but didn't have the energy.

THE DAY of the funeral was muggy, with rumbles of thunder.

'I have to say, in all my time living in France, I've never got used to this custom of burying people so soon after they've died,' Cerys said at breakfast, sniffing hard. 'Now, you're sure you'll be okay managing Philippe in addition to our brood? Weird it is, Véronique wanting him to come here when there must be other people to take care of him. I suppose they all want to attend the funeral.'

I nodded. Since learning about Richie's death, one thought had occupied my mind – how to find out if Philippe was my son. Martin's advice had been to ask Véronique straight out, but I didn't feel I could do this. My best chance, I reckoned, was seeing if there were any clues in the Bruhman house, and this meant going there after the funeral service. But I hadn't been invited.

It was raining when Renée appeared with Philippe. In a grey dress, her dark hair lank round her ears, she seemed younger, vulnerable. He looked wan. When they reached the door, I bent to hug him, one question dominating my thoughts. Was he *mine*?

'*Maman* is saying that you must bring Philippe to the house at twelve o'clock when the guests will arrive,' she said. 'You can bring also the other children.'

Phew!

Philippe was clutching a green piece of cloth.

'What's that?' I asked.

She glanced at him. 'It is the handkerchief of Pascal. He does not let anyone take it.... I must go now. *Maman* waits in the car.'

When I closed the door, Odette and Henri appeared, each taking one of Philippe's hands and leading him to the playroom. Having checked he was okay with them, I flopped onto the sitting room sofa, aware of orange peel and crisp crumbs on the rug, but too tired to tidy and vacuum. How could I best use my time at the Bruhmans? There was no one to safely question about his parents: Marie-Beatrice and

Renée would report anything to Véronique, and Clara was probably too young. If possible, I'd search his room for photo albums or photos of Alice. If there *was* one of her, this would be my answer.

Closing my eyes, I practised one of Seth's meditations. But my mind refused to declutter, so I gave up. On the table lay the latest edition of *Marie Claire*, and flicking through it, to my surprise I found myself smiling at Cerys's scribbled comments – beside a long skirt, "could try this, probably not tall enough"; under a layered bob hairstyle, "?forehead too small for fringe, ask André".

Half an hour later, I woke to see a forlorn figure by the door.

'What is it, Philippe? Are you hungry? Do you want a drink?'

'I want to go home.'

I went over to him, clasped his hand. It felt small and cold. As for his lost expression, it was painful to witness.

If only I knew he was mine.

Véronique's home seemed even more imposing today, with its rust and gold walls and parquet floors, its caterers settling trays of wine glasses and silver salvers of finger foods. Public rooms bore the heady scent of Oriental lilies, vases of the salmon-flowers gracing tables, bureaux and the grand piano. The solemn ticking of an antique grandfather clock in the hall lent additional gravitas.

'Let's build a Lego space ship,' Henri suggested.

Philippe's face lit up. 'I have Lego. *Papa* gave it to me.'

He rushed off with Henri and Odette.

Minutes later, Henri bounded downstairs, announcing, 'Me and Odette'll take care of Philippe.'

After speaking to Marie-Beatrice, I carried the sleeping Frances upstairs to the spare room and placed her buggy by the window. Ten minutes until the guests arrived. I paced the ground floor rooms, imagining the storm that had killed Richie – waves hurtled against rocks, white foam tinged with brown; dark, angry clouds. And today the scenes would be similar. Suddenly I longed to be perched on these slippery rocks, howling, my voice competing with the roar of wind.

The need to uncover Philippe's identity drove me upstairs once more. Tentatively, I opened a door. Posters of film stars, a clutter of lipsticks and nail gloss, clothes and magazines littering the unmade bed, suggested this was Renée's room. An ashtray contained a cigarette stub smelling of cannabis. On a chest of drawers was a photograph of an olive-skinned man, probably her father. Nearby, Christmas and birthday cards, all reading, "*Gros bisous, Papa,* lots of love, *Papa*", festooned a cork wallboard. About to leave the room, I spotted a photo of Richie on the dresser, with "Pascal" scribed in different styles on the back. Had he been flattered by his stepdaughter's crush? I wondered.

Next, I inspected what was obviously Clara's room. The pine bed was covered by a Superman bedspread, beside it, a chair contained a pair of jeans, neatly folded. A large basket accommodated dolls, furry animals and toys. As I lifted a one-armed teddy with an eye patch, a tear snaked down my cheek. Propped against a laundry basket, a rucksack bulged with ordnance survey maps, binoculars, and a biscuit tin labelled "*les réserves*'", "emergency rations". The bookcase was crammed with Spider-Man, Batman and Spy Kids books.

At the sound of crunching gravel, I moved to the window. Three black Mercedes were halting near the front door. A middle-aged man appeared first, helping Véronique out, then Clara and lastly, a tearful Renée. The occupants of the following two cars emerged.

When I popped my head round Philippe's bedroom door, I scanned the room for photos of him with Richie and Alice. There were none. The small bookcase housed a few books but no photo albums.

In the hall, Marie-Beatrice was relieving guests of their coats and explaining where the bathrooms were. Caterers dispensed wine and canapés. Véronique, pale but elegant in a tailored black dress, was circulating, saying little.

Now she turned to Renée, '*Va chercher les verres de rechange dans le bureau. Il nous faut six.* Collect some glasses from the study. We need six.'

'I'll help,' I offered, ignoring Véronique's disapproving expression.

The study overlooked the back garden. By the window, a desk contained papers, a laptop, printer and scanner. Metal bookcases overflowed with box files, journals, textbooks. On the one free wall hung a portrait of a woman in a saffron dress, her dark hair loosely gathered into a chignon – Véronique. She sat on an antique dining chair, legs crossed, the slit in the dress revealing a toned calf. With its detail, its sharp, clean brush strokes, the painting could have been a photograph. I blinked back tears, visualising Richie gazing uninterruptedly at the portrait.

Something prompted me to move closer to the desk, where a white envelope poked out from underneath the printer. Deciphering the first few letters 'Ol', my heart leaped.

'*Qu'est ce que vous faîtes?* What are you doing?' Renée asked.

'I was wondering what the desk is made of.'

She scowled as she handed me three glasses. Desperate

to have another look at the envelope, I indicated she go first, but she stood back to let me pass.

In the sitting room I hovered, overhearing comments about Richie's professional ability and his family qualities, all the while awaiting an opportunity to slip back unnoticed to the study. The grandfather clock chimed twelve-fifteen, twelve-thirty.

'I'll check on the children,' I informed Véronique.

In the hall, near the study, Bertrand was conversing with a short-skirted, high-heeled woman. I couldn't risk him asking questions or following me into the room. When I returned to the dining room, Cerys approached me.

'Bertrand still talking to that tart? What an outfit for a funeral.'

Upstairs, having looked in on Frances, I entered the one unfamiliar room – Richie and Véronique's bedroom. The space was dominated by a mahogany sleigh bed, sheets and duvet cover half removed, a lacy bedspread draped over a chair. Packing boxes crammed with shirts and trousers littered the floor. By the window stood an empty shoe rack, its contents nearby: golfing shoes, several pairs of slip-ons, unused trainers, leather sandals.

I pulled out a wardrobe drawer, fingered a pair of crimson silk knickers and matching bra, held a beige satin camisole over my blouse. Everything smelled of rose. I shoved the lingerie back in and rammed the drawer shut, glancing at my flushed face in the wardrobe mirror.

While backing away, I knocked over the wastepaper basket. As I replaced its contents, I spotted the black *Paloma Picasso* perfume bottle and slipped it into my pocket.

It was raining heavily again, so automatically I went to close the window. Then I noticed the suitcase, half-concealed under the bed. I opened the door and listened. A babble of children's voices from Philippe's room indicated they remained absorbed in their play, and there was no sound of crying from the spare room.

Kneeling by the suitcase, I raised a linen shirt to my face, inhaling Richie's smell. I examined the golf club logo on a tie, glanced at a crumpled pocket Italian dictionary, tugged at his toilet bag zip then halted – this was masochistic. As I skimmed through an Uffizi Gallery brochure, some business cards fell out: Hotel Brunelleschi, Firenzi; Nadine Lingerie, Lungarno degli Acciaiuoli, 22/red, 50123 Firenze. Jealousy seared me as I studied the card for the lingerie shop.

Straightening to stand, I honed in on a travel wallet. In frenzied manner, I emptied out its contents: baggage stubs (dated two days before the Paris conference); a fifty-euro note; a letter from the Università di Firenze and a passport. My fingers felt like bananas as I looked through the maroon booklet. No mention of Philippe.

To make sure I hadn't missed anything, I examined the passport again, carefully turning over every page in case two of them had stuck together, lingering over each one as if the information I longed to see about Philippe might magically appear before my eyes. Nothing. Despair surfaced once more. When I returned the contents to the wallet, however, I discovered another passport, covered in soft green leather.

The bedroom door juddered and I squeezed under the bed, heart thundering while I waited for someone to enter. After a minute I slid out, opened the passport, damp fingers fumbling for the last page. It displayed a photo of a small boy – name: Phillip Williams; date of birth: 31. 8. 2006. A date I'd never forget. My heart contracted with joy. A baby who had survived. Philippe!

24

Fleetingly, like the protagonist in a drama series, I considered grabbing Philippe and running for it. But I couldn't. I must retrieve the letter, take it from there. And there was someone who could help.

As I paused on the landing, Clara emerged from her bedroom. I grasped her arm and pulled her back in. 'I need to talk to you.'

'Is it a mission?'

'Yes, and it's important you don't tell anyone, right?'

She jiggled up and down. 'What is it?'

I explained about the letter in Richie's study, how, for important reasons, I needed her to intercept it.

'I understand,' she said, and rushed off.

I heard Frances cry, so I changed her nappy and fed her expressed milk. Then I went into Philippe's room where the children were now setting up his Playmobil fire station. He glanced at me briefly, Henri and Odette remained absorbed in the task. I lingered, gazing at my son. My son...

Shortly after, I went downstairs again, thunder reverberating across the sky, prompting a collecting of coats, a searching for car keys. Perspiration gathered on my back as I realised that both Clara and Renée were absent from the public rooms. Had I been foolish entrusting such an important task to a child I barely knew? What if Clara confided in her sister? Or Véronique?

Cerys indicated we were leaving, so I rounded up the children, hoping to bump into Clara and receive the envelope. There was no sign of her. However, to my relief, soon after we left the house, she ran along the drive and hovered by me.

'Cerys, you seem shattered,' I said. 'Why don't you go with Bertrand and Odette and Henri, and I'll take Frances with me in your car?'

When Bertrand had pulled away, I turned to Clara. 'Did you get the letter?'

Face wreathed in smiles, she produced a crumpled envelope from her pocket.

Not until evening did I have the time or privacy to read Richie's letter. After returning from the Bruhmans, I'd prepared a late lunch for the children, put on a wash, and helped Henri tidy his room. When I returned to the kitchen, Cerys had prattled incessantly about Véronique, intermittently muttering about needing a nap.

'Why don't you go and sleep?' I'd suggested, after she'd abandoned emptying the washing machine and switched on the iron, stopping ten minutes later to select rubbish for recycling, ruminating yet again about how Véronique would manage single-handedly with three children.

When Cerys finally went for a nap, I'd been about to read the letter when Odette burst into my room to complain about Henri. I'd then resigned myself to waiting until guaranteed uninterrupted time.

Now, letter in hand, I stood by the open window, inhaling the scent of jasmine – pungent after the thunderstorm – hearing the reassuring chirping of crickets. In the fading evening light, Bertrand opened the car bonnet and peered inside, swivelling round when a pyjama-clad Odette and Henri arrived to say goodnight, Odette bending to sniff a rose, Henri imitating a plane swooping and circling. Cerys then appeared, imploring them to hurry.

I lingered while the children kissed their Papa, and Henri sprinted round the lawn, Cerys scampering after him, remonstrating. I listened to their footsteps on the stairs, to the opening and shutting of bedroom doors and to Cerys padding downstairs once more to the balmy August evening.

Carefully, I detached the flap of the envelope and edged the letter out. *'Dear Olivia,'* it read, *'It was such a shock to see you this evening and I haven't been able to think about anything else since. I'm not even sure why I'm writing to you when we're meeting tomorrow. But I can't sleep. Guilt, I suppose. It's so difficult to write this. I am guilty of the worst kind of deception, you see – the separation of a mother from her child. And I wonder if you'll ever be able to get over this, let alone forgive me.*

'You are aware of the pressure Alice put on me to ask you to let us bring up the baby. About five weeks after our babies were born, your mother contacted me to say that the hospital in Tangiers had been in touch with her to let her know that the little girl had survived – your father was the contact on your passport. Obviously, I had no idea you were in Morocco, or that you were having twins. Your mother explained that you'd been ill and couldn't possibly bring up a child on your own, and that she'd prefer the baby to be raised by one of its natural parents, than be

adopted. At first I did nothing, just pondering the situation. Unfortunately, Alice, always intuitive, sensed something had happened and insisted I told her.

'She suggested I went to Tangiers to fetch the baby, make an excuse to the hospital about my wife/you, being ill, and that we raise the child as ours. I was unhappy about being involved in such a deception, but she threatened to report me to the University Faculty if I didn't go along with her idea. I convinced myself that I should do what she wanted. She was so desperate to be a mother, but please believe me, Olivia, when I say I took no pride in what we did. When I got to Morocco, I found out that it was the boy who had survived.

'I loved Philippe from the start and Alice bonded with him quickly once we got back to London. But we felt anxious about being discovered. Neighbours noticed we suddenly had a baby and friends were baffled. We'd said nothing about adoption before then, you see.

Moving abroad was the solution. Being bilingual, France was the obvious choice. I found work in Perpignan and we moved soon after. In Perpignan we worked hard at rebuilding our marriage while becoming used to being parents. When my contract ended, I found another one in Paris. By this time, I'd changed my name by Deed Poll, to Pascal Vernay.

'Shortly before Philippe's second birthday, Alice developed ovarian cancer. We returned to London because I knew a specialist there. She fought hard but none of the treatments worked. Her final words were that she'd been so happy being a mother. I could almost forgive myself, us.'

I dropped the letter and clutched my stomach, picturing Richie arriving at the hospital in Morocco, tired and hot, still absorbing being a father. I saw him cuddling Philippe on the flight to London, giving him a bottle, relishing the charmed expressions of stewards and passengers. The twisting sensation in my abdomen increased as I imagined Alice listening for the taxi, placing a prepared infant feed in the fridge, checking the nursery one last time

I conjured up her first experience of Philippe, cradling him and studying his face for resemblance to Richie. Amazed to finally have an outlet for her maternal instincts, at the same time worrying about what the neighbours would think. Had she been conscience-stricken, even fleetingly? Or had desperation to be a mother overridden any moral considerations?

Had Richie really swallowed my mother's story whole? Had he ever sat bolt upright in bed, horrified by what he'd done, to be soothed with hackneyed lines from Alice about their actions being in the child's best interest? Had he ever panicked on seeing a policeman at the university? Stopped mid-sentence during a lecture or conference presentation, perceiving his behaviour in a new light? Had he – even once – considered contacting me to check out my physical or emotional state? Been prepared to compromise on our son's upbringing?

I returned my attention to the letter.

'After Alice's death I returned to Paris. It was hard. I missed her more than I'd anticipated. Then I met Véronique who'd recently become divorced. We married six months later and moved to St Jean Cap Ferrat, so that the children could see their father regularly. Shortly after, I established my consultancy business – as a visiting lecturer, doing research, the occasional teaching.

'Although Philippe has been a joy, the guilt has never disappeared. And there were so many occasions, especially during the first year, when I was tempted to contact you to tell you what had happened, to see how you were. By the time Alice died, Philippe had been "ours" for almost two years and I convinced

*myself that too much time had elapsed and that I would cause
you more pain than happiness if I got in touch. In the midst of the
shock of seeing you again, there was almost a sense of relief. I
don't know what will happen when we meet, but although the
way ahead will be difficult, I won't prevent you having access
to him.*

*'And now I must explain all this to Véronique. Please forgive
me, Olivia. Yours, Richie'*

～

IT WAS NEARLY ten that evening when I arrived at Laurent's
apartment block in Beaulieu. I parked the moped, scrutinised the names on the entryphone system and pressed the
buzzer. No reply. As the air was warm and fragrant, the
cicadas in full flow, I plonked myself on the grassy patch,
willing his early return. Half an hour later, his grey Fiat
appeared. Not until then did it occur to me he might be
accompanied. He wasn't.

'An amazing thing's happened,' I told him in the lift,
updating him on finding Philippe's passport and Richie's
letter.

'You *are* a mother!'

He unlocked the apartment door and ushered me into
the sitting room. 'Would you like some coffee? Or should we
celebrate with a bottle of wine?'

'I hope you don't mind me coming round like this, I did
try to phone you at work.'

'There was a meeting all day,' he called from the kitchen.

While looking around the room, my eye was drawn to
the mantelpiece and a black and white photo so arresting
that I stepped forward to study its subject. The dark-woman
had almond shaped eyes, short, spiky hair, and a sensual

mouth. She wore a scoop neck sleeveless top and no jewellery.

When Laurent entered the sitting room, I stepped away from the fireplace, feeling as if I'd been caught doing something underhand. He handed me a glass of wine and I gave him the letter which he read, standing at the window.

'This is an important letter. It is the evidence that Philippe is your son. You must make copies. It is possible that you will need proof.'

'If it goes to court, you mean?'

He nodded. 'You must find a lawyer. We must presume that Véronique now knows the truth.'

I thought of Véronique's elegant home and her daughters' private school. Compared her situation with mine – a modest flat and a precarious future, job wise. But, invested wisely, my inheritance would make a difference.

'You must prepare yourself, Olivia. If she wants to fight for Philippe, she must find a lawyer that will help her to make a case to obtain legal custody – *une garde d'enfant*. It is also possible that she will apply for the shared custody, so that Philippe will live with her in his country of residence – *une garde de résidence*.'

I leaned back, trying to stem my anxiety. 'When you say "build a case", do you mean they will try to prove that... that Philippe would be better off with her?'

'*Exactement,* exactly. She will ask that the social services department will write a report about you.'

'In other words, find proof that I wouldn't be a fit mother... Would they... will they contact the UK, dig out my psychiatric record?'

If my eating disorder were revealed, would anyone consider me fit for motherhood? In more negative moments, even I questioned my ability to raise a child.

He shook his head. 'They are not permitted to look for evidence outside of France.'

'Bertrand's always snooping around – I'm sure he knows I've seen a psychotherapist.'

Laurent waved a dismissive hand. 'But he cannot be certain. And you have not talked to Cerys?'

'I'll have to – sooner or later – if I want a reference from her.'

He refilled his wine glass, offered me more. I shook my head. 'Can't risk being done for driving a moped when under the influence'.

He sipped his wine. 'The City Hall in Tangiers will have records of all the births. The embassy can perhaps help you to contact them. If there is a doubt, a DNA test can be made. However, with the birth record, and especially with Richie's letter, it will be difficult to challenge.'

'What if Véronique doesn't know about Philippe, if Richie didn't manage to tell her before he died?'

Laurent thought for a moment. 'I have met her brother, Jean. I could talk to him. It would be easier for her to hear this from someone that she is close to.'

'But what, oh God... what if she's already adopted Philippe?'

'Under French law, she will not be permitted to do this. But if the case goes to court then the judge will consider the best interests of Philippe when he decides about custody.'

Was I resilient enough to cope with this? In two weeks' time, my contract with the Chevaliers would end and I'd lose my anchor. I'd have many obstacles to overcome.

As I noticed Laurent's gaze lingering on the photo on the mantelpiece, I asked, 'Was that your fiancée?'

His expression told me it was.

'So, what happened?'

He clutched his chin, as if bracing himself. 'She died – she killed herself.'

'I'm so sorry, Laurent... What went wrong?'

He cleared his throat several times. 'On the day she graduated, her father told her that she had been adopted... For years she searched for her biological mother, she looked so hard for her.' Laurent wandered over to the window, gazed out for a moment. Then he turned round, expression impassive. 'When Brigitte found her, the woman was not interested to know her. It was at that time that she met me and soon after, we decide to marry... Two months before the wedding, her real mother contacted her and they arrange to meet.'

He paused. I looked away.

After a moment he continued. 'It was all that Brigitte talked about... I drove her to the hotel for the lunch. Her mother does not appear. After two hours, Brigitte left. Then she discovered that her mother had a heart attack. She was dead... Dead... Brigitte could not accept that nearly has she met her mother... She became depressed. I tried to help her but the week before our wedding, she took her life. This is the reason why I have wanted to help you to find your child.'

DURING MY JOG along the beach the following day, phone conversations with James occupied my thoughts: his mother's death, the detailed description of her funeral and his ruminations over whether he could have done more to support her. Poor James... To his credit, however, he'd responded positively to my subsequent apologetic call asking him to check the registry office for Philippe's birth registration.

At least I had James's assurance that under British law, without proof of my death, Véronique would have been unable to adopt Philippe. This knowledge, and Laurent's declaration that she wouldn't have been permitted to adopt my son under French law, reassured me. The weeks ahead would test my strength. But I must keep going. I remembered Seth, could hear him telling me to take it one day at a time.

WHILE CERYS UNPACKED the picnic lunch, I gazed around the Parc Mercanteur. Three days had elapsed since learning Philippe was mine. Three days of heightened reactions – the music on my iPod emitting an enhanced richness and warmth, the fragrance of domestic products like shower gel and washing up liquid, potent as the finest French perfume. And now, the purple distant Maritime Alps, the foreground of brilliantly blue gentians, provoked further emotion. As I watched Henri and Odette flying their kite, the images changed to Richie and Philippe.

Frances cried and Cerys lifted her. 'Probably needs feeding.' She stared at her breasts. 'I will be flat as a pancake if she continues like this, I will. Pity, I did enjoy being better endowed.'

'You've been quiet these last few days,' she said moments later, transferring Frances to her other side, helping her attach.

I'd postponed confiding in my employer long enough. 'There are things you should know, about me, I mean... I knew Pascal. I was a student of his.'

'What a coincidence... But why didn't either of you admit this at the dinner? It must have been weird seeing him again, very weird. Don't think I could have kept silent, no.'

'Actually, there was more to it.'

'More? A relationship. You had a relationship, did you?'

'And a baby.'

'A baby! A baby... Where is he... she, your child?'

I relayed my story once more, everything, including Richie's letter.

'This is bizarre,' she said when I'd finished. 'And you had no idea Philippe was your son?'

'Until the Bruhman's dinner. I mean, I believed it was the baby girl who'd survived, and I didn't know Philippe was only Véronique's stepson. When Richie opened the door... well...'

'It's the sort of thing you read about ... but for it to happen. What you've been through...'

I fiddled with my necklace. 'I'm not out of it, you know?'

'No, of course not. But I'm so glad. Glad for you, for Philippe. Véronique has never bonded with him, according to Antoinette. It was the one thing she and Pascal argued about. Devoted to Philippe, he was.' Cerys adjusted the angle of the sun umbrella shading Frances. 'No wonder you were so weird at the Bruhmans. What a lot to take in.'

'Come and play with us, Olivia,' Henri called.

Relieved to break from an emotive conversation, I joined the children, helping them decide when there was enough wind to launch the kite, rescuing it from a tree, helping Odette become untangled from the bridle lines and tail. When they tired of kiting, we retrieved a football from the car boot, and played with it until we were all exhausted. I then fetched them sandwiches before rejoining Cerys.

'If this goes to court, I'll speak for you,' she said.

I retrieved my half-eaten baguette. 'Thank you... I'm

waiting to see if the Moroccan embassy can get a copy of the birth registration from Tangiers.'

'You have Richie's letter – it should be proof enough you're Philippe's mother, at least. But it wouldn't do any harm to have a DNA test. You can get a test kit online and send off a sample yourself. Speed things up, it might.'

She made it sound so easy that my spirits lifted. Pleasantly drowsy, I stretched out on the picnic rug.

'Will you be okay when I'm away?' Cerys asked eventually, packing away the picnic things.

I sat up, rubbing my eyes. 'You're going away?'

'I'm sure I told you. Back to Wales – retirement dinner for my mother. Bertrand isn't going. I'll take Frances, of course, she's longing to meet her. But you'll have to get Odette and Henri ready for *La Rentrée*, the start of the school year. Will you manage, with all this going on?'

I nodded. 'There's another thing you should know. After it all happened, once I'd returned to London, I wasn't well – I had an eating disorder, but I'm fine now.'

Silence.

As I was about to ask Cerys if she was uncomfortable with this - not that there was anything she could do about it now, she spoke. 'We should get going. Bertrand wants to take the children fishing this evening, although I expect they'll be too tired. Henri, Odette, come here. Make sure Henri practises while I'm away – he's hardly been on his clarinet all summer.'

～

FROM MY RESTAURANT seat I could see the water sparkling in midday sunlight, boats bobbing in the gentle breeze. Elderly men perched on the harbour wall, smoking pipes, chatting, and a steady stream of beachgoers strolled past.

'I love this time in the year,' Laurent said, scrutinising the menu. 'It is hot but it is also like autumn. All the good things happen to me at this time.'

I wondered which season Brigitte had died. How much he'd recovered from losing her.

'Shall we order?' he asked.

'You choose for me,' I said, ignoring his raised eyebrows.

When our food arrived, he smiled at me and my pulse quickened. For a while we ate in silence. Then he reached for my hand. 'I met again with Jean last night. He has spoken with Véronique about Philippe. You were right – she did not know the truth. He has tried to convince her that Philippe should be with you. He has told me also that a Trust fund is already arranged for the child. I understood that there are financial considerations and–'

'She wants his money, you mean?'

'She has the power of the Attorney for this Trust. It is different from an inheritance. Pascal – Richie – has left a lot of money to Philippe... Work must be done to the house.'

Of course, Richie would have been Alice's beneficiary, and if he'd sold both their homes, his Estate would be considerable.

'For God's sake, you mean she's planning to use Philippe's money for her house?'

He shrugged. 'It is possible. She has a lawyer with an excellent reputation. For you, I have the names of three lawyers with the speciality of working with custody issues.'

I glanced at the photo of the male lawyer on the first business card, then scanned the other ones. 'Christiane Gerboni-Gouron – I'd prefer a woman. And someone fluent in English. There's no way my French could cope with legal speak.'

'It will be wise to speak to several of them before you choose one... Jean has managed to obtain an *écouvillon* – I do not know the word in English – from Philippe for the DNA test.'

'A swab. That's great, thanks. Oh, if only I could see him...'

With each passing day, the longing to reclaim my son increased, sharpened.

'You must be patient, Olivia. There is a procedure to follow.'

'Someone's visiting me from Social Services next week. Then I might be allowed to spend time with him. Supervised, naturally.'

When we left the restaurant, Laurent hugged me. 'I will contact you when I have more news. Be brave.'

25

I paused on the steps to the ruins of the ancient Château de l'Anglais, relieved to find shade. Beneath me, the city of Nice shimmered in early evening heat. While climbing, I'd mulled over the afternoon's visit from the social assistants attached to the High Court. Predictably neutral, they'd observed me supervise baths for Odette and Henri who'd fallen in the river while fishing with Bertrand, and hovered while I'd prepared the children a snack. Knowing that the assistants – one male, one female – would report back to Véronique's lawyer made it impossible to relax.

How impartial were they were allowed to be?

When I reached the top, I bought coffee and chocolate cake. Shortly after finding somewhere pleasant to sit, however, I noticed a bank of dark clouds, so I finished my coffee, wrapped the cake in a serviette and scampered down the 213 steps. The first fat drops of rain appeared as I parked Laurent's moped in the garage and let myself into the house.

Despite the downpour, the air remained heavy and I

turned the fan in my bedroom to maximum. As thunder rumbled and forked lightning cracked the sky, I gazed through the window at the church under repair, its plastic sheeting flapping in the escalating wind, like sails in a storm. This evening, the dramatic weather failed to excite me.

What if the social assistants had misinterpreted my conversations or behaviour with the children?

During the night I woke to notice a figure by the door.

'Ssh,' Bertrand said.

'What's wrong? Is it the children?'

As he approached my bed, the full moon revealed his green dressing gown, his gold neck chain. My alarm clock read three o'clock.

'What is it?' I asked, hugging the duvet to me.

He perched on the bed and reached for me.

I scrambled out. 'What are you doing?'

'I know English women are cold. But I think that you are different. I see how you watch Pascal at the dinner.'

'For God's sake...'

'No one will know.'

I sprang back. 'Please go.'

'You are beautiful.'

Several feet away, even, and his breath stank of fish and garlic.

'Leave.'

He stood. 'You make a mistake.'

After he left, I locked the door and crept back to bed where I lay trembling. Cerys must have told him about my eating disorder and now he'd badmouth me to Véronique.

Asleep again, I dreamed about walking along a country lane on a snowy day. Noticing a child in the distance, I quickened my pace. Simultaneously, it moved away. The more I hurried, the more it did. Eventually I stopped to rest against a tree, closed my eyes. At the sound of a gloating laugh, I glanced up to see the child six feet away. I stretched out my arms but it scurried off. When I awoke, my face was wet with tears.

One fact claimed my attention. It was August 31, Philippe's sixth birthday, and I couldn't spend it with him. Would anyone help him celebrate his day?

Ribbons of light streaked the sky before I returned to sleep again, waking finally to the front door slamming when Bertrand departed for work.

'I DIDN'T THINK you'd let us go to McDonald's,' Henri remarked during the drive into Nice that morning.

'If you behave while we shop.'

Noticing the queue ahead, I drew to a halt, switched off the engine and opened the window.

The warm air reeked of petrol, so I closed the window again and turned on the air conditioning. Still no movement.

'You've been yawning all morning,' Odette pointed out.

'It's the heat,' I said, noting the forward movement, switching on the engine. 'So, trainers first, then haircuts. After lunch, we'll shop for schoolbags, and *Maman* said you need crayons, Odette.'

At least such activities would keep me busy, stop me from worrying too much about possible outcomes from my rejection of Bertrand's odious advances.

When we approached McDonald's several hours later, Henri said, 'It's *Papa*!'

Sure enough, across the street was Bertrand – with Véronique.

'*Papa*,' Henri called out.

Odette clasped my hand more tightly. 'I don't like that lady.'

'*Papa*,' Henri called again, before dashing across the road.

A car swerved to avoid him. 'Henri!' I yelled. 'Stay here, Odette.' I rushed to the other side where he stood, shaking. 'What were you *doing*? You could have been killed.'

He blinked back tears. 'I guess.'

Bertrand had reached us.

'I'm sorry,' I said. 'He ran out and I...'

Bertrand spoke quietly. 'You must be more careful.'

I glared at him, then marched Henri to the traffic lights and across the road, where an ashen-faced Odette waited for us.

'It's okay, sweetheart,' I said, bending to hug her.

I felt sick as I ushered the children into McDonalds. Not only had Bertrand obviously contacted Véronique immediately after the bedroom incident, but he could use Henri's near accident to demonstrate my incompetence.

The restaurant heaved, its odour of French fries and grilled meat making me queasier. At the counter, staff were urging a boisterous mob to queue. Remembering the salad bar four doors away, I turned.

Henri was eying me. 'You promised we could come here if we behaved, and we did, sort of... I'm sorry about running across the road.'

'Look, there's Philippe,' Odette said.

I looked over to where she was pointing – he was with Renée and her friend. The girls were retrieving clothes from carrier bags, and texting. He was chewing a straw. Quickly I found a table.

'I'll be back in a moment,' I told the children. 'I want to speak to Philippe – it's his birthday.'

When I reached Philippe's table, Renée recognised me and muttered a greeting. My heart sank. Was this how my son would spend his birthday? Traipsing round Nice with two self-absorbed teenagers? Had anyone noticed the shadows under his eyes? How thin he'd become?

'Happy birthday, Philippe,' I said. 'Do you want to speak to Odette and Henri?' He nodded, I told Renée we'd be back in a minute and clasped his hand to took him to our table.

'How old are you?' Odette asked. 'I'm seven and three quarters.'

He raised six fingers.

'Did you get lots of presents?' Henri asked.

'I got a car. A little car.'

Henri nodded. 'What else?'

Philippe thought. 'A football from Uncle Jean.'

'We could get trainers like Henri's for Philippe,' Odette suggested.

Henri scowled at her. 'It's Philippe's mother who buys his clothes, isn't it, Olivia? Why do I have such a stupid sister?'

Odette stuck her tongue out at him.

'Henri, you don't need to be rude,' I said.

Once I reclaimed Philippe, I'd buy him trainers with flashing lights. I could give him everything.

Except his early childhood years.

Noticing Véronique entering the restaurant, I returned him to his table.

'Come, Philippe,' she said. 'It is time for the party.'

After they left, I forced myself to concentrate on Henri and Odette, ordering their lunch, afterwards shopping for school things. The better I performed these chores, the more I'd believe in my competence.

Neither the exercise nor the sea relaxed me as I ran along the beach that evening. What if Bertrand persuaded Cerys not to give a reference? And if he sided with Véronique, how weighty would a doctor's opinion be in court? If my medical history were revealed, I'd be considered fragile. Nothing worse. But it was one thing when the vulnerable parent already cared for the child, quite another when she fought for custody. Should the court learn of my psychiatric stay, what were the chances of it ruling that Philippe live with me, rather than have continuity?

And, of course, events surrounding Philippe's birth would become public. How might a judge regard a mother who'd abandoned her babies before they died? With this revelation, Véronique's advocate could reduce me to rubble, portraying my actions as callous. The scary truth was that it would require a skilled lawyer to paint me as distraught and unwell, not monstrous. I must ask The Priory to confirm my diagnosis of postpartum psychosis, help depict me in a better light.

Suddenly I heard Dorothy's voice: *You can do it.* Then it came to me – there was one thing I *could* do to help my case. I'd rent an apartment here. This would provide Philippe with some continuity.

∿

AT THE KITCHEN TABLE, Cerys was marking pages of *Marie Claire* with Post-it notes. She grinned when I appeared.

'There's fresh coffee and croissants... It's lovely to be back again. Thank you for holding the fort... Oh, there's a letter for you, somewhere in this mess.'

I peered at the postmark, tentatively opened it, scanned the contents and frowned.

'What is it?' she asked, yawning.

'The social workers want to speak to me again.'

'Standard practice, I'm sure. And remember, you have my total support. I've written a reference and a testimonial. I'll get them. I want you to see what I've said.'

'Cerys, I need to ask you something.'

She lavished upon me the smile of an appreciative employer. 'Ask away, do!'

I sat down. 'Did you tell Bertrand about Philippe and me?'

'You didn't say not to.'

'How well does he know Véronique, Bertrand, I mean?'

'Why?'

'I saw them together... when I took Odette and Henri shopping.'

She yawned again. 'They probably bumped into each other.'

I hesitated. In tired mode, Cerys was less likely to be sympathetic. 'I think he may have criticised me to her. Told her I... that I see a psychotherapist. And that won't help my case.'

'A psychotherapist? You didn't tell me this, did you?'

'I did tell you I'd had an eating disorder.'

'But how would Bertrand know this? I didn't tell him. And why would he want Véronique to think badly of you?'

When I hesitated again, Cerys narrowed her eyes, her expression a mix of warning and a need to know. To backpedal now would leave her wondering, perhaps quizzing Bertrand.

'You know she wants to find evidence that I'd be a bad mother. She'll be trying to dig up dirt about me.'

'Bertie knows I've agreed to be a character witness for you. Why would he want to make things difficult for you?'

I opened the back door to check the children weren't about to appear. They were playing in the den, t-shirts discarded in the September sun, making the most of the last day of the summer holidays.

'Something happened while you were away... I need you to understand that I've never done anything to encourage him.'

Cerys's tone was scornful but her eyes conveyed concern. 'What *are* you talking about?'

'He came into my bedroom... during the night.'

'What exactly are you saying?'

'He... came on to me.'

Eyes flashing, she leant over and jabbed a finger at me. 'Bertrand would never do such a thing.'

'I know it's difficult to hear this, but he was in his dressing gown and–'

'STOP! Stop right now.'

Flinging me another hostile look, she scuttled from the kitchen. Minutes later I heard her on the bedroom phone.

I chucked my half-eaten croissant in the bin, berating my stupidity – her knowing of Bertrand's behaviour wouldn't affect the outcome with Philippe. Better simply to have asked her to find out what he'd told Véronique.

My heart raced when Cerys reappeared.

'I've spoken to my husband, see,' she said, head nodding vigorously. 'He told me that on Tuesday night he heard you call out to him and came in to see what was wrong. He said you talked to him in a... a suggestive way. But once he knew what your intentions were, he left immediately.'

'No, that isn't what happened, I swear.'

She grabbed her plate and mug, stomped over to the dishwasher. 'If you expect me to believe you over Bertrand, you've got that wrong. I won't have you accusing him of doing such things, I won't.'

I tried to moderate my tone. 'Why would I lie?'

She twisted round. 'I know you're worried about Philippe, but I can't have you accusing Bertrand.'

'I need to know what he's said to Veronique about me. It might affect my chances of getting Philippe back. Bertrand's angry because I rejected him.'

'Not another word, I won't listen to this.'

'Will you at least ask him what he said to Véronique?'

'If you admit you've... you've fabricated this nonsense, if you apologise to Bertrand when he gets home. Retract all this nonsense, this ridiculous fantasy.'

Despite the frenzy she'd whipped herself into, I detected a lack of conviction.

'Cerys, I can't.'

She snatched my barely finished coffee mug, rammed it into the dishwasher, added detergent and shut the machine door. Then she turned to face me, now the voice of reason. 'Olivia, you've admitted you have a psychiatric history, and I accept this, but accusing my husband of something so... so disgusting, is not on. You leave me no option but–'

'It's all right, I'll be away by this afternoon.'

Trying to appear dignified, I left the kitchen and trudged upstairs to my room.

Two hours later, I'd packed, bade farewell to a tearful Odette, a stoical Henri, and a tight-lipped Cerys and booked into a small hotel on the outskirts of Villefranche. In happier circumstances, I'd have chilled out on a lounge chair in the garden, relishing the afternoon sunshine, the vineyard workers harvesting grapes. Instead I crawled into bed.

I woke to the ring of my cell phone.

'This is Laurent. Philippe has disappeared.'

26

'What do you mean, disappeared?' I fumbled in my bag for my inhaler.

'Jean has told me that he disappeared from the garden.'

Ringing in my ears distorted my words, reflecting them back in a high-pitched voice.

'Come and get me, Hotel Beausoleil, 26 rue Pertois, outside Villefranche.'

'You have moved?'

'Come now, please.'

'The police will search for Philippe–'

'I have to do something.'

'*D'accord*, okay, I will collect you and we will then drive to Véronique's house to see if there is news.'

Humming replaced the ringing while I paced my room, hands over ears. Philippe was too young to run away. To cross busy roads. Get on a bus. What if he'd been abducted?

We arrived at the Bruhman house to find Clara and Renée in the garden. Clara's eyes were puffy and even the sullen Renée appeared shaken.

'Any news?' I asked.

They shook their heads.

Laurent introduced himself to the children and asked where their mother was.

'She is in her bedroom,' Clara said.

He focused on Clara, 'Do you know what has happened?'

She wrestled her tears. 'Philippe was playing in the garden. When I went to tell him that lunch was ready, I could not see him. I searched in all the places. Yesterday he–'

Renée grabbed her sister, whispered something I didn't understand.

Laurent's tone was stern. 'Clara, this information might help us to find Philippe.'

She hesitated before turning to Laurent. 'Yesterday he was sad. He said he wanted to find his Papa and bring him home. He said–'

'*Arrête!* Stop!' Renée cried.

Clara thumped her sister's arm. '*Je te déteste, je te déteste*, I hate you.'

I visualised two men monitoring the grounds, awaiting an opportunity to grab Philippe. I saw them bundling him into a car. Heard the tyres screeching on hot tarmac. Saw the car hurtling along the autoroute to Italy. *Cut, cut, cut...*

A police car halted in the drive and a man and woman emerged.

'Is there some news?' Laurent asked.

The gendarmes shook their heads. '*Nous avons besoins d'un photo d'enfant. Où est qu'on trouve Madame Bruhman?* We need a photo of the child. Where can we find Madame Bruhman?'

'Elle est dans sa chambre. She is in her bedroom,' Renée said.

The policewoman conferred with her colleague, slipped an arm round Renée's shoulder and they walked towards the house. Clara ran after them.

I grabbed Laurent's arm. 'We're wasting time, come on.'

'Olivia, wait. The police will have a plan. When they have a photograph they will search.' Another police car pulled into the drive and four men got out. They consulted with their colleague, and started combing the grounds.

Clara ran out of the house in tears. *'Maman* cannot find a photo of Philippe.'

I retrieved the one from my purse. 'Use this.'

The policeman spoke rapidly to Laurent.

'They are contacting the airport and the railway stations,' he told me.

I retrieved my inhaler. Philippe couldn't have travelled so far on his own – they must fear he'd been kidnapped.

Véronique was approaching us.

'If anything's happened to my son, I'll never forgive you,' I shouted at her.

Clara's eyes widened. *'Maman*?'

'Olivia,' Laurent warned, gripping my arm.

'They think he's been abducted, don't they?'

The policewoman placed a calming hand on my arm. 'This is a routine procedure. It is more likely that he is close to here. We must think of the places where he might have gone.'

'How could he cross roads on his own? We need to try hospitals and–'

'They have contacted the hospitals.'

'We should check La Plage Marinière, but he couldn't have got there on his own.'

Despite the gusty wind, sweat trickled down my back. The policemen were conferring.

One of them spoke to Laurent.

'They will separate,' Laurent explained. 'Some of them will continue to search here, some will go to the beaches, some will go to the parks. We will go to La Plage Marinière.'

My legs wouldn't move, like one of those nightmares where you need to dial 999 but your fingers won't work. He noticed and supported me round the shoulders.

There was no sign of Philippe at La Plage Marinière, nor at the adjoining Plage de l'Ange Gardien, either on the beach itself or the rocky cliffs and pine trees. Hearing a helicopter circling overhead, I grabbed Laurent, 'Is this connected to Philippe?'

He consulted with a policeman and reassured me it wasn't.

At sunset, when most people had left the beach, the unrelenting and unnerving static of walkie-talkies was all I could hear. When darkness fell, the police cars drove away.

'EAT YOUR OMELETTE,' Laurent said.

I shoved my plate aside. 'I'm not hungry.'

He selected an Inti Illimani CD and soon the combination of flickering candlelight, and guitar and bamboo flutes wafting around the room calmed me. Later, on the sofa, I leant against his shoulder, his shirt fabric soft and comforting. A crescent-shaped moon rose into a starless sky. From the garden, I heard an owl.

During the night, I woke, shoved aside the rug, and stood on the balcony. It took considerable willpower not to go and wake Laurent, insist we search for Philippe. I tossed and turned on the sofa, waiting for dawn, wondering where my child could be.

The whishing of the shower and aroma of coffee woke me at eight o'clock.

'You're working?' I asked Laurent, when he appeared in smart trousers and short-sleeved shirt.

'This morning only. You can stay here, if you prefer.'

'I'm meant to be seeing a lawyer but I don't know if I can go through with it.'

'You must,' he said, appraising me. 'Jean will contact me if there is any news. I will drive you to your hotel, if you want to change your clothes.'

IT WAS POURING when I arrived at the lawyer's office, the sea a murky grey with choppy waves. While looking round the harshly lit reception area of Cabinet Morel, I noticed a boat zooming out to sea. Only someone on urgent business would undertake a trip in such weather. Oh God, Philippe couldn't be on it, could he? On his way to Spain. South Italy. Morocco. I pictured him being handed over in the alley of a souk in Fez. *Cut...* A cruel twist of fate – born in Morocco, returned there. Ensnared in child trafficking. *Cut, cut...* Sexual exploitation. *Cut, cut, cut...*

Instead of talking to a lawyer, I should be searching for him.

'Mademoiselle Bowden?'

The woman by my side was small and thin, with short straight dark hair and black-rimmed spectacles. Her grey blouse buttoned to the neck.

I peered out of the window again but the boat had disappeared.

'I am Christiane Cerboni-Gouron. This way, please.'

I followed her into a large room furnished in chrome, leather and glass. It smelled of paint.

'How can I help you?' she asked, indicating a chair with a sweep of her arm.

I opened my mouth but my rehearsed information eluded me.

She gestured impatiently. 'Sit, please.'

'I am trying to get my son back.'

'Where is your son?'

'I should tell you everything,' I said, willing her to smile, help me relax. 'I gave birth to twins six years ago, they were ill when they were born and... and I thought they were going to die.'

She checked the wall clock. 'What was their condition when they were born?'

'I don't know... it was in Morocco... Tangiers. They were premature.'

'How premature?'

'Thirty-one weeks and three days.'

'This would be described as thirty-two weeks.'

'Whatever, thirty-two weeks. I believed they would die and so I left the hospital.'

She removed her spectacles. 'You did not wait to see what happens?'

'I panicked... I had a bad reaction to the drugs. It was a difficult birth – they had to do a forceps delivery. I was... I wasn't thinking clearly.'

How could I expect this woman to understand my actions?

'You assumed that your babies will not live and so you leave the hospital. What happened after?'

I hesitated, selecting my words. 'I went to Marrakech... then I returned to London.'

'And the father of the babies, he was not with you?'

This sterile room mocked my weakness, my lack of staying power. Even the clock's ticking rebuked me. I hadn't realised how distressing it would be discussing my situation with a lawyer. It was one thing telling a friend or a sympathetic employer, quite another talking to a robot.

'He was married. He and his wife wanted to adopt the baby... I mean, they didn't know I was having twins, a girl and a boy.'

My throat constricted.

The lawyer tapped her pen on her notepad. 'Mademoiselle Bowden, if this will go to court, it is necessary to control your emotions.'

'You don't understand – he's missing. He disappeared yesterday. He–'

'I am confused. You are searching for your son but not for your daughter? When did you search for your son – soon after he was born or... when?'

I studied her expressionless face – someone like this shouldn't be working with people. She jerked her head forward, waiting for my answer.

'I believed the baby girl had survived. My aunt wrote me to me before she died, telling me. So I started off looking for my little girl. I found the father... then I found out the girl had died, then the father, Richie, was killed in a sailing accident.'

'Excuse me. I do not understand. You are telling me–'

I stood. 'I need to go. Sorry.'

AT THE HOTEL, the receptionist admired my dress. I managed a smile and a bland remark about the lovely hotel grounds. She was of similar age, had recently transferred from a hotel in Bologna, and possessed a warmth so absent in the ice maiden lawyer that fleetingly I wanted to confide in her.

In my room, I phoned Laurent. 'Have you heard anything?'

'Not yet. Did your meeting with the lawyer go well?'

'She was odious. I need to look for Philippe.'

'I will finish working in one hour. Then I will come to your hotel.'

When he arrived, I dragged myself to the door. 'I'm so frightened I'll never see him again. It's been twenty-four hours.'

He placed his arms on my shoulders. 'Listen to me. There is a big chance that Philippe will be found. You must believe this. What happened at your meeting with Madame Cerboni-Gouron?'

'I don't want her representing me.'

'*Alors*, then perhaps you should talk with Monsieur Lefèvre.'

'Perhaps. Phone Jean, see if he's heard anything.'

When Laurent had finished his call, he said, 'The police have not found evidence that a stranger was in the Bruhman house or in the garden. Jean has assured me that Philippe will not go away with a stranger.'

'He's so young... Wait, I've remembered a beach. I should have thought of this before.'

'We must inform the police. Where is this place?'

'Very near here. La Petite Plage. I've never been there but Richie used to take him, Philippe told me... He could have walked there.'

'Olivia, the police have been to all the areas with beaches.'

'But he loved the boats. Perhaps they didn't search them. I mean, there are boats coming and going all the time. Phone and tell them, but we must get moving. Come on, please...'

As cars crawled along the road, I drummed my fingers on the dashboard. The odour of petrol in the warm air stung my eyes and made my head ache. Then the traffic thinned out and Laurent changed gear, his Fiat leaping into action, like a dog off a lead.

When we arrived at La Petite Plage I jumped out before he'd applied the handbrake. Policemen were scouring the pebbly beach and rocks, questioning sunbathers, circulating Philippe's photo. Another car arrived and Véronique and a dark-haired man emerged.

'This is Jean,' Laurent introduced me.

I nodded. 'We should search the boats.'

'The policemen are doing this,' Laurent said.

Maybe Philippe had been brought here before being transferred to another car. He could have been drugged and left in a boat. I rushed to the pier, clambering from dinghies, yachts, and catamarans, searching in galleys, in sleeping quarters and storage spaces. Soon after, Laurent joined me. No one ordered us off, the few people we encountered understanding the situation when they noticed the police.

A voice shouted, '*Ici*! Here!'

A policeman had appeared from a boat, carrying a wriggling figure. I splashed my way to the shore. When he reached the beach, the policeman lowered Philippe to the ground, steadied him as he staggered. Philippe was now running towards me. I bent to pull him close, reluctant to let him go. His face and hair were grubby and his knees grazed, but otherwise he seemed unharmed. He smelled of oranges, bits of peel clinging to his t-shirt.

Tightening my grip, I became alert to the surrounding silence. The policemen were staring at me, Jean had his arm round his sister, Laurent's expression was guarded.

'Go to *Maman*,' I whispered to Philippe.

He kept his arms round me, so I gently disengaged him and led him over. When we reached Véronique, however, he ran off and began digging furiously on the beach, pebbles flying everywhere. I clenched my palms. Jean was talking with Véronique, she was remonstrating. Irritation barely suppressed, he then spoke to the policemen. Philippe now sat trembling on the beach so I draped my jacket round him.

Jean approached me. 'May I speak with you?' We moved out of Philippe's earshot.

'Laurent has explained to me the story. My sister is fragile but I will speak with her again. I will try to persuade her that Philippe must live with you.'

That evening I went running, the only way I knew of decompressing. Philippe was safe: the most important thing. Even if the court didn't award me custody. *Pant, pant.* Even if restricted to occasional visits, he'd be in my life. Part of me. And when older, he could choose if he wanted to live with me. *Pant, pant.* And I could appeal. And if unsuccessful here, I'd apply to a British court.

I increased pace, entered another orbit. I was flying.

～

'PLEASE SIT,' Monsieur Lefèvre said. 'Would you like coffee?'

The lawyer had a rugged face, wavy dark hair and a relaxing smile. Adorning his desk was a photo of two golden labradors, which he explained he'd adopted from a shelter.

'Please tell to me your story. I will make notes.'

I relayed the events: the circumstances of my pregnancy and birth; Richie's death and his letter; the DNA test results proving officially that Philippe was mine; Véronique's determination to retain custody, and lastly, Philippe's Trust. Monsieur Lefèvre remained silent while writing.

When I finished, he went over to the window to water the cacti. Then he re-established eye contact, and I realised he'd been allowing me time to compose myself.

He smiled reassuringly at me. 'I will repeat to you what I know regarding your situation. If I am making a mistake, please tell to me.'

He repeated my story. 'Are these the main points?'

I nodded.

'Is there anything else?'

'I developed an eating disorder after Morocco. I was in a psychiatric hospital for four months.'

'Fortunately, this does not prevent a children's judge to rule in your favour. In these cases, if the mother is not considered to be stable emotionally, social support will be provided. In most situations a judge will decide that the child must live with the biological mother. What is the condition of your health now?'

I hesitated. 'After hospital, I continued the psychotherapy. Then I went through a difficult time last month when... when my employer here had another baby. So I went back to London to see my therapist.'

'Do you take any... medication?'

'Not now.'

He spoke gently. 'When were you in the hospital?'

'Five years – five and a half years ago.'

'And you have not been in the hospital after?'

'No.'

'Did the doctors believe that your eating disorder was connected to what happens with your babies? I am asking this, because this could help your situation. If it is possible to connect it to grief it will... I don't know how to say it in English...'

'Help to portray me in a better light?'

'Yes, I think this is what I mean.'

'We discussed the link, but there's something else I forgot to tell you that might help.

When I returned to London after Morocco, my GP diagnosed me with postpartum psychosis – I think it is the same expression in French: *psychose post-partum*. It was only mild, but it partly explained why I left the maternity hospital when I did. I can ask my doctor to send a letter with this information.'

'This could help.' Mr Lefèvre's smile communicated acceptance, understanding. My spirits rose.

'The Social Services will watch you with the child to see how it is. This will happen if the current guardian does agree or does not agree to give custody. You must decide soon if you wish that I represent you, if this case will go to court.'

I leant forward. 'I would, please.'

'*D'accord,* okay, I must see now the original copy of the letter from Richie, and the results of the DNA tests. Have you received some visits from the social workers who will support Madame Bruhman?'

I handed him Richie's letter and the DNA test results and explained about the visit.

He walked over to the window again. 'The case will go to the Children's Judge at the High Court. It will be a civil court hearing. There will be no *contra-interrogatoire,* cross-examination. There will be no jury. The lawyer of Madame Bruhman will present a case for her.'

I found myself trembling and Monsieur Lefèvre smiled at me sympathetically.

'I will present your case. If Madame Bruhman will learn about your health problems, her lawyer will show that you are not suitable to be a mother. I will, of course, argue against this lawyer, but you must prepare yourself for a difficult time.'

'I thought they weren't allowed to use evidence outside France.'

'This is true. But...' he shrugged. 'The judge will consider the interests of the child. Will your employer give a reference to you?'

I described the incidents prior to my leaving the Chevaliers. To my relief, he didn't think this would make a huge difference.

'How will I manage when I'm being asked questions? My French isn't great.'

'We will provide for you a translator.'

THREE AFTERNOONS LATER, needing a change of scene, I went to La Plage Marinière. To the east, the wooded peninsula of Cap Ferrat dozed in the afternoon sunshine. Nearby, boys were flinging themselves off rocks into the sea, whooping with laughter; girls were guddling in the water with nets, peering at the contents. Younger children lay by the water's edge, letting the waves bring them in, parents hovering.

I recalled the previous day's visit with Philippe. We'd met at the social services department, in a beige coloured room with chipboard bookcases and crates of dilapidated toys. The weather was awful and intermittently he had gazed wistfully out of the rain-spattered window at the slide and swings. We'd played with a train set and a farmyard, then I'd read to him, always conscious of the social worker's presence, her sporadic note taking.

After she'd whisked Philippe away, questions beleaguered me: had I connected appropriately? Been spontaneous and affectionate enough? What would happen if he hadn't enjoyed himself?

I now joined the food stall queue for a chocolate mint ice cream, returning minutes later for a hot dog. After eating, I left the beach. It was too crowded today.

Too many families.

As I WAITED at the park, my spirits were lifted by the unblemished blue sky and invigorating breeze mixed with wood smoke. I felt even happier when I saw a woman and small boy approach me.

'We are here,' the social worker said, her hand in Philippe's.

I bent to kiss him.

'You play now with Olivia,' she said.

Flinching at her use of my name, I imagined him saying "Mummy" or "*Maman*". Then it came to me – I'd never heard him address Véronique as "*Maman*". I must tell Monsieur Lefèvre. This was a powerful illustration of Philippe's lukewarm relationship with his stepmother.

'So, what do you want to do?' I asked him.

He ran over to the sandpit where we constructed a wall and laughed when it collapsed. Then, brow furrowed with concentration, he crammed sand into a bucket to build another wall. I remembered our first visit to a play park, when our bond had formed.

'Can I play on the swings?' he asked, when the second wall collapsed.

I pushed him, delighting in his cries of, "higher, higher". When two middle-aged women passed us, studying him, studying me, I experienced pride, despite my precarious situation. The sun had shifted, shards of light darting amongst the trees, and his tousled curls shone.

'What do you want to do now?' I asked, when he descended from the swing.

He pointed to the sandpit. We immersed ourselves in filling plastic shapes with sand.

'I like the dinosaur best,' he said, tipping out the brown mould onto the sand. 'It's a T-rex. My *Papa* told me about it. It was enormous. It ate meat. I've got a picture of it in my animal book.'

I ruffled his hair. It smelled of pine shampoo.

'Can we come back tomorrow, Libbia?'

Before I could think of a response, the social worker dumped her baguette packaging in the litter bin and replaced her kindle in her bag. 'We leave now. It is necessary that Philippe is home before five o'clock.'

Two hours had flown.

'I hate it when he goes. The more time I spend with him, the more I love him... I know I'm meant to be calm, but it's hard – he's so young.'

She smiled. 'You are being good with Philippe. It is evident that you love him and he cares with you. I will recommend that you gain custody. Please, tell no person that I say this to you.' She produced a photo from her wallet. 'My son has six years, also. This is a special age.'

'Oh, I forgot to tell my lawyer that I'm renting an apartment here. Will you put this in your report?'

She nodded. 'Of course, but you should phone or email him about this. It will certainly help your case.'

THE FOLLOWING EVENING, as always, I paused at the top of the road down to Place Amelie Pollonais to absorb the salmon and ochre-coloured restaurants with their giant palms and wrought-iron lanterns. Tonight, peddlers were selling hand puppets and garish dolphin-shaped balloons, and children frolicked in the pedestrianised area although darkness had long fallen. As always, I imagined the scene in a storm: water heaving over the harbour wall; people rushing to the boulangerie for bread; boat hatches battened down and sails reefed in.

My thoughts returned to the upbeat meeting with Monsieur Lefèvre earlier today. He was very positive when I told him about the apartment and it was then I had a strong sense that he cared deeply about what happened with Philippe. My case would be heard next Wednesday, he'd explained, and in the absence of a legal claim for Philippe, and supported by the report of the social assistants attached to the High Court, (however favourable their findings), Véronique's lawyer would argue for continuity of care. If he mentioned my psychiatric record, presenting me as unfit to care for my child, Monsieur Lefèvre would remind the court of the help available to vulnerable parents. We'd rehearsed the answers I should give to certain questions.

Since the meeting, I'd vacillated between calmness and confidence, and negativity and anxiety. Now, at the harbour

front, in the comfort of darkness, calmness reigned. If the
court case failed, he had assured me I could appeal.

From my bag, I retrieved the card that had arrived
yesterday.

'*I wanted to let you know that I will give you a reference,*'
Cerys wrote. '*I will also speak for you in court, if necessary.
Please let me know what is happening.*'

Relief flowed through me. One thing less to worry about.
But what did this imply about Bertrand?

ON THE DAY of the trial, I woke with a racing heartbeat. I
tried to meditate, I tried to read, but it was impossible to
concentrate. Despite dreading the court case, knowing the
outcome had to be more manageable than this transient
state. Eventually I took the bus into Villefranche where I
strolled through backstreets, gazing at houses with red
pantile roofs and bougainvillea straddling the walls; gardens
of hibiscus and pale blue flowered plumbago; alleys lined
with terracotta pots of yuccas and ferns. I heard birds chirping, a piano accompanied by a flute, a child being taught
Italian. The peaceful ambience helped.

When the taxi drew up outside the courts in Nice three
hours later, my body felt like one great tremble. It was one
thing imagining the procedure, quite another being in the
situation. Nearby were Laurent, and Monsieur Lefèvre in his
black gown. Moments later, Véronique arrived. Dressed in a
beige trouser suit, with her hair hanging freely and her face
ostensibly devoid of makeup, she appeared almost moth-
erly. Tripping down the steps to greet her, was a distin-
guished-looking man with silvery hair swept back and
wearing a black gown. I turned away, wishing now I'd

agreed to Dad or Roz coming over. There was no sign of Jean.

I exchanged a few words with Laurent, then Monsieur Lefèvre said, '*Courage!* Be brave! Come, we must go in now.'

In the court, a smaller and less imposing room than I'd expected, I sat down beside him, relieved to notice Laurent's appearance. Shortly after, a woman in her late thirties appeared, conferred with him, then sat on my other side, introducing herself as Susie, the translator. Her New Zealand accent and the warmth of her smile provoked the emotion I was struggling to suppress.

The judge entered the room, bowed to the court.

'He will explain what the case is about,' Susie told me.

The judge spoke for a few moments. Then Monsieur Lefèvre rose.

'He's explaining what happened when your babies were born,' Susie said. 'That you weren't well and left the hospital, presuming both of them were on the point of death. That as soon as you learned from your aunt of your son's existence, you started searching for Richie, and never lost focus until you found him. Monsieur Lefèvre is also saying that although he has known you only for a short time, he believes that you would make a good mother.'

I remembered Cerys and her reference. Had my lawyer contacted her to see if she would testify on my behalf? If only I had a better grasp of the French legal system

When Monsieur Lefèvre finished, Véronique's lawyer stood up.

'He is describing the stable home Philippe has with her family, how settled he is at school, how he has a good relationship with her and her two daughters.'

'Yeah, well he doesn't get on with her,' I said.

Before Susie could reply, I heard a commotion behind

me and turned round to see Jean, clutching a brown envelope. He approached Monsieur Lefèvre and they conferred.

Monsieur Lefèvre then addressed the judge.

'What is he saying?' I asked Susie.

She listened, then turned to me. 'He is saying there's
new evidence. A letter from Richie has been found which
states that if anything happens to him, all efforts must be
made to find you, and you must be given care of Philippe.
His brother-in-law found the letter when he was collecting
Richie's possessions from his office in Nice.'

The judge was speaking again.

'He is suggesting an adjournment of twenty minutes for
Véronique's lawyer to consult with her,' Susie told me.

'For him to advise her to give up her claim, you mean?
And if she doesn't?'

Monsieur Lefèvre placed his hand on my arm. 'No judge
will rule in her favour now. There will only be a problem if
she will challenge the authenticity of the letter, but I do not
think that this will happen.'

IN THE HOTEL GARDEN, I lay on a sun lounger, watching
leaves swirl to the ground. The beginning of October and
autumn had stamped its presence.

Events of recent weeks circled and recircled, each detail
under examination: calls to Mr Minto and the bank about
my rented apartment; meetings with Richie's lawyers about
the Will and Trust fund, the latter transactions made more
arduous due to my gender.

And in between, time with Philippe – a final supervised
visit, two afternoons on our own. Despite having been
awarded custody, however, I still worried that something

would go wrong, that another piece of evidence would appear. Sometimes, exhausted from the day's events yet incapable of sleep, I pictured how things might have been if Richie hadn't died or if I'd been refused custody. Calling at the Bruhman home to take Philippe to the beach or play park, arranging the occasional sleepover, negotiating a visit to London to introduce him to his grandparents.

Shadows now enveloped the garden as the sun descended, the aroma of frangipani and lavender pervasive. A car pulled up, Jean emerged and extracted a child from the car seat. A six-year-old boy lingered, clutching his toy monkey. A boy who needed a mother. As I went to greet them, I saw a vision of Dorothy smiling.

Printed in Great Britain
by Amazon